Here We Sta
Infected

(Surviving the Evacuation)

Frank Tayell

Dedicated to Tom

Published by Frank Tayell
Copyright 2016
All rights reserved

All people, places, and (especially) events are fictional.

ISBN-13: 978-1532734915
ISBN-10: 1532734913

Other titles:

Strike A Match
1. Serious Crimes
2. Counterfeit Conspiracy

Work. Rest. Repeat.
A Post-Apocalyptic Detective Novel

Surviving The Evacuation
Zombies vs The Living Dead
Book 1: London
Book 2: Wasteland
Book 3: Family
Book 4: Unsafe Haven
Book 5: Reunion
Book 6: Harvest
Book 7: Home
Book 8: Anglesey
Book 9: Ireland
Book 10: The Last Candidate

Here We Stand 1: Infected
Here We Stand 2: Divided

For more information, visit:
http://blog.franktayell.com
www.facebook.com/TheEvacuation

Prologue - Inauguration
January 20th, Washington, D.C.

"Another bomb went off, did you hear?" Max asked. The aide closed the door to the Oval Office, leaving Tom Clemens alone with Grant Maxwell, the newly sworn-in President of the United States. Despite himself, the reason he was there, and what his friend had said, Tom couldn't help but stare in wonder at the room. Somehow it was simultaneously larger and smaller than he'd imagined.

"It was in Tulsa," Max continued. "A crowded shopping mall."

Tom turned back to his friend. "I watched it on the news, in the residence with Claire," he said, belatedly remembering to add, "Mr President."

"Mr President? I don't think I'll get used to being called that," Max said.

"I imagine every occupant of this office has said the same thing," Tom said. "Do you know the death toll?"

"In Tulsa? That's what's puzzling. The bomb was planted in a unit that was being refurbished. Two painters died, but that's all. Dozens were injured, and hundreds have been hospitalized after the attacks in Richmond and Carson City, but it could have been worse. A lot worse."

A door opened. Charles Addison, the president's chief of staff, entered. "Sir, it's time," he said.

"Already?" Max asked.

"The press are in the briefing room, sir," Addison said.

"Give me a minute, Chuck," Max said. Addison left, shaking his head in frustration.

"You're going to address the nation?" Tom asked.

"I have to," Max said. "We've cancelled the inaugural balls. Unfortunately, someone announced it was out of respect. The truth is that it's a security decision and there's no point trying to hide it. The truth will get out, and I don't want to start my presidency on a lie."

Tom winced. That comment hit too close to the reason he'd been waiting all day to speak to the president.

"I have to allay the nation's fears," Max continued. "Although there is precious little reason to think this crisis is over. You know my predecessor called? He told me that this, today, is the job. Hell if I know what that means. But I'll tell you this, I'm not going to let education reform get sidelined because of domestic terrorism."

"You think it's domestic?"

"I don't know what to think, not yet, but the FBI believes it's home-grown. There's something to do with some intercepted emails and a bomb profile that I didn't begin to understand. If education is our first priority, replacing the director of the FBI just became our second. And now," he added, "I have to go on television and reassure people so that, tomorrow, they go to work. Not that we know this is even over." He picked up a leather-bound folder from the desk. "Take a look."

Tom took the folder. Inside was the president's statement. "Gregson wrote this? There's nothing about the first-responders. Single out their heroism. Say that their devotion to their job is second only to their concern for their fellow citizens. And at the end, finish with something like 'Here we stand, bloodied but unbowed, together, united'. Or something like that."

"Is this the time to use the election slogan?" Max asked. "Wouldn't that seem as if I was making some statement to those that didn't vote for me?"

"Or that you hadn't forgotten the reason that the majority did."

"Maybe." Max sounded unconvinced. He took out a pen and made a note. "Can't say 'citizens'," he added. "The bomb in Richmond was at a convention hall. An international symposium on the history of democracy and the American dream. Historians, Tom. How does killing them help a terrorist's cause?" He sighed. "Some first day. I know I promised we'd talk over dinner, but that's not going to happen. I don't even think dinner's going to happen. Can you say what you need to in a minute?"

3

Tom could, but it wasn't news of the bombings that made him hesitate. He'd planned, schemed, plotted, and broken dozens of laws to ensure that his friend was elected. Once he made his confession, and explained why he'd done it, everything would change. Not just his life and the direction of Max's presidency, but the entire world. Yet staying silent wouldn't halt the conspiracy.

"It's a long story," he began. His mouth was dry. He coughed. "The short version—"

The door opened.

"Mr President," Addison said. "It's time."

"Mr President," Max repeated. "No, I really don't think I'll ever get used to being called that. Walk with me, Tom." Tom fell into step beside the president as they left the Oval Office and headed toward the press briefing room. "What was it you wanted to tell me?"

"It can wait," Tom said. "There'll be time after you've addressed the nation."

"There won't," Max said. "I've got to decide whether the stock market should open tomorrow, and then take calls from world leaders. Apparently they'll need reassuring. Not sure why since it's our country that's under attack." Max stopped walking. There was a murmur from the lead agent in his security detail as this was relayed to the control room.

"I can see this is eating you up, Tom," Max said. "Whatever it is, tell me now."

Tom looked at the secret service agents blocking the corridor. This wasn't how he'd imagined it. He couldn't simply *tell* Max, he needed to *explain*, and this wasn't the place for that.

"Is it that bad?" Max asked. "It is. I can tell from your expression. Tell me. Please."

Tom saw genuine concern in his friend's eyes. All that he'd planned to say, and how he'd planned to say it, was forgotten. The words came out in a rush, and in the wrong order.

"There's a conspiracy," Tom said. "It's wide-ranging, and its members are in the highest of offices. They tried to take control of the White House. That's why I asked you to run, and why I made sure you won."

Max's face crinkled in puzzlement. "What are you talking about?"

"The election was rigged, Max. I won you the nomination. I had to make sure America was being led by someone honest and untainted by the conspiracy."

"Is this a joke?"

The weight of history exuding from the walls, the stress of waiting, not just today, but for years, the presence of the agents, it was making Tom babble. He pushed on, knowing that time was running out, that he had to finish, had to find a way of making the president understand.

"The Super-PAC who ran those 'who can't you trust' ads, I paid for them. I hacked Farley's email. The recording where you asked General Carpenter to be the VP, I leaked it to the press. The photographs of Claire, I—"

Max's fist smashed into Tom's jaw. He staggered back a step. Before he'd time to take another, two secret service agents grabbed his arms, and a third stepped between him and the president.

"Get him out of here," Max said.

"Max, I—" Tom began.

"Get him out!" Max yelled, before turning on his heel, and storming down the corridor.

Barely a minute later, Tom was outside. He stared at the hulking secret service agent. Had they heard what he'd said to the president? Could they be trusted?

"You should go home, sir," the agent said.

Tom sighed. It was tiredness. It was stress. It was the exhaustion that came with having lived a life of secrets. He'd said it all wrong, but there was no point arguing, at least not with the suited figure standing before him.

"My car," he said, "it's parked in the residence."

"Maybe you should leave it there until tomorrow," the agent said, in a tone that made it clear that wasn't a suggestion.

"I suppose I'll get a cab," Tom said. "Tell him, I'll… I'll wait for his call."

The agent's expression cracked. "He's the president, sir. He doesn't need to call. If he wants you, he can send in a SEAL team."

Tom forced a smile at the reference to a line from the final presidential debate.

"Go home, sir," the agent repeated.

But when he got in the cab, Tom gave the driver the address of a restaurant to which he'd never been.

Tom Clemens was a political fixer. Under other names, and he'd had many, he was a criminal who'd stolen, bribed, and blackmailed in pursuit of his own ambitions. He'd discovered the conspiracy by accident while testing the effectiveness of a set of stolen passwords. At first, he'd thought he'd stumbled across another black-book project, and one that wasn't even operating in the United States. He'd kept investigating because of the link between it and the British politician Tom held responsible for the deaths of his family. As he'd untangled each thread, he'd uncovered a widespread plot that stretched far beyond the web of that particular MP.

Though its origins were in Britain, the cabal was truly transatlantic. Its members cared nothing for policies, parties, or people, but only in acquiring enough power to impose its dystopian doctrine upon the world. Those who wouldn't submit would be destroyed. At first, Tom hadn't believed what he'd found. As he'd pieced the fragments into a coherent picture, he couldn't believe he was the first to have discovered the plot. Then he'd learned that he wasn't. Some had had their silence bought. Others had been killed.

He'd dug, searching for the names of all the conspirators. Even now, he hadn't found them all. During those early years, he'd been lulled into a false sense of the cabal's influence. Each name he'd discovered belonged to an elderly politician whose power was waning. Had he learned of this terrible truth twenty years before, even ten, his instinct would have been to wreak a murderous vengeance on each conspirator as soon as they were identified. Experience had taught him there was a better way. He'd planned to expose the conspiracy for what it was: a lunatic fantasy of power-mad vultures, unaware that the world no longer wanted their blood-drenched vision of the future. And then, Senator Paul Farley had announced his run for the presidency.

No, he still didn't know the identity of all the conspirators, but Farley was at the dark heart of the vile group. As the campaign season began, and candidates in both parties announced themselves, Tom finally understood how wrong he'd been. The conspirators' influence hadn't waned. They'd ensured Farley would face no credible opponent. He would walk to the nomination, stroll to November, and civilization would be crawling on its knees before the midterms.

Tom had considered killing Farley, and might have done it if he'd been able to guarantee that there wasn't another candidate ready to pick up the torch of the dead senator. Martyrdom would make their victory easier. The only solution was to field a candidate against Farley, and so steal the nomination from him. That was what Tom had done. Yes, he'd rigged the election, but the contest had been fixed before he'd persuaded Max to throw his hat in the ring. That didn't excuse his actions, but he'd seen no other course open to him. No matter how ham-fisted his attempt, he'd been right to tell Max the truth today. Out of a sense of party unity, Farley had been appointed secretary of state. There had been no effective way of dissuading Max without telling him of Farley's involvement in the conspiracy, and no way of doing that without revealing the truth about the nomination, the election, and every other dark secret. Out of fear that his honest friend would refuse the oath, he'd waited until after Max had been sworn in.

Perhaps Max would resign, and this would become the shortest presidency in history. Perhaps not, but it wouldn't alter what was going to happen to Tom next. Tomorrow, or more likely later tonight, Max would summon him. Tom would tell him everything and every name he'd been able to discover. That would only be the beginning. Max was a truly good and honest man, and there was no way Tom would avoid a federal prison. So be it, a life in jail was far better than a world of ash, where there was no one left to even dig a grave.

"I think the police are following us," the cab driver said, cutting through Tom's thoughts.

He turned around in the seat. Sure enough, a police cruiser was fifty yards behind. "Is it flagging you down?"

"No, sir."

"Then they want to make sure I go home," Tom said.

"Who does?" the driver asked, his tone suddenly anxious.

Tom had wanted a last meal at an absurdly expensive restaurant. Something to remember during the years of imprisonment that stretched before him. It wasn't to be.

"Change of plans," he said. "Take me to Kensington." He'd bought a house in that Maryland suburb because the name had kindled memories of his youth. Not that he'd ever lived in that central London borough, but he had visited and dreamed of living in one of the grand houses. He'd bought this house shortly after he'd decided that Grant Maxwell *had* to stand for the presidency. He'd known then that his dream of living in Britain was just that: a fantasy that had kept him company during the three decades since, as a teenager named Thaddeus, he'd fled to America. This house was as close as he'd get. He knew it was likely to be the last one he'd ever own, and that he wasn't likely to own it for long.

He stood on the curb, watching the cab's red lights disappear. The police cruiser had followed him home and was now stopped a hundred yards down the quiet street.

"Maybe I should have told you sooner," Tom said, rubbing his jaw. "I guess today's lesson is that there's a time and a place, and that I'm not much good at picking the right one. Still, it'll make an interesting anecdote for the history books."

He raised a hand, waving at the police. They'd been sent on Max's orders, he was sure. He could imagine the two officers speaking to their control room. There, the duty officer would be standing ramrod straight, awaiting instructions relayed from the White House.

"Go on, Max. Let's end this now."

The officers stayed in the car, and he began to feel ridiculous. He gave the cops another wave before walking up the path to his house. Whatever tomorrow would bring, tonight he'd make the most of his freedom. A cold drink, a comfortable chair, and that documentary about how Max had won the election. He enjoyed listening to the pundits with their oh-so-wrong conclusions. His smile froze. The light above the door hadn't come on.

He'd replaced the bulb... when? It was after the election. Christmas, that was it. When he'd gone looking for a bulb, the stores were all closed. He hadn't realized it was Christmas Day. He looked up and down the street, but other than the police, he was alone. It was a busted bulb, he told himself. He grabbed the key from his pocket, opened the door, and his heart skipped a beat. The hall lights didn't come on. That was wrong. Very wrong. He'd rigged it so the wall-light to the left of the door flickered. Anyone entering would glance toward it and so present their face to the camera hidden in the fitting.

"It's the fuses," he said, trying to believe it. He stepped inside and flipped the switch. The hall lit up. The polished floor, the ornate mirror, the solitary cabinet; it was all unchanged from when he'd left that morning, yet old instincts told him not to believe it.

Shifting his weight to the balls of his feet, bunching his fists, cocking his head, listening not just for sound but for its absence, he crossed to the cabinet. It had the appearance of a baroque antique, but he'd designed it himself. The ornate curls of the elaborate fretwork had been fashioned to conceal the hidden panel. He slid it back. The compartment inside was empty. The gun was gone.

His mouth went dry. Some part of his dark past had caught up with him. He'd lived a life of aliases, all of which had more enemies than friends. As he inched along the polished floor, memories came back to him of the people he'd been and the names he'd used. Above all the others, there was one that had caused more trouble for more people than any other: Sholto.

His heart beat faster and became all that he could hear. Wanting to get the confrontation over with, he ran into the living room. He spun around, fists raised. There was no one there. He slammed a hand against the light switch. The room lit up. No, there was no one there. No one living.

He recognized the body instantly. It was Imogen Fenster. She was a journalist and, at twenty-six, already ran one of the world's largest networks of independent reporters. They'd met on the campaign. In her search for an angle that no one else had covered, she'd turned her inquisitive eyes to him. Ostensibly, he was an old friend of the candidate, and most of the press had bought that line. She hadn't. She'd dug into his past and discovered a few breadcrumbs. Not enough to sink the campaign, but enough to destroy him. He'd had no choice but to tell her about Archangel, Prometheus, and the conspiracy. Without naming names, he'd revealed enough that she'd wanted to look for more. It had been a test. His way of assessing whether she could be the backup plan he'd been seeking. Someone on the outside, in case everything went tragically wrong.

She'd been shot once. The bullet had entered above her right ear. Blood had pooled around her skull, turning her blue-dyed hair a dark, matted brown. It was obvious why she'd been killed. Not killed. Murdered. Here. Tonight. And then he saw what he'd been looking at all along. His gun lay next to the body.

His phone was already in his hand. He swiped the screen, bringing up the keypad. He tapped in a six-digit number and pressed dial. Instead of placing a call, an app opened, one that he'd had specially written. It showed the security cameras inside the house. Half of those streamed static. That was as it should be. Those were the cameras they were meant to find. He scrolled back through the others until he watched Imogen enter the house. She wasn't alone, but with a man dressed in the government uniform of a dark suit and tie. The man was in his thirties with a boyish face framed under a shock of white hair. Imogen wasn't a prisoner; she marched into the house with a smile. She stopped in the den. There was enough time for puzzlement to furrow her brow before the white-haired man drew the revolver and fired. She collapsed. The man put the gun on the floor, and left.

The time stamp said it had happened while he, Tom, had been in the residence with the first lady. This wasn't the time and place to consider the full implication of that. He put the phone away. Precisely who that white-haired man was, Tom didn't know. He could guess the name of the man he worked for: Farley. Proving it would take time, but he could now rely on the full might of U.S. security services to do that.

There was the sound of an engine outside. Blue and red lights danced through the window. The police. He crossed quickly to the front door and looked out. It was the cruiser that had followed him from the White House.

He'd already turned the latch before he checked himself. He glanced at his phone. Max hadn't called. The secret service agent was right. If Max wanted him, he didn't have to call, but nor would he send a couple of uniformed cops. They got out of the car. The officers wore bulletproof vests over their uniforms. It didn't seem right. The vests had no police markings and seemed bulkier than standard issue equipment.

Of course it wasn't right. Farley's agents had discovered and disabled some of the cameras. They would have assumed there were others. The body had been left and the gun dropped, but they hadn't finished staging the crime scene. A vital element was missing. They couldn't risk him speaking to a lawyer, or even being seen entering a police station. No, they would kill him here. The police report would state that the two officers responded to the sound of gunfire, forced an entry, and shot him dead. The coroner would be bribed, the time of Imogen's death faked, witness statements forged, and the whole thing would get forgotten.

The cops were on the path, approaching the house. There was no more time. He had to escape.

He went to the rear of the house, opening the sliding glass doors that led to the garden. He'd prepared for this. If he'd chosen the neighborhood because of the name, he'd selected the house because of its ease of escape. That had been two years ago, and he'd not thought about it in the time since. Mud had drifted up around the loose section of fence. Splinters dug into his hands as he dragged the wood free. He let the panel fall conspicuously on the lawn.

11

There were no lights on in the neighboring house, and no easily stolen car left in the drive. That was frustrating, but not an insurmountable problem. He pulled out the phone and opened the app that would summon a cab.

He walked quickly, but didn't run. It would attract too much attention. He'd been pursued often enough to know that you didn't run until you had to, and he knew he'd have to soon enough.

When they found he'd gone, Farley's men would call in for orders before they began their pursuit. That gave him time, not much, but more than he needed. He would call Max and send him the video of that man killing Imogen. After that, it would be a long night of questioning and the rest of his life in jail. Perhaps he'd get a presidential pardon. Perhaps.

A car pulled over to the curb fifty feet ahead. His phone chimed. It was the cab. He didn't relax, but his muscles fractionally unclenched. He'd make the call from the car. Not to Max, since he no longer carried a phone, but to the First Lady, Claire. He'd send the video to her. She would give it to Max, and by the time the cab reached the White House, his innocence would have been proven.

He was level with the cab, reaching for the passenger door when he saw the driver's reflection in the side mirror. The hair was hidden under a hat, but that face was the same one he'd seen marching Imogen into his home. He took a step back, and another. The driver's door flew open. The assassin stepped out. Now was the time to run if it wasn't already too late. He darted down the sidewalk, glanced back, saw the face, the hand, the gun.

As a bullet pocked against concrete, he leaped over an ornamental hedge, rolling across the lawn on the other side. There was another muffled retort. Grass flew a few inches from his hand. The gun was silenced, not that it mattered. A barrage of artillery might bring police uniforms, but he couldn't trust the people wearing them. He picked himself up and sprinted for the edge of the house. A flowerpot exploded as he ducked out of sight. He heard glass breaking. He didn't look back. The house lights came on, illuminating the rear garden as he ran across it. There was an indistinct yell that turned to a scream, and was abruptly cut short. He stopped, but there was nothing he could do. He shoulder-charged the fence, knocking it down.

He was in an alley, about five feet wide with a brick wall immediately in front. The next house had a wooden fence. He ran over to it, kicked until a panel came free, and dragged it out of the way. He didn't cross into the garden. He kept running down the alley until he was hidden behind the bulk of a white oak. He waited, watching. The assassin bounded into the alley, but barely paused before running to the gap Tom had kicked in the fencing. The white-haired man disappeared through it.

When he was sure the man wasn't coming out, Tom doubled back on himself, running soft-footed down the alley. The alley led to a road. The road to a park.

He stopped and took out the phone. It was broken. He cursed. On the other hand, the white-haired man *had* been in the cab, he'd probably been tracking the phone. He dropped it on the ground.

What he had to do was obvious. He had to get online, retrieve a copy of that video, and get it to Max. He began walking. It was many years since he'd been on the run, but old habits came back to him. He picked up his pace, determined that the conspiracy had claimed its last victims.

Chapter 1 - Outbreak
February 20th - Lower Manhattan, New York

Tom hesitated with his hand over the keyboard. For the umpteenth time, he searched for an alternative. He knew there wasn't one, but from the moment the call was made, there truly would be no turning back. It was a month since the inauguration, and his pursuers were closing in. At best, they were only hours away.

After he'd fled from his house, it had taken nearly twelve hours before he'd found a phone, downloaded the video of Imogen's murder from the cloud, and sent it to the First Lady. It had been eleven hours too many. When he'd followed the message with a call, it hadn't been Claire who'd answered but some anonymous agent from an unknown agency. He'd called the White House. Max wouldn't take his call. Instead, he'd spoken to Chuck Addison, the chief of staff, and been told that his video he'd sent was a fake. Apparently, they'd already seen other footage that showed Tom firing the fatal shot. That recording had been taken from *his* house, from his *very own* security system. Before he'd been able to protest his innocence, Addison had continued listing the evidence against him. It included a computer that contained files implicating him in the bombings in Carson City, Richmond, and Tulsa. That computer had been recovered from the car he'd left in the White House residence. According to an unsent email on Imogen's phone, she'd been investigating Tom since the campaign, suspecting him of being the one behind a conspiracy to undermine the government.

He'd been stitched up, sent down the river, and thrown over the side of the boat before he'd realized they were on to him. Not only had they discovered his plans, they'd concocted a way of neutralizing him without his ever noticing. Paranoia had him checking and re-checking every communication he'd ever sent and every channel he'd used. His systems hadn't been compromised, but it was his increasing reliance on technology that had been his downfall.

Max had appointed Farley as secretary of state one week after the election. That had been a signal to the cabal that Tom hadn't revealed what he'd learned about the conspiracy. It had been no great leap for the conspirators to realize that he was waiting until after the inauguration. They'd acted first. The bombings had been planned to distract the president long enough for Imogen to be lured to Tom's house, be murdered, and for the evidence to be planted. Even if Tom had confessed everything to Max on January 20th, it wouldn't have mattered. Any suspicions against Farley would have been shrugged off when the evidence against Tom was discovered. It was clever in a very old-fashioned, low-tech way, and he should have expected it.

He'd been on the run for the last month, alone, and cut off from most of his resources. Most, but not all. There was one way left in which he could get word to Max, but words weren't going to be enough. To him, the planted evidence was proof that the cabal was behind the bombings, but it had damned him in Max's eyes. He'd tried to come up with an alternative plan, but he'd run out of time.

Large pieces of the conspiracy were still hidden from him, but the cabal had moved their plans forward. Tom had done the same. Everything now rested on this last, desperate throw of the dice. The world would be saved, or it would be in ruins before the year was out.

Still, he hesitated.

Later today, he would leave America. There was a chance they might never find him. If he continued, he would be hunted by the intelligence services of every nation on the planet. That fear was replaced with a memory of his dead parents and the infant brother stolen from him. He pressed enter. The VOIP software placed the call. He tapped a button so the conversation would be recorded. The phone rang. Once. Twice.

"This is the White House," a woman said. "How may I direct your call?"

"Charles Addison, please," Tom said.

"And who's calling?"

"Lionel Kendrick," Tom said, naming one of the campaign's major donors.

There was a click, a pause, and Tom waited for the call to be picked up.

"Office of the chief of staff. How can I help you, Mr Kendrick?" a young man said.

It was now or never.

"Hello? Mr Kendrick?" the aide prompted.

"This is Tom Clemens. I need to speak to Chuck," Tom said.

There was a short intake of breath, followed by a stuttering, "I… I…"

"I'm going to stay on the line for thirty seconds," Tom said. "After that, I'll hang up. He'll want to take this call."

"Please, um… please hold."

Tom clicked a button on the tablet. A timer began counting down. On the laptop, he brought up a window split into four boxes. Each showed the view from a different camera: a section of road; the entrance to an apartment; a hallway with a door at the end; the inside of a room. Other than a couple pushing matching baby-strollers along the sidewalk, there was nothing to see on the screen. Not yet.

"Tom?" Addison's voice sounded weary, edged with skepticism.

"Hi, Chuck. It's really me."

There was silence followed by a slow intake of breath. "Why are you calling?"

"I need to speak to Max," Tom said.

"He's not going to talk to you, Tom. He can't. You know that. The president can't get involved in a case of domestic terrorism."

"I was set up, Chuck. I sent you the evidence."

"And I got it. I saw it. I'm not sure what it proves. You fled the scene of a murder, Tom. In your own house! What do you think that looks like? We have the maps of where those bombs went off, and the emails you sent, and the information that journalist collected on you. Whoever your accomplices are—"

"Chuck, do you think I'm a murderer? You know me."

"I don't know, Tom. I don't think I know you at all. I do know that Tom isn't your name."

Tom winced. He'd been wondering how much Farley and the rest of the cabal had learned, and how much they'd share. It didn't matter. Not now. He glanced at the tablet, making sure it was recording. Of course it was, but after a month of looking over his shoulder, paranoia had truly taken hold.

"If you won't let me speak to Max," Tom said, "I need you to give him a message."

"Turn yourself in, Tom. Maybe you can… speak to him when you're in custody." From the stilted sentences, Tom guessed someone else was in the room. It would be one of those anonymous suits, gesturing for Chuck to keep talking, while they awaited confirmation that the call had been traced. Did that agent work for Farley, or not?

"It's not going to happen," Tom said. "Not yet."

"Where are you, Tom?" Addison asked.

"A non-extradition country."

"No, I don't think so. You're close, aren't you?"

Tom glanced at the timer. It had been long enough. "Tell Max this is about Prometheus and Archangel," he said. "There are people in his administration who've spent decades plotting to bring about their own vision for global domination. The bombings were part of it; so was killing that journalist and framing me for murder. There are plenty more deaths I can lay at their door and—"

"Conspiracy theories, Tom. You're losing it. You know how many calls like this we get every day? We've had twenty this morning warning us of shadowy forces wanting to create a new world order. Seriously, you're losing it. You need—"

But it was Tom's turn to interrupt. "I'll call back tomorrow. Pass the message on."

He hung up.

The call had gone as he'd expected. He'd never dreamed that he'd actually be put through to Max. Speaking to Charles Addison was the second best thing. Like the VP, Max had known Chuck since high school, and Tom knew he could be trusted. The call's purpose was to lay the groundwork for what was going to happen next.

He picked up the tablet, plugged it into the sat-phone, brought up a window, and entered a password. A dialogue box came up. There was no written prompt. He'd not bothered putting one in, just a simple yes or no option. Before any more doubts could beset him, he pressed yes. It was done. There really was no turning back. Not now, not ever.

Then doubt returned, not that what he'd done was right, but that it hadn't worked. The tablet buzzed, alerting him to a new email. It was the one he'd sent. His receipt confirmed that it had gone to all ten thousand accounts on the list. Some were in America. Others were spread throughout the world, in nations considered both allies and foes. There were military commanders on that list, diplomats, politicians, scientists, and journalists. The content was short and simple: a statement of the conspirators' plans with a few facts that would pique the recipients' professional curiosity. Not all would open the email, and fewer would believe it. Like Addison had said, conspiracy theories were commonplace, but hopefully enough would read it for questions to be asked. Tom's plan depended on getting a copy of the answers. To that end, he'd had a busy month.

He'd gained access to Farley's email accounts during the campaign. The man was a creature of habit. For a former spy, those habits were bad. He changed his passwords once a week, always on Sundays, and always from the computer in his home office. A small camera hidden behind the Revolution-era musket hanging on the wall recorded his every keystroke. Unfortunately, there had been nothing incriminating in any of those accounts since the man's bid for the nomination had imploded. That was why Tom had come to New York. The email he'd sent should have diplomats talking, arguing, and threatening one another. Where was the greatest concentration of international politicians? The U.N.

Tom drummed his fingers on the desk, his eyes glued to the camera feeds. He was growing impatient, but he couldn't rush, not now. Everything had been planned to the last detail and timed to the last second. He'd created a web in which he'd catch all the conspirators. Should any of the strands break, and he failed, a new era of darkness would be ushered onto the world. What if he didn't get proof? What if no one talked, at least not in places to which he'd gained access? What if the email was ignored as the product of a fantasist? What if—

In the window on the laptop, a car drove into view. The time for doubting introspection was past. Red and blue lights flashed behind the grille, but there were no markings on the vehicle. Out of it jumped four men, all wearing black tactical gear, with bulletproof vests marked FBI. So far, so unsurprising. They didn't enter the building. Instead, they lingered on the curb, waving pedestrians away.

"What are you waiting for?"

The answer came ten seconds later when another SUV pulled up. The figure who got out wasn't wearing black, but a blue suit and brown overcoat. The clothes screamed detective even without the badge hanging from a chain around the man's neck. Tom played around with the camera's controls, enlarging the image until he was certain that it was a New York detective's badge. He knew it was a fake. The face underneath that shock of white hair had haunted his dreams for the last month.

The man's name was Powell. At least, that was the name he'd given the police in Maryland. His cover was good, but Tom had created enough false identities that he could spot a fake. In Maryland, after Powell had opened fire on Tom, and Tom had fled, the police had arrived on the scene. The *real* police. The white-haired man had presented credentials identifying himself as Agent Powell of Homeland Security and explained he was on a matter of classified national interest. Powell was the cabal's hatchet man.

On the camera feed, he watched the armed group enter the building. Tom picked up the sat-phone, unplugged the tablet, and placed both in his pockets.

The armed group had reached the door of the apartment. Tom brought up a command line prompt, tapped in a few lines of code, and paused. He watched the group take a collective look at Powell. The man held up a hand, signaling they should wait. Powell held a hand to his ear. A puzzled expression crept across his face. He took out a phone. Odd. Tom wished he'd installed microphones along with the cameras. He could try to trace the call later. Powell hung up and motioned agitatedly with his hands. The group broke into the apartment. Tom turned his eyes to the final screen and smiled as he watched the men storm an empty room.

He took a moment to enjoy their confusion. The call to the White House had been routed through an empty apartment, six blocks from the partially constructed office building he was now in. He tapped the keyboard. The laptop's screen went blank as almost all the contents were erased. He grabbed the hard hat and the paint-splattered rucksack and made his way to the bare concrete stairwell.

So far, everything was going to plan. Powell's presence in New York was a surprise, but it wouldn't be a problem. Within the hour, they'd have found the construction site and the laptop. It would take them at least a day to recover the files. Those would lead them to Mexico City, by which time Tom would be on a fishing trawler, out on the Atlantic.

The street-level traffic was more frenetic than usual, even for downtown New York. Bumpers ground into one another as cars shunted back and forth, trying to break free of inescapable gridlock. The sidewalk wasn't much better. People barged along with their eyes fixed to their phones, or ran blindly, barely pausing to curse as they ran into one another.

There was no choice but to let the crowd carry him along. He waited until he was a block from the construction site before he pulled out the sat-phone and dialed a number he'd memorized long ago.

"Si?" a voice answered.

"Julio," Tom said. "I'm calling in the favor."

"You want your favor *now*?"

That seemed an odd thing to say. "I'll need a flight. Today. One way," Tom said, adding, "As we agreed."

"I'm not surprised," Julio said. "After this, you won't be the only one. Do you know what's going on?"

"What are you talking—" Tom began, then almost dropped the phone as a sprinting woman knocked him into the curb. She was shoeless. "Julio, I'll be there in six hours."

"Yeah. Sure," Julio replied distractedly.

Tom hung up. That hadn't gone entirely as he'd expected. Julio had a farm with an airfield from which he ran a flight school. It was his retirement job, the career he'd moved into when being a commercial pilot had become too dangerous. Julio had been in the wrong place at the wrong time, and seen something that he couldn't ignore. He'd offered himself as a witness to a series of brutal kidnappings, and had become a target himself. Tom had arranged for a new identity and a new life in North America. In exchange, Julio had agreed to take him on a one-way flight. No questions. No manifest. No trace that Tom had ever been on the plane.

It would take six hours to get to the airfield. Six hours after that, they'd be at a landing strip in Canada. From there, he'd drive to the coast. Now he had to call Sophia Augusto and arrange for the boat that would take him on the final leg of his journey. Of course, he still wasn't… wasn't…

His single-track obsession with escape was finally derailed. Something *had* happened. Something big. He turned around, trying to see what all these people were running from. All he saw was a sea of faces, all wearing the same expression of disbelieving fear. His first thought was of those bombs on the day of the inauguration. Had Farley again guessed what Tom had planned, and organized something similar here in New York? No, he couldn't. Not today. Surely not. There was no smoke in the sky, but, barely audible over the crunch of plastic and metal, the blaring of horns, and the yelling of hundreds of people were sirens and… were those screams?

On the far side of the road, a cyclist dodged through the stalled vehicles at an insane speed. She raised a bloody hand, waving it in a circling motion above her head. Turning in the saddle, she looked behind, and realized that whoever she'd been signaling to was no longer there. She didn't see the cab driver open his door and didn't have time to brake. The front wheel hit the door, and she went flying. Tumbling over the hood, she disappeared from view.

Tom tried to push his way through the dense crowd toward the woman.

"Out of the way!" an obese suit bellowed, elbowing Tom in the ribs. The pain cut through that treacherous instinct. No matter what had happened in New York, he was on the run. Suppressing a wave of guilt, he let himself be caught up in the throng. As his legs concentrated on moving, and his arms on pushing the jostling crowd away, that old instinct kicked in. He was escaping. Getting away was good, but now was the time to think of his destination. Maintenance crews were working on the Brooklyn Bridge. His plan had been to mingle with them before disappearing into an underground parking facility on the far side. He had a car there, and so would drive to Staten Island, change cars, head to the mainland, and then to the airfield. It was twenty minutes since he'd left the construction site, and he was heading in the wrong direction. Powell would have traced the call to that location in another forty minutes. Not long after that, he'd have accessed the satellite feeds and seen the guy in the hard hat leaving. He'd wanted Powell to waste time inspecting the work crew on the bridge, knowing that for each question asked, he'd get at least two in reply. He wasn't going to make it.

He pulled off the hat and let it fall into the road. Head bowed, he pushed his way through the surging mob and into the relative calm of an alley. He took out the tablet, but hesitated before using it. If they traced his activity, they might link it to the call he'd made to Julio, and so be waiting at the airfield. But unless he found out what was going on, he'd never catch that flight.

He opened the browser and loaded a website. The entry of a stolen password later, he had access to the city's transport management system. After one more click, he was looking at traffic-camera feeds for downtown Manhattan. It was chaos. The island was at a standstill. Where people weren't running, they were supine on the ground, or staggering from spot to spot, clearly injured and suffering from shock. No one was helping them. Though he could hear sirens, there were no first-responders in the feeds. Three clicks later, he had a southbound view of Brooklyn Bridge. It was gridlock. As to what was causing this panic, he still couldn't tell. The screen was small and the images indistinct, but he saw a man staggering through an intersection toward a school bus. His arms were outstretched as if he was seeking help. Tom closed the browser and opened the newsfeed. One word was common to all headlines: terrorist.

Detail and fact were missing from the hastily written articles, but twice he saw Grand Central mentioned. He swore. That was his plan B, to be used if Powell was close on his heels. He wasn't going to catch a train, but he wanted to be seen going into the station. There was a spot, halfway down a platform that wasn't covered by any cameras. It led to a service tunnel, the exit of which was opposite the fire door of a gym. In a locker was a change of clothes, and a rudimentary disguise that—

An animalistic scream cut through his thoughts. He looked toward the alley's mouth, but couldn't see what caused it. No matter. There was always plan C. He put the tablet away and set off down the alley, heading north.

When he was sure he was out of sight, he ducked into the lee of an emergency doorway. The lock was easily broken, and he entered the building. He opened the paint-splattered backpack. The reflective vest went inside, along with the work-stained overalls. Out came a pair of generic blue jeans, a thin black jacket, and an I-heart-NY cap. He splashed a small bottle of solvent on the boots and wiped away the paint. The last thing to come out was a compact red and black rucksack with an airline luggage-tag still attached. The paint-splattered backpack and clothes went inside. He slung the bag in front of his chest and hoped, at least to a casual observer, he looked like a tourist. He walked up the narrow stairs, and into a corridor. It was an apartment block. A small group had gathered near the door. Ignoring them as they ignored him, he went back outside.

The traffic here was just as bad. Bewildered drivers stood by open car doors as pedestrians ran past. There was another scream, and this one was far closer. It came from ahead. He clambered onto the roof of a freshly washed sedan.

"Hey! Hey! Get off my car!"

Tom ignored the irate driver as he scanned the roads. He knew he was being stupid, drawing attention to himself and thus negating the thin disguise, but he'd survived the last three decades thanks to information. If life was a puzzle, data was the key. It had become his lifeblood, his tool, his weapon, and without it he was feeling worse than unarmed.

A gunshot echoed around the towering buildings. Another. The screams grew louder, edged with fear and panic. He jumped down and kept walking. Another junction, another block, and another crowd too dense to push through forced him further away from where he wanted to go. Alleys and roads, doubling back, heading north, then south, east then west until he was on Kenmare, two stores down from the junction with Elizabeth Street. Here, the people had stopped running. They stood in clusters, not talking, but all with their heads glued to their phones, oblivious to the woman staggering across the junction.

Blood poured down the bespoke blue overcoat from a wound on her neck. Tom was halfway to her when she collapsed. By the time he reached her, there was no pulse. Part of her throat was missing. It was a miracle she'd made it this far. Shrapnel, he guessed, although there were no other wounds, nor was her clothing scorched from being in close proximity to an explosion. There was nothing anyone could do for her. He stood and backed away, walking into the opening door of a cab.

"Watch out!" a suited-man said, getting out of the back, dragging a suitcase with him.

"Yeah. Sorry," Tom said, instantly ignoring the guy. He turned to the driver. "Do you have any idea what's going on?"

"The radio says terrorists," the driver said, pointing at his dash. "I'm going back to the depot. I can take you there, but nowhere else. Not today."

Tom looked at the traffic. Part of him wanted to get inside the cab, to close the doors so he could rest, think, and find out the meaning to all this chaos, but it would be hours before the vehicles were moving freely again.

There was a shout from behind the cab. It turned into a horrified scream. The cab's passenger was in the middle of the junction being attacked by… It was impossible. Tom stared in frozen shock.

The woman, the one he'd been sure was dead, was clawing and pawing at the man. Tom took a step toward the pair. The man was trying to push the woman away, but her hands had caught in his clothes. Her mouth opened, snapping up and down, getting closer and closer to his face. The man yelled a desperate plea for help.

There was a crash of metal as the cabbie tried to shunt the car in front out of the way. The sound brought Tom out of his daze. He ran to the fighting couple, reaching them as the woman clamped her mouth down on the man's neck. An arc of bright red blood sprayed across Tom's chest as he wrestled the woman off the injured man. She fought with an inhuman strength, flailing her arms and kicking her legs in an uncoordinated frenzy. He let go, jumping out of reach of those clawing hands. She staggered sideways, moving jerkily, as if each limb was moving independently of the others. Her right arm swiped around in an arc, and that motion pivoted her around.

It was like nothing he'd ever seen before. He backed off a pace, and she took one toward him, and another. Her hands reached out. Her fingers caught in the rucksack slung across his chest. With a surprisingly strong tug, she pulled him toward her. Her mouth opened. A gobbet of flesh she'd ripped from the man's throat fell out. Horrified shock brought him out of frozen immobility. He shrugged off the pack. The woman sagged forward as the weight of the bag dragged her arms down. A low hiss escaped those bloody lips.

Tom kicked. There was a crunch as his boot smashed into her kneecap. Her leg buckled. She collapsed, jaw first onto asphalt. A tooth flew out, but she didn't scream and her arms didn't stop flailing. Tom ran. This time he paid no attention to where he was going.

It felt like seconds. It felt like hours. That woman's bloody, blank face filled his vision until it was all he could see. He stopped, leaning against a wall. His heart was pounding, his vision blurred.

A month on the run, sleeping little, eating quick and cheap meals, it hadn't prepared him for this. Nothing could have. But what was *this*? Some kind of drug, he supposed. A dirty bomb primed with an airborne hallucinogen. Did those even exist? They had to. The alternative was impossible. Forget the impossible, he told himself. Focus on the immediate. That, clearly, was reaching safety. Where that might be wasn't an easy question to answer. He checked the sat-phone and tablet were still in his pockets. What he needed was a few minutes of calm so he could find out what was going on. There was the apartment in Harlem where he'd been sleeping for the last month. That prospect of safety evaporated when he remembered Powell. Wouldn't the man have more immediate problems to concern himself with? Unless Farley and the cabal were behind this, whatever *this* was. No, that was fear speaking. What he needed was to get inside long enough for his heart to stop racing. Somewhere he could think.

A gunshot came from somewhere far too close. Ahead was a coffee shop. Inside, two customers were helping a barista upturn tables against the floor-to-ceiling glass doors. That would do.

He was ten feet away when a siren burst into life behind him. Fear of impossible horrors was again replaced by that of Powell and capture. Resisting the urge to turn around, he kept his head bowed, but his eyes on the people inside the coffee shop. The siren drew nearer. A police motorbike overtook him, weaving a path down the road.

The police officer didn't see the man, and Tom didn't see from where he came. One second the bike was slowing to pass a cement truck whose driver-side door hung open; the next, a blood-soaked man tumbled out, onto the cop. The bike slewed into the side of a stalled limo. The rider fell off. Cop and man tumbled across the road in a jumble of arms and legs that kept on thrashing even after the two bodies had come to a halt.

Without thinking, Tom ran over to the pair, grabbing at the back of the snarling, thrashing man's coat. He hauled him up and off, and tried to hurl the man away, but he was a dead weight. All Tom succeeded in doing was dragging the snarling man to his feet. The man's arms swept out. A jagged white sliver of bone protruded from his forearm. A dark red ooze seeped from the wound, splattering droplets against the stalled truck each time the man flailed his arms.

Not a man. Not anymore. Tom shook his head, trying to clear it of a horrified fog conjured by being feet away from the impossibly inhuman.

"Get up!" he yelled at the cop. "Get up!" The woman's hands twitched, her head moved back and forth, but she was dazed.

Tom kicked, aiming at the man's legs. It had no effect. He crooked his hand and slammed his palm into the man's chest. The monstrosity staggered back a pace, but then snarled again, swiping his one good arm at Tom's chest.

Tom screamed, not in pain, but in tormented frustration. He reached down, grabbed the sidearm from the officer's belt, aimed, and fired. The bullet smashed through the monster's thigh. He fell. He didn't scream. On one working arm and leg, he pushed and clawed his way closer.

"Stop!" Tom yelled. "Stop! You have to stop!"

Somehow, Tom knew the man couldn't hear him, not anymore. He fired again, two shots, straight at the man's chest. The force of the impact flattened the man against the road, but still he didn't stop. A bubbling snarl hissed from blood-flecked lips.

Tom fired again, this time into his head. Finally, the man was still. Except, he wasn't a man, not any more. It was a—

"No." He wouldn't even think the word. It was adrenaline, that was it, that was what had kept his assailant moving. He had a vague memory of a late night conversation with the VP, soon after Max had asked the retired general to join him on the ticket. Stopping power was a myth, the general had said. People could be shot in the chest and still keep going. They could be shot in the head, only for bullets to ricochet off the skull. Unless you were using a grenade launcher, stopping power was a myth. It had been an odd conversation, but then the vice president was an odd man. Tom stared down at the corpse, trying to convince himself that his two shots to the chest had missed the vital organs. He didn't believe it.

There was a groan from behind him, and a weak, solitary, "help."

The cop. He couldn't leave her out in the road, not now. He put one arm under her shoulders, lifting her up. Now what? The coffee shop. He staggered over.

"Let her in!" he yelled at the three occupants. They stared back, unblinking, their faces pale with shock.

"Let her in!" he repeated, before lowering the woman so that she was leaning against the door. He held up the gun. "You see this? You see it?" He waited until their eyes focused on the sidearm. "You'll need it," he said, and slid it back into the officer's holster. "Let her in. Please."

The barista nodded and reached for the bolts. Tom took that as his cue to leave. He jogged along the sidewalk, barely registering the shop windows, often crowded with people who'd taken shelter from this... what? A hallucinogen that turned people into rabid, cannibalistic monsters that could only be stopped by a bullet in the brain? There was a word for that. A word from fiction, yet here they were, in the streets of New York. He needed to find what had caused this, and how far it had spread. He could do that in the apartment in Harlem. Whatever answers he found, however, wouldn't change the reality of what he was facing; zombies.

Chapter 2 - Zombies
Harlem, New York

Tom closed the door to his apartment, threw the deadbolt, added the chain, and felt no safer. Zombies. It was impossible, but during the journey back he'd been unable to think of anything more plausible. Speculation was useless. He needed facts!

As he pulled out the tablet, he caught sight of his boots. They were covered in blood. So was everything he wore. Infected, contaminated blood. Hurriedly, he stripped, leaving his clothes in a heap by the door. He peered at his flesh, looking for cuts and scratches. There were a few bruises, but no abrasions. What could he have done if he'd found any? Nothing. He collapsed onto the bed, giving in to despair.

It wasn't quite an efficiency apartment; there was a folding plastic divider that could be drawn across to separate the sleeping area from the living space. To be more accurate, it separated the bed from the desk. The entire room was barely sixteen feet across, with an alcove-kitchen and a bathroom that wasn't much bigger. It was anonymous, and he'd claimed a bad divorce was the reason for his sudden need for new accommodation. The landlord hadn't cared about anything other than the three months rent, paid in advance. Tom had haggled a little, for form's sake, but knew the place wasn't worth half what he'd paid.

What he'd done began to register. Not the flight, nor the fight in which he'd killed a man, but his actions on entering the apartment. He sat up and stared at his hands again. What would it matter if there were cuts? Infected blood was, like the name he'd given to the creatures, a concept from the movies.

Wanting to fill the room with noise to drown out the fearful voices in his head, he stood, walked over to the ancient television, picked up the remote, and pressed the button. Nothing happened. As he'd not planned on coming back to the apartment, he'd unplugged the set. Powered on, the screen showed the news. He collapsed on the bed once more. Slowly the words of the anchor cut through the veil of shock.

"We don't know what it is," the anchor said. "People are attacking each other—"

"Biting. They're biting people. Eating them," a male voice, off-screen, interrupted.

"No, we don't know that, and it's criminal to speculate," the anchor said, displaying more restraint than was usual from the news media. Tom sat up, watching more closely.

"The facts are… the facts are…" The anchor faltered. She glanced to one side of the screen. "Okay, yes, people are attacking one another. Violently, and with hands and teeth. The people doing this are ordinary people. There are… they're just rumors. We don't have any confirmation for any of this. It's phone footage recorded in the street. Other stations are saying that this was a terrorist attack. We don't know, we just don't! And we shouldn't say that until we do."

Tom switched to a different channel. The woman's rationality would be comforting if the argument with someone off-screen wasn't preventing her reporting what was actually going on.

"Terrorists have attacked downtown Manhattan," the anchor of the next station said. Sweat had dissolved the gel keeping his comb-over in place. Lank strands hung limply across the man's left eye, but he spoke with the same absolute certainty with which he'd reported every story for the last decade. "They've deployed a biological agent of unknown origin. People who have been exposed collapse, seemingly dead, then rise again to attack others. Obviously this is a neurological agent of some kind, but…"

But the man was guessing. He knew no more than what Tom could deduce from all he'd witnessed. In the corner of the screen, behind the man, was footage taken from… a helicopter? Yes. It was an aerial shot of a mall. From the field visible in the distance, it wasn't in Manhattan. Whatever this was, either it hadn't started on the island, or it had already spread to the mainland.

Next to the TV was the cheap laptop he'd brought from a pawnshop two blocks away. Like the computer in the construction site, he'd left this one here in case Powell somehow found where he'd been staying.

"Powell." It seemed an age since that man was his most pressing concern. He'd thought it highly improbable that the cabal would discover the apartment. On the other hand, zombies were more than just improbable. He glanced out the narrow window. Smoke rose above the towering buildings. He couldn't concern himself with Powell, not now.

He powered the laptop on and opened a browser. An error message came up. There was no network connection. Of course there wasn't. He walked over to the pile of clothes and gingerly retrieved the tablet and sat-phone. He opened the window, propping the sat-phone outside where it could find a signal. The blast of cold air reminded him he was naked. Clothes could wait. He had to know.

He began with the traffic cameras, watching people stumbling through intersections, slamming fists on car windows as they fled in every direction. No matter which direction they chose, there were always these… these…

"Zombies," he said aloud. "Zombies." He felt a little better until he realized that it wasn't true. That wasn't what they were. With the name came a definition based on fiction. He needed facts. He found the depressing first of those in a video from Grand Central Station, recorded nearly an hour before.

A group of twenty police officers had formed two lines around the front entrance. They stood ten to either side of the doors, the front rank kneeling, the other standing, both ranks firing into the darkened ticket hall. The firing stopped. A cop waved her arms. A man and two children ran through the gap between the officers. The firing resumed. It was careful, measured, methodical. There was no sound, but Tom could imagine them calling out targets to one another. It was reassuring. He began to relax. For all the horror he'd witnessed, this crisis could be controlled.

"There are plans," he murmured, thinking back to the records he'd accessed, years before. "What was it called? Operation Green Garden." Yes, that was it. A national strategy to deal with a pandemic. They'd even run a simulation that assumed the outbreak started in New York. They only needed to dust those off, and this could all be managed.

That momentary confidence vanished as he glanced at the television and saw that footage of a mall still playing to the left of the anchor's head. Again seeking reassurance, he returned his attention to the laptop. The officers had stopped shooting. Their arms were waving another unseen civilian toward safety. No one appeared. An officer raised her gun. She fired. Another did the same, and then the barrage recommenced. Something was wrong. Very wrong. Not all the officers were firing. Two had drawn their nightsticks. One in a rear rank was slowly backing away. Another lowered his weapon. They were running out of ammunition.

A zombie, its legs missing below the knees, crawled into frame. Bullets thudded into its arms and shoulders. It twitched, but continued crawling, leaving a gory trail, until a shot blew its head apart. Tom's attention had been on that creature. So, it seemed, had that of the officers. Three more zombies lurched into view. All were still on their feet. The volley that met them was ragged, aimed at the center mass. The zombies staggered back, and then kept on, another four appearing in the edge of the frame. There was a final, desultory fusillade, and the thin line broke. Three officers ran forward, nightsticks raised, and Tom turned the screen off. He didn't want to know how that had ended.

"It's not a hoax. It's not a dream. There are zombies in New York." And slowly, he was adjusting to this new reality. New York? The footage on the TV suggested they were already far beyond Manhattan.

He hunched over the laptop, his fingers working furiously. They needed information. Not just him, but everyone. Proper, reliable information on which solid deductions could be based. He went online and began altering the parameters of an application he'd commissioned during the campaign. The programmer had thought he was writing software that would sift the internet to find, file, and copy to the cloud any mention of buzzwords Max used during specific speeches. The real purpose was so that Tom could search out disinformation created by the conspirators. He changed the parameters once more, this time setting it to search out 'zombies', 'virus', 'outbreak' and, after a brief hesitation, 'undead'. But were they? Was he sure that woman who'd collapsed in the junction had been dead? All he could say was that he'd found no pulse.

There was the legless zombie in that video from Grand Central, but again, that wasn't proof.

"A head shot kills them. That's all I know," he murmured.

But he needed to know more. Where had they come from? How had they been created? Was it a virus? The ticker on the television still claimed this was a terrorist attack, but there was no clue as to who was responsible.

An icy gust came through the open window. He shivered and realized that he was still naked. A tepid shower did nothing for his concentration. Having not planned to come back to the apartment, he'd thrown out the soap, toothpaste, and the towel. He dripped his way back into the main room.

Laundry was more time-consuming than buying new clothes, and he'd had no time to spare for either in the last few weeks. All that was in the wardrobe were a pair of suits and some new shirts. He'd left them there so Powell would assume those were the type of clothes he'd been wearing during his escape. He used a shirt to dry himself. Donning a suit, he couldn't imagine himself more ill-prepared for what lay ahead.

"As to what that is, start with how and where this all began."

People talked about zombies a lot. It took twenty minutes before he found the point where the references weren't to the episode of that television show broadcast the previous night. He began refining the parameters for the algorithm, dumping the useless information. Slowly, a picture emerged. It had begun in Manhattan that morning. Precisely when, he was uncertain, but it had reached the streets, and social media, between ten and eleven a.m. Twenty-eight people had been…

"Infected? Contaminated? Twenty-eight people were contaminated in four separate incidents in downtown Manhattan. Okay. So what can I tell about the people who infected them? Is that…?" He peered at the photograph on the screen. "Yeah, those are hospital scrubs." He glanced at the TV. If this had begun in a hospital, surely that would be easy to confirm. The television station was still broadcasting vague hints about terrorism to a background of the same shaky camera footage.

"Okay. It began in a hospital. So patient zero is someone who was sick. Maybe someone who came in on a plane? No. Don't guess. Check that." How? He'd have to access the air traffic control logs. That would take time. He paused with his hands above the keyboard. Everything would take time, and he wasn't sure how much of that he had.

"Find out where they are, how far they've gotten." Yes, that was more important. Then he could plan his escape. The twenty-eight took the infection in almost every direction, but the story was the same. The infected person staggered through the streets, onto public transport, or sometimes into a car. Inevitably, they collapsed. Others would come to their aid. The person turned. A zombie came back and attacked those dutiful Samaritans, and so the virus spread.

"There's no consistency," he realized. Some turned almost immediately. For others, it took far longer. One woman made it to Grand Central. Another all the way off Manhattan, to a mall north of the city. That was the footage he'd seen on the TV, a recording from a news chopper that was being shared, unedited, on thousands of accounts.

He glanced at the clock. It was already half past four. What was he doing? Wasting time. He'd learned nothing that he couldn't have guessed. He forced his hands off the keyboard, stood, and went into the kitchen. He opened the empty cupboards, knowing he'd find nothing there. Like the damp towels and dirty clothes, he'd thrown out anything that might start to smell, and so have the landlord come and investigate. And he'd done all of that because of Powell. The conspiracy.

"Is it connected?" That was the real question, the one he'd been avoiding thinking about because the answer terrified him.

This morning, he'd sent a warning about the plans for Archangel and Prometheus to people across the world. Minutes later, the zombies started attacking people.

"Minutes. It happened too soon. Even if one of the recipients was a conspirator, they couldn't have organized a viral outbreak that quickly."

Unless they'd been planning it all along. Powell *was* in New York, after all. Perhaps he was here to do more than search for Tom. Even so, releasing this type of virus didn't fit with what he knew of the conspirators. In fact, it went against everything he'd discovered about Project Archangel.

Archangel was a super-vaccine designed to combat some of the most deadly viruses on the planet, and which, it was hoped, could be adapted to respond to any new virus in a matter of months. The project had its roots in the Cold War, created at a time when there was a very real threat of biological attack from the Soviet Union. The early trials were a disaster, a financial sinkhole that could only be justified by that era's fanatical paranoia. When the Iron Curtain was pulled back, Archangel was mothballed. It wasn't forgotten.

The original research had taken place in Britain. It was there that an ambitious politician secretly resurrected the plans. He'd turned to his ideological brethren in the United States for support, and thus the conspiracy was born.

When Tom first discovered it, he'd found the concept of politicians plotting to end disease intriguing. He'd only continued monitoring it because one of those involved was the man he held responsible for the deaths of his family. Tom had dedicated his life to murderous revenge. Exposing this scheme would allow him to destroy the politician's reputation before he took the man's life.

Then he discovered the other part of the plan, the reason these self-centered, power-obsessed politicians were acting in an uncommonly altruistic fashion. The vaccine was nearing completion. There had been some limited trials that showed it worked, at least in theory. A demonstration had been planned. Representatives of the world's major governments had been summoned to New York. This was why Tom had scheduled the release of that email, and why he'd broken into the U.N.

He knew the conspirators had agents in foreign governments, but he didn't know how high up they were. What he did know was that after the demonstration, after proof had been given that the vaccine worked, the ultimatum would be issued. The vaccine would be made available to those countries that adopted policies 'friendly' to the West. Those that didn't would be destroyed.

part of the plan was called Prometheus. It was a distributed, nuclear strike against technological infrastructure. Population _____ would be left standing so that hungry millions would be left without power, water, communications, and food. That was the insanity of the cabal. The ultimate in join us or die. And the worst part was that this plan bypassed the usual command-and-control protocols. It was instituted by presidential order under a previous incumbent. Having it rescinded was one of the reasons Tom had wanted to get Max elected.

It was an insane plan, an utter nightmare that he wouldn't have believed if he'd not seen the bodies. Yet, however the conspirators might describe their motives, they were the megalomaniacal fantasies of old men who *needed* history to remember them as saviors. Unleashing zombies on the streets of New York went against everything he'd learned of them.

Tom stalked back to the computer. He brought up a video, watching someone's phone recording of a zombie attacking a cop.

Sending that email had nothing to do with the outbreak. That was the coincidence, and it left two possibilities. This virus had been created in a U.S. or British lab as a weapon to be used against nations who refused the vaccine. A toe the line or be destroyed device that had been accidentally unleashed here. That wasn't likely. He'd spent years tracking down black sites and off-the-book projects. The conspirators didn't have the resources to organize two secret biological research projects. The second possibility was that some foreign power had unleashed the virus as a pre-emptive attack.

He knew for a fact that both the Russians and the Chinese had learned of Prometheus, though he'd been unable to find out precisely how much they knew. However, they had far greater resources than he did, so it was reasonable to assume they knew as much, if not more, than he. Perhaps this virus was some Cold War weapon, left unremarked but not forgotten. Perhaps.

What mattered was that this crisis increased the chances that Prometheus would be initiated. If he couldn't warn Max, he had to warn off the cabal. It was an Anglo-American project, and he knew someone on the other side of the Atlantic who could get word to the British government. He gathered all the information he had on Prometheus, the files he had on the vaccine, and the lab that had created it, and sent them to a remote server to which only one other person had access, Bill Wright. He was a speechwriter, spin doctor, and the confidant of a rising star in British politics. He'd be able to get word to their prime minister.

It was a start, but it didn't feel like enough. He needed proof. Something he could take to Max that would finally convince the president. There was one logical place to look: Farley's personal email accounts. So far, he'd not found anything incriminating. Today was different. Someone had emailed him a video. He didn't recognize the name, but it came from an official NSA account. It was an uncompressed video that would take too long to download, so he sent it to the remote server, with a copy to the online drop box he shared with Bill. As an afterthought, he copied the rest of Farley's inbox, outbox, and his contacts.

His stomach growled. He blinked. It was eight o'clock. The background footage on the television had changed, and so had the anchor. He didn't recognize the woman at the desk. Behind her, more graphic scenes of impossible violence played out. The ticker read 'America under attack. Stay inside. You are safe in your homes. Await further announcements.' Despite the message on the screen, he wasn't safe. Was anywhere?

He opened the tablet and began accessing the traffic cameras, this time checking the bridges. The ones to the south were filled with stalled traffic and fleeing people, except they didn't look like people. Their movements were too erratic. The tunnels were worse. To the north, the George Washington Bridge was being cleared of traffic. Giant yellow bulldozers were moving from the New Jersey end, pushing vehicles into the Hudson River. That might be a way out, except it looked like there were military checkpoints at the bridge's far end. It was unlikely they'd be keeping a specific watch for him, but he didn't want to end up in a quarantine camp.

There was one other way out of the city: by boat. He'd discounted it as being too slow and conspicuous when he'd thought he'd be fleeing from Farley and Powell.

He dialed one of the other few numbers he knew by heart.

"Sophia?"

"Why are you calling?"

"You remember the favor you owe me?"

"Now? Absolutely not. The FBI came looking for you. Do you know that? They came asking questions. They said you were a terrorist."

"I'm not. Was this a guy with blond hair?"

"No. A bald man with an absurd little goatee."

Not Powell, then, perhaps he worked for him. "When was this?"

"Two weeks ago. He said you were behind those bombings."

"I wasn't. I've been set up."

"Huh. And now you are calling me. And today."

"I'm in New York, Sophia. In Manhattan. I'm trying to get out. I was hoping… well, I thought you might be off the coast, somewhere nearby."

"I'm in Puerto Rico," she said.

"Oh. Why?"

"What business is that of yours? Why does the FBI think you were behind the bombings?"

"It's a long story," he said.

"Tell me."

"I can send you an email with some files that will explain everything," he said. "Is the internet still working there? Do you still have power?"

"Of course."

"The files will explain everything."

"And then you want me to come north and sail into New York?" she asked.

"How about you look at the files, and if you come this way, you call me. And if I make it out to sea, I'll call you."

"Maybe. Or maybe I'll call the FBI and they'll be the ones to collect you. Except after today, I think they'll be too busy to do anything."

"Just look at the files," he said, and hung up.

She might not show up, but she wouldn't betray him. Sophia was a fisher; so were her parents, her grandparents, and as far back as any history had recorded. She'd borrowed money from the wrong people to expand her business. When the ships were sunk in a storm, those people came asking for a repayment she had no way of making. He'd dealt with them partly with violence, but mostly by ensuring that they were arrested in possession of so much uncut cocaine that they were all still in jail. He'd funded Sophia's trawlers himself, using funds he'd taken from the same thugs that had threatened her.

No, she wouldn't send the FBI. She might not come at all, but if she did, it would be days before she arrived. He had to get out of the city and couldn't wait that long to do it. Get out? And go where? Like Julio, Sophia was part of his plan for getting out of America. He doubted distance offered safety any more.

The clip behind the anchor changed. This footage was shot in Times Square. Six of those inhuman creatures were clustered on the ground, tearing and ripping at some unseen body. One cricked its head. Its empty, lifeless eyes stared right into the lens. Slowly, it stood. The camera didn't move. The creature staggered closer. Behind it, the others began to rise. The zombie's red-stained mouth gaped open. The image abruptly changed to an aerial shot of a road crammed with cars.

The anchor didn't say what had happened to the person who'd shot that footage. Since someone had uploaded it to the television network, Tom assumed they'd survived, but for how long? How long would anyone survive in this city? Where was the official response? Where was the CDC?

And then he knew where he had to go. Max needed proof of the conspiracy, but he also needed answers as to what this outbreak was. Tom tapped at the laptop, cursed the slow connection, and finally found the file he was after, the one that contained information on Dr Ayers.

She was insane, though a court had ruled she wasn't. He'd first come across her when looking for the scientists behind Project Archangel. A decade ago she'd been employed by the CDC. During a viral outbreak in West Africa, she'd smuggled infected tissue samples back to the United States. She'd found a cure and tested it on her grad students. That they'd knowingly volunteered for it, and that the anti-viral had worked, had kept her out of prison. It had also led to her being barred from going within five miles of a high school laboratory, let alone anything more complex.

The address was near the Allegheny National Forest, on the western edge of Pennsylvania. Would she still be there? From outside came a long, high-pitched scream. She might not be there. She might be unable to help. She might already be in some government lab. Her house wasn't so much a destination as a direction in which to head. On the way, he would look for a refuge where he could go through all the files, and attempt to decipher what was going on.

It wasn't a great plan, but as if to underscore the need to get out of the city, there came another scream from outside. It was time to leave Manhattan, and the best way out was still going to be by boat.

Chapter 3 - Supplies
Harlem, New York

The suit was barely warm enough for a summer's evening, let alone a wintery trek across the city before a midnight boat ride into the unknown. However, it was what he had, and almost *all* he had. The sat-phone and tablet were in one pocket, with five thousand dollars in another. The money was another breadcrumb. The bills were marked, in the hope that Powell would take and spend them. With access to most of his bank accounts cut off, it had been a real hardship not dipping into the fund during the lean days of the last month.

There were no weapons in the apartment. Though he'd identified Powell and a few of his goons, many of the people hunting for him were legitimate officers of the law. If he had a gun, he might use it, and suspected that was what Farley wanted. Now he regretted that prudence. He pulled his collar up and left the apartment building.

The streetlights worked, but the road outside was quiet. The silence was unsettling. Where were the sirens? The police? Where was the National Guard? Halfway down the block, a delivery truck had crashed into a parked sedan. There was no sign of the passengers, nor, unsurprisingly, any towing service. A narrow stretch of road was visible between the erratically parked and abandoned vehicles on this street, but he knew gridlock was only a few blocks away. Opposite, a couple hastily loaded a beat-up hatchback. He thought of warning them that there was no way of driving out of the city. He doubted they'd listen. Instead, he crossed to the bodega on the corner, pushed at the door, and was surprised when it opened. Rami, the middle-aged co-owner of the store, was behind the counter, just as he always was during the evening shift.

"Hey, are you open?" Tom asked.

"Cash only," Rami said, not taking his eyes from the small television next to the register.

"Fair enough." Tom grabbed a six-pack of vitamin water from the shelf, and placed it on the counter, adding a box of candy bars that claimed to have thirty-three percent more nuts. He wasn't sure what they were using for comparison, but that gave him protein, water, vitamins, sugar, and carbs. It was almost a balanced diet.

"Do you have bleach?"

"What? Bleach? Yes, over there." Rami jerked a thumb toward the back of the store. The clerk's eyes stayed glued to the screen, on which military uniforms were setting up a checkpoint. The ticker read 'City In Lockdown', but the footage wasn't of Manhattan. Tom wasn't even sure it was in America.

He wandered through the store, vaguely looking at the shelves. His brain switched gears from the mystery of what had happened to the puzzle of what was going on. More precisely, to why no official response seemed to be going on anywhere that he could see or hear. Did it change his plans? No. He picked up a bottle of bleach, then another, wondering if any commercially available disinfectant would be strong enough.

The bell above the shop's door jangled. Tom moved a few inches, so he could see who'd entered. Two men, in their early twenties, both dressed in dark denim, black hoodies, and bulky sneakers that were more logo than style. One had a baseball cap covering his eyes, the other a gold chain so large it was obviously fake.

"Rami, how are you?" the one in the baseball cap said, with menacing cordiality.

"We're closed," Rami said. Tom could sense what was coming. He looked around for another way out, but the only other exit was behind the counter.

"Good," the one with the gold chain said, Eastern Europe clear in his accent. "We're taking payment in advance. Two years in advance."

"I can't pay that."

"Then we'll take goods," baseball cap said.

There was a moment's silence. "Fine," Rami said. "Take what you want."

Tom relaxed. There was a limit to what the two thugs could carry. As soon as their arms were full, they'd go, and then he could do the same.

"You don't understand," gold chain drawled. "We're taking your store. Everything here is ours."

Baseball cap walked to the door, and slid the bolts at top and bottom. He glanced toward Rami, gave a feral grin, and flipped the sign to closed. Tom mentally cursed. This was the last thing he needed.

"I don't... I don't understand," Rami said.

"You seen the news?" gold chain asked. "The city's in lockdown. No food's gonna come in for days. Maybe weeks. It's like my man says, he who controls the supply controls the demand."

This wasn't going to end well, but Tom didn't panic. He'd been in far worse situations than this. His family had died when he was a child. He'd spent his teens helping smuggle drugs and guns through a heavily policed city. That life ended when he walked into a bloodbath and was the only one to walk out alive. He'd taken a bag of cash, and another of forged passports, and fled to America. Though in recent decades information had been his weapon of choice, it hadn't always been his final resort. Two callow youths could be swiftly dealt with. No, he wasn't worried, not until the man with the gold chain pulled out a revolver.

Tom swore. Perhaps it was exhaustion, or perhaps it was an angry externalization of all that had happened that day, but he swore out loud.

"Who's there?" baseball cap called, drawing a weapon of his own.

Tom stepped out from around the shelves, bottle of bleach in one hand, nothing in the other. "Just buying some bleach," he said. "It's good for infections."

"Infections? You infected?" gold chain asked, taking a step back.

"What do we do? What do we do?" baseball cap asked. He was shifting agitatedly from foot to foot, the gun's barrel drawing a circle in the air. If he fired, there was a good chance he'd miss. Tom wasn't willing to take the bet.

"Glass windows like that aren't going to offer you much protection," Tom said. As he spoke, he extended his arm toward the front of the store, using the movement to take a surreptitious step closer to the two men. "You need to take the supplies and find somewhere high up. The top floor of a building with at least two stairwells would be my recommendation." He shifted his stance again, sliding another step forward. Another three feet and he'd be able to topple the set of shelves onto the pair of them. "And," he added, "you need to act quickly, before the army comes rolling down the street." He'd said something wrong.

The man with the gold chain sneered. "Army's not going to come. Not here. No cops, neither. Ain't you heard? They've gone."

"What do we do?" baseball cap asked again.

Gold chain shifted aim. "The cops won't care. We kill—"

There was a shot. Gold chain flew backward, slamming into the aisle. Baseball cap pulled the trigger, but Tom was already diving forward. The bullet sailed past him. He reached out, grabbing the man's wrist, twisting the hand up and back. The gun fired again, the retort muffling the sound of bone snapping. The thug screamed. Tom jabbed his left hand into the man's throat. The screaming stopped as the man collapsed, sobbing for air. Tom grabbed the revolver from the ground. He took a step, and another, backing around the shelves so he could see the thug with the gold chain. The man was dead.

"Okay," he began, uncertain what to say next. "Okay, I—"

There was another loud boom. The face underneath the baseball cap disintegrated. Tom turned around. There was a young woman next to Rami, a shotgun in her hand. She looked terrified, but her hands were steady, and the gun was now pointing at Tom.

"It's over," Tom said, slow and calm. "It's over."

Rami came out of whatever shock had been gripping him. He grabbed the gun from the girl. "I shot them," he said. "Me. Not her."

"It won't matter," Tom said. "That man was right. The police won't care. Fire another shot into that man's head and say they were zombies. Like on the news." He walked over to the counter and picked up a tote bag. The water went in, and then the box of candy. "If I were you, I'd drag them outside, turn the lights off, and lock the doors." He slung the bag over his shoulder. "Then paint the windows so no one can see in. Barricade them. The police aren't coming." He took a step back. "Not for days. Maybe weeks. You've got food here, and water." He took another step back. "Enough to last you until this is all over."

Rami nodded. "You think weeks?"

"I really do," Tom said. "But you can keep your family safe. Take the bodies outside." He took another step, and now he was at the door. "Block the doors." He raised a hand, pointing at the shelf behind the counter. "Do those cameras work?"

"What?" Rami turned around to look. Tom opened the door and stepped outside before the spell had a chance to break.

He began a slow jog along the sidewalk, wanting to put distance between him and the store. He took the first alley he came to, then kept on jogging down the next road, only slowing when he was three blocks away.

He could be wrong. The police might come. Part of him hoped they would, that any minute now, he'd hear sirens. He didn't. The streets were deserted. There were lights in some windows, but just as many were dark. From the occasional glow of a screen, he could tell there were people in there. Watching. Waiting. Hoping that dawn's first light would bring an end to the nightmare. He knew it wouldn't.

Chapter 4 - Leaving
Manhattan, New York

The Seventy-Ninth Street Boat Basin was a marina on the west of Manhattan where people could live in their boats year-round. Thanks to a city ordinance a few years before, those boats had to be sea-worthy even if their live-aboard owners never untied them from their moorings.

He'd taken a walk down to the basin during a tense afternoon two weeks ago, when he had nothing to do but wait to see if his plans would work or collapse. He'd looked at the boats – some new, some old, some desperately in need of repair – and imagined sailing away to someplace warm. He'd turned around and walked back to the small room, knowing that if he stayed there looking at the boats for too long, he'd succumb to the ocean's siren song.

Now the idea of a boat was more beguiling than ever. It was almost twelve hours since the outbreak had hit social media. Untold thousands must already have fled Manhattan, joining ranks with the tens of thousands on the other side of the Hudson. With the zombies already ahead of them, theirs would be no orderly migration. The safest course of action was to hunker down, but that wasn't an option for him. Like the old adage said, the best way to get somewhere was to start from somewhere else. A boat would take him up the coast, beyond the densest of the suburban sprawl orbiting New York, and perhaps ahead of the refugees. A long night of driving, and he might reach western Pennsylvania soon after dawn.

Behind him, something wooden banged against something metal. A plaintive cry came from above, followed by the slamming of a window. Music momentarily blared from an unseen speaker before being abruptly turned off. Compared to the previous day, compared to any of the days he'd spent in New York, it was as quiet as the grave.

A clattering rattle of metal came from an alley to his right. A soda can, blown by the wind, he decided. Except there was no wind. The rattle came again, and with it something else. Something more guttural, almost a moan. He crossed the road and picked up his pace.

One block west and one south, a bright yellow van had crashed into the window of a shoe-store. Sneakers of every lurid color had spilled into the road. There were no staff or security guards, and from the look of it, no one had come to steal the merchandise. Somehow, that was more troubling than anything else he'd seen.

The rear of the van had been levered open. The inside was coated in a dusting of soil and a few broken wooden crates. From the fragments, he pieced together the logo of an organic grocery, but all the produce was gone. He thought of the two men who'd tried to rob that store. Had society really collapsed so swiftly? Had the perceived value of goods changed so fast?

A cab had crashed into the side of the van, reducing the road to a single lane. As he continued south, he passed more wrecks, and more abandoned cars behind them. The complete absence of people was getting to him. New York was a city of millions, and Manhattan was one of the most densely populated areas of real estate on the planet, and yet it was almost as if he had it to himself.

The ground under his foot changed, becoming sticky. He'd stepped in something. Blood. He heard a noise, similar to yet different from the moaning sigh he'd heard before. With it came a rustling bang as if someone was dragging themselves along a wall. He drew the revolver he'd taken from the now-dead thug and crossed to the middle of the road. Get to a boat. Put out to sea. He'd be safe. The idea lodged in his brain, going round and round, growing in appeal.

A hand slapped against a car's window, an inch from his side. A face appeared, a snarling, snapping apparition absent of all humanity. The hand banged against glass. Tom backed away. Something pulled on his coat. He spun around, tugging it free from the arm reaching out through an open window. The banging continued in stereo as it was joined by others. Not near, but not far enough away. He ran, sometimes in the road, sometimes along the sidewalk, only slowing when he reached a street almost clear of traffic. Something big had passed this way, shunting the stalled and abandoned cars away from the median. With some distance between himself and those steel tombs, he told himself to relax. There had been only four zombies. Maybe five. That's all. Perhaps six. Seven at the outside. Maybe ten. Twenty. A hundred. A million. An undead city in which he was the only one left.

He was running again. He forced himself to stop. Stay calm. Stay rational. There was no way *not* to think about the surrounding horror, so he tried to think about it constructively. How had those people ended up in the cars? They were in the southbound lane, as if they'd been heading toward the outbreak. Had they been infected by some passing refugee after they'd decided to flee? The questions were pointless and based on an assumption for which he had no evidence. He was assuming that the virus was passed on by blood and saliva because that was what the television had said. Sure, he'd seen video footage of people being bitten, but that wasn't proof. It was an assumption, because that's how it worked in the movies. The virus could be airborne, but only a fraction of the population was susceptible. Or only a fraction was immune. Or it could be somewhere in between, or almost anything else. There was no way of knowing, not right now, but that ignorance would kill him.

Ahead came the sound of breaking glass. With it came voices. At any other time, he would have taken a different direction. After what had happened in the bodega, he knew he should. Right now, and above all else, he wanted to know that other people were alive. Not wanting to look openly hostile, he put the revolver in his pocket, but kept a hand on it as he approached.

They were looters, and they were organized. A group of at least twenty were systematically emptying a grocery store. Two more stood guard to the west, with three, near him, to the east. Those five were all armed with long guns, though the weapons were held casually.

One of the three walked over to the broken window and took the arm of a young woman carrying something outside. The woman looked down, and then gave a short laugh before heading back into the building. Tom was about to turn away and find another route when the man spotted him.

"Hey!" he called. "Something moving!" The four sentries raised their weapons. Tom raised a hand. The guns were lowered. The sentries even seemed to relax. Curious, Tom stepped forward.

"You shouldn't be out here," the leader said. "It's not safe for anyone."

"I'm just passing through."

"No," the man said. "You need to get inside and stay there. Where do you live?"

"The Upper West Side," Tom said, naming somewhere not far from the marina.

The man shook his head. "Do you have food? Water? Enough supplies for at least two weeks?"

Tom raised the tote bag.

The man gave a rueful shake of his head. "You're going to need more than that. What are you going to do when the water's cut off?"

"You think it will be?" Tom asked.

"Don't you know what's going on?" the man asked.

"You mean the… the zombies?"

The man grimaced. "Yeah, everyone's calling them that. It doesn't matter how many times I tell them it isn't true. But no, that's not what I mean. I was talking about the police. Didn't you hear?"

"Hear what?"

"Yeah, how could you? We were called back, told to leave Manhattan."

"You're a cop?"

"Detective. I live here. This is my city. There's no way I'm going to leave on the say of some politician, but most did. All our support's gone. Can't get through to the chief. Hell, I can't get through to anyone. They left us to ourselves, to fester and tear one another apart. You've got to go home or find somewhere safe. Fill every container with water. Start breaking your furniture for firewood. Speak to your neighbors. Work together. Secure the building, and the block. Together we can beat this. Alone we'll die. There's more food here than we can take. Get your neighbors, come back, take what you can. Or find somewhere else. Take anything that'll go bad from any store unlikely to open tomorrow."

49

"Right, sure. Yeah, maybe I'll come back," Tom said. "Thanks. Good luck."

"And to you."

Tom threw an occasional glance at the group as he went past. It was somehow uplifting seeing people work together. On the other hand, the news that Manhattan had been left to fend for itself was contrary to everything Tom knew about Max. That was something else to think about when he was on the water, heading away from the island.

Chapter 5 - Blockade
The 79ᵗʰ Street Boat Basin, New York

The Seventy-Ninth Street Boat Basin wasn't so much up and coming as came up and went. Where the boats had gone, he couldn't guess, but only one was left. A thirty-foot yacht with a mast and motor, and reddish stains he knew were rust, but which he couldn't help but think of as blood. Two lamps cast dim shadows on the boat, the jetty, and the small group of people. He should have thought this through. Of course the boats would be gone, and this last one was spoken for. Twice over, judging by the confrontational nature of the scene.

A woman stood, legs braced, on the jetty. Ten feet from her were two men and two women, dressed in expensive outdoor clothing that looked too clean to have ever been worn outside a dressing room. In contrast, the boat-woman's faded jeans and bulky jacket looked far more suitable to a life at sea. Tom stepped into the shadows, moving slowly and quietly, assessing his odds of getting to the yacht.

"You can come with us, Helena," one of the women in the group of four said.

"No. I told you," the boat-woman, presumably Helena, said. "This boat isn't going anywhere."

"The boat is," one of the men said. "With you, or without you."

"Enough talking, Trent," the second man said. "Let's go."

"I told you," Helena said. "You can't."

There was no fear in her voice, just mild exasperation, and clearly she knew these people. Tom's hand strayed to the gun. He could take the yacht easily enough. From what that detective had said, even if the 911 call was answered, no one would respond. Except stealing the boat at gunpoint was unnecessary. Whether she realized it or not, this woman, Helena, *would* be safer off the island, and in the company of others.

He took a step forward, sizing up the group, deciding that it was the man, Trent, who needed to be reasoned with. How to do it? Pretend to be a cop?

From somewhere inland came a trio of shots, a brief squawk from a siren, a burst from an automatic weapon, and then silence. It lasted only a second before the air was pierced by a scream.

"It's time to go, Trent," the second man said.

"Last chance, Helena," Trent said. "See reason. Come with us." The man spoke as if he was absolutely certain he was going to get what he wanted. Tom drew the revolver, but kept it behind his back as he stepped out of the shadows, whistling a few bars of the first song that came to mind.

"A bad night to be out," he said. "There's looting and worse throughout the city. The police have been called back to checkpoints on the mainland. This isn't a safe place to be."

"Who are you?" one of the women said.

"Just a guy looking for a way out," Tom said. "And that yacht fits the bill."

"Don't you understand?" Helena said. "Don't any of you understand? No one's taking the boat!"

"We are," Trent said, but his eyes were on Tom.

"We all should," Tom said. "I doubt there's much fuel for the motor, but that sail should carry us a good way along the coast. We can get ahead of the people who fled during the day. That would be safest for all of us."

"Trent?" the blonde said, a warning tone to her voice.

"Go away," Trent said to Tom. "And get out the way," he added to Helena.

"No!" Helena cried. "Why won't you listen?"

The blonde swore, half turned around, and turned back with a small gun in her hand. Tom ducked as she fired in his direction. The round went wide. She fired again as he rolled away from the light. He pushed himself to his knees, raising the revolver. Helena was on the ground. The four of them were running onto the yacht. The blonde fired again. Tom hesitated and did it too long. The rope was cut. The boat began drifting out into the Hudson.

Slowly, he stood.

"No," Helena said, from her knees. "You have to come back. You have to! I tried to tell you. I tried to warn you!"

The engine chugged into life, and the yacht drew further away.

"I tried to warn them," Helena called again, though this time she was speaking to the sky.

Tom walked over to her. "You need to get out of here," he said, pulling her to her feet. "It's not safe."

She shook his arm free. "I tried to warn them," she repeated.

The words sank in. "Warn them of what?" he asked, looking out at the yacht's blinking lights. Helena didn't need to reply. The boat was lit up by a pair of searchlights. Tom peered out across the water, trying to see from where they came. Ships, obviously, but he couldn't make them out.

A voice echoed across the water. "Unidentified vessel. Turn back. Return to shore." A moment later the message repeated.

The people on the yacht made no attempt to turn around.

"I told them," Helena said. "I tried to warn them."

"Unidentified vessel. Turn back. This is your last warning."

Was it turning? Before he could tell, there was a flash of fire, an echoing boom, and the yacht was gone.

"I tried to warn them," Helena whispered. "They came here this afternoon. Said no more boats could leave. Freddie didn't listen. Joan got sick, you see. Attacked by someone. Freddie couldn't get an ambulance. The roads… He thought it would be easier to go across to New Jersey. They sunk the boat."

"And the other boats?" Tom asked. "There were dozens of craft here a couple of weeks ago."

"Most left this morning. The rest tried to leave after dark. They were all sunk. I said they shouldn't. I said they should listen to the Navy. People don't listen."

The searchlights played across the burning wreckage as if highlighting the good sense of her words. They went out. Now he knew where to look, Tom thought he could make out the silhouette of a warship. It was too dark, with too much light coming from the shore, to identify what kind.

"Who were those four people? They knew you."

53

"I worked with them. I didn't like them much. Especially Chloe, but…" She trailed off into something halfway between a sob and a sigh. "I'm Helena Diomedes," she said, holding out a hand.

"Tom Clemens," Tom said. Only after the words were said did he remember he should have used one of his other aliases.

"You didn't shoot them," Helena said, gesturing at the gun in Tom's hand.

"I wanted the boat. I didn't want to murder for it."

"And now they're dead."

There was another scream in the distance.

"Where do you live?" Tom asked.

"On the boat," Helena said.

"Ah. Do you have friends near here? Someone you can stay with?"

"What? Oh, yes. Tammy, I suppose. She's not far. Just a couple of blocks."

Had he taken the boat, he wouldn't have turned back when ordered, and so would now be dead. In a small and accidental way, this woman had saved his life. Escorting her a few blocks seemed the least he could do. "I'll walk you," Tom said.

She looked skeptically at him. Her gaze dropped to the revolver, and skepticism changed to outright suspicion. There was a third, louder scream.

"Okay," she said, with evident reluctance. "It's over there." She waved a hand to the north. "What about you, where do you live?"

"Harlem. But I was trying to get back to my family."

"Oh. Right. That's why you wanted the boat?"

"The bridges and tunnels were blocked. I thought a boat might get me further, quicker."

"Do you think they'll stop it?"

"Stop what?" he asked.

"The virus. That's why they're not allowing boats off. They said there was a quarantine, to stop the virus from getting out of Manhattan."

"You don't know? It's already beyond the island," he said. "It's spreading throughout the country."

Chapter 6 - The Bridge
Manhattan, New York

The naval blockade and the police withdrawal had kicked Tom's paranoia into overdrive. He wanted to check the tablet, dreading that he'd have his worst fears confirmed, but knowing that was better than traveling in ignorance. Yet he couldn't, not while Helena was with him. He made a few attempts at conversation, but they were cut short by the sound of distant gunfire.

"That's it," Helena said as they turned a corner, pointing at an apartment building. "So, um, thanks, I guess. I'll—"

"Wait," Tom hissed. Outside the apartment door were a group of figures. Three? No, four. Their arms moved up, down, raising and falling, as if they were knocking at the closed door. He pulled Helena back into the shadows.

"What is it?" she asked.

"Didn't you see?"

"I think that's Mrs Kenton," Helena said, taking a step forward. "She must have forgotten her key."

"It's not her," Tom said. "Not anymore."

"What? You mean…" She trailed off.

"Is that the building?" he asked.

"Mrs Kenton has the apartment below Tammy," Helena said.

The figure at the back of the small group jerked around. It moved as if its limbs were on wires being pulled by an unseen hand. Arm and then leg, each movement was disjointed and unnatural as it staggered into the pool of light from a streetlamp. Its mouth slowly opened, letting out a low, breathy hiss.

"We need to go," Tom said, pulling Helena's arm. She was immobile a second longer, and that was long enough for the other two creatures to turn toward them.

"Now," Tom said, dragging her back down the alley up which they'd just walked.

"But…" Helena began. "But…" She didn't seem to have any other words to add to her protest at this sudden horror.

"They're zombies. That's what the news said," Helena said when they were two blocks away.

"It's as good a word as any," Tom said, staring at the empty street.

"But it's impossible," Helena said.

"Whatever they really are, think of them as zombies for now. We don't have the luxury of worrying about being accurate." It was the road the detective and his gang of looters had been on, he was sure of it. The grocery store window was broken, but there was no sign of the group he'd passed on his way to the marina. Had the detective said where he lived? No, and no clue had been left to suggest where the group had gone.

"Who's Tammy?" he asked, hoping he might be able to prompt her into remembering some other, nearby friend.

"What? Oh, she's the deputy principal at the school."

"You have kids?" Tom asked, suddenly horrified at the thought of who else might have been on the yacht.

"No. I'm a teacher," Helena said. "Last semester, I was sick. Flu. Tammy came round to pick up some papers I'd been grading. She saw my apartment, heard my neighbors. Said I couldn't stay there. She said I could stay in the boat. It was kind. Or mostly kind. She knew I was thinking of leaving. I'd mentioned it a few times. I like New York, but it—" She stopped, as if remembering Tom was a complete stranger. "What's happening? What are these things?"

"Zombies is as good a word as any other," Tom said. He started walking north.

"Yeah, but they're not, are they? I mean, not really."

"This isn't the time to overthink it. Do you know anyone else?"

"In Manhattan? No. I mean, yes, of course, but not where they live. I should go to the police, I suppose. To report it, I mean. You know, that they stole the boat, and that they're dead."

"The police are gone," he said. "The only authorities left are the ones who sunk your yacht."

56

"Gone? You said something about that before. What did you mean?"

"They were overwhelmed, so they pulled back to the mainland. I don't know on whose orders, but we're on our own for now."

They walked on in silence. Every rustle, every rattle, every little sound seemed to presage one of the undead.

"Where are we going?" Helena asked.

"I have an apartment about a mile from here. There isn't much there, but it'll be safe for you until dawn. Maybe by then…" And now it was his turn to trail off. He couldn't bring himself to lie and say things were going to get better.

"And you?" she asked.

"The George Washington Bridge," he said. "They were setting up checkpoints earlier, but it was clear of traffic. It might be a way out." And if it wasn't, he was running out of options.

"Why? I mean, if I'm going to be safe in this apartment, then wouldn't you be?"

"Shh!"

There was a sound from nearby, and he couldn't place where. It was getting closer, more distinct. A rasping, coughing wheeze. A figure staggered out of a doorway, collapsing to the ground twenty feet in front of them. Tom paused. Helena didn't. She ran toward the figure. Tom tried to stop her, but she moved quickly, bending down, looking for a pulse. From his clothing, Tom guessed he was a vagrant. He raised the revolver, taking aim.

"There's no pulse," Helena said.

The tramp's clothing was more stain than cloth, any one of which could have been blood.

"There's nothing we can do," Tom said.

Ignoring him, Helena pulled out her phone.

"No one's going to come," Tom said.

"That doesn't mean we shouldn't try," she said.

"That's not—"

There was a loud bang of wood hitting stone. Tom managed to turn around just as a clawing, snarling figure tumbled out of the doorway. Its flailing arms knocked the revolver from his hand. He grabbed one arm, then the other, but the creature's momentum pushed him to his knees. The mouth snapped. Its dark, gaping maw got closer and closer. He tried to turn and twist the creature away. He had a grip on each of its wrists, but it was flailing and shoving, and he didn't have enough purchase to push it clear. Its mouth jutted forward, biting, nearer. Nearer. Tom let go of the arms, ducked his head forward, butting the creature in the stomach. He grabbed its legs, one at the thigh, and the other by the knee. He pulled, dragging the zombie from its feet. It tumbled down into the road.

The thing moved in a completely inhuman fashion. Trying to stand, it didn't use its arms to push. They flailed, slapping and clawing at the road as it rolled to its side, and then its knees, all the time the teeth kept snapping up and down, up and down, up and—

There was a roar of a gun. The creature's head disintegrated.

"Zombies," Helena said. "Zombies." Her voice shook, and so did her hands as Tom took the gun from her.

"They're real," she said. "Really real."

"Yes," Tom said. "Yes, they are."

She took a sudden, terrified step back. "What about him," she asked pointing at the vagrant. The man hadn't moved.

"Heart attack, maybe?" Tom said. It was a guess, and as much of an explanation as either of them needed. Walking more quickly, jogging every time they heard a sound, they kept moving.

Outside his apartment building, blue and red lights danced across the puddles.

"Finally!" Helena said. "Normality."

Tom quietly cursed. The clerk in the bodega must have called the police. Well, he'd done his duty, he'd found somewhere safe for Helena. He could retreat back into the shadows, and head to the bridge. No doubt she'd tell them whom she'd been with, and when he'd introduced himself, he'd said his name was Tom Clemens. That was a problem, but reports would have to be taken and processed, crosschecked and filed. That would all take time, and he'd be long gone before they were after him. Except the two cars were unmarked, black SUVs, and they were parked on the wrong side of the street. They were outside his apartment building. A figure stepped away from a vehicle. He had a hand holding a phone to his ear, but there was no mistaking the shock of pure white hair.

He grabbed Helena's arm. "It's not safe. Trust me."

"What? Why? That's the police."

"Okay, the short version?" he said frantically searching for a believable lie. He could only come up with the plot of a book he'd read the previous week. "I was in the bodega. A group of crooked cops came in. They were running protection for a money-laundering outfit. They'd decided to seize the store and all its supplies. The clerk opened fire. I got out of there, and that's why I went looking for a boat. I mean, if you can't trust the police, what do you do? You get as far away as possible."

Helena looked between Tom and the flashing lights. Her expression was a study in disbelief.

"Look," Tom said. "How many other cops have you seen tonight? That lot are using this crisis to clear house. You can go over to them if you want, but they're not going to offer you refuge. At best, they'll drive away, leaving you here, alone. They probably won't hurt you, but what will you do then?"

"Then what am I supposed to do?" she asked. There was genuine desperation in her voice as if it was finally sinking in that the world she'd known was never coming back.

"Get out of Manhattan," Tom said. "While we still can."

"If we still can," Helena said, but she let him lead her away.

It was barely four miles to the George Washington Bridge, but traveling in a straight line was impossible. Shuffling zombies effectively blocked some roads. On other streets, snarling, captive creatures reached through the broken windows of cars abandoned fender to fender. They tried clambering over trunk, roof, and hood, but that set off a kicking, punching cacophony beneath their feet.

It was approaching one a.m. when Tom realized they were further from the bridge than the apartment. They stopped to rest on the stoop of a crumbling apartment building. Tom fished out the sat-phone and tablet.

"I thought you said there was no point trying to call anyone," Helena said.

"I did. I want to access the traffic cameras," he said. "Maybe there's another way. The subway tunnels or—"

"Hey!" The yell came from above them. A moment later there was a gunshot. They ran, not stopping until they came to the edge of Central Park. There was barely enough time for Tom to reach into his bag for a bottle of water before the sound of shuffling, irregular feet had them moving again.

Tom was exhausted. There was no escaping the fact that he was approaching fifty. He'd tried to stay fit, but exercise had taken a backseat during the campaign, and the last month had been filled with junk food and little sleep. Whatever reserves of nervous energy he'd stored up were ebbing away. His eyes were heavy, his breathing the same. Helena didn't look much better. Shock had carried her through the first hectic hours after they'd left the marina, and now the reality of all the death and horror was sinking in. She'd become silent, and Tom saw no reason to draw her out.

They almost walked straight into the band of looters. Unlike the group organized by the detective, these were far from friendly. Two gunshots had them running randomly again, though dark, ominous streets, but ten minutes later, they saw a sign pointing to the bridge.

A door slammed shut ahead of them. A man pushed a bicycle down the steps of a seven-floor apartment block, and out into the road. Tom raised his hand in what would have been a greeting if it hadn't been holding the revolver. The man hurried away, half-pushing, half-dragging his bike.

"I guess he thought I was trying to rob him," Tom said.

"A bike would be handy," Helena muttered. She pulled out her phone. "Four a.m. Dawn will be here soon." She tapped at the keypad as she'd done at least twice an hour since they'd left Tom's apartment behind. "Still no signal."

"Who are you trying to call?"

"My sister. She's not close, but—" And again she stopped, as if remembering that Tom was an unknown, and armed, stranger.

He gestured at the sign pointing toward the upper deck of the double-decker bridge. There was no logic to the choice. Once they were on the bridge there would be no escape except forward or back, but after all he'd been through, he wanted the illusory comfort of being able to see the sky.

What, on the traffic cameras, he'd thought was a checkpoint had been a roadblock. A bus had crashed through it, and into the side of an armored personnel carrier. Other vehicles had tried to drive through the gap. It was impossible to know whether any had made it further onto the bridge, but the two cars wedged in the gap had their tires blown out and bullet holes in their engines. As to who had fired those shots, there was no sign. Beyond the APC were two yellow diggers.

"I saw those clearing the bridge," Tom said as they walked past.

"You did?" Helena jumped up the steps of the nearest. "The keys are still in here."

"Do you know how to drive it?" Tom asked, looking down the length of the bridge.

"No," she said, jumping down.

"Pity."

They crossed the bridge, no longer walking together, but not yet walking apart, though soon they would each go their own way. They were just two more refugees, like the others crossing the bridge with them. There were around thirty, and there was enough light to make out the silhouettes of a few dozen more ahead. The cyclist overtook them. Too many bags hung from the crossbar for him to ride it properly. Instead he had his left foot on the right-hand pedal and was pushing it along as if it were a scooter.

They were alive. That was all that mattered. But what had he really achieved? It had taken most of the night to cross a few miles of city. Ahead lay a vast continent in which he had no real refuge, few friends, and which was now peopled by the impossible undead. The temptation to run and hide was strong. The desire to travel far, far away was stronger. Perhaps Julio would still be at the airfield. He could call him and… An image of the diggers came to mind.

"Yellow," he muttered. They were civilian models taken from some construction site, not the type used by the military. He looked down the length of the bridge, seeing it properly for the first time. The pre-dawn light added weird shadows and curving shapes, but there was no mistaking how empty it was. They'd set up a roadblock, not a checkpoint. Why? Why had they cleared the bridge? There were no lanes marked out for the millions of refugees who would descend upon it in a few short hours. Nor were there any military personnel ready to organize and control that exodus. So why clear the bridge? There were hundreds of people behind them now. A long ragged line that would only grow as the day wore on.

"No helicopters. No checkpoints. Helena, what was it you said about the boat? A quarantine?"

"What?" she asked, her face showing nothing but exhaustion. It didn't matter. He knew what she'd said, and he knew what it all meant.

"We need to run!" He grabbed her arm, dragging her along until her feet overruled her brain. They ran, and some of the other refugees copied them. A few called out questions. Tom ignored them. He should have realized. She'd practically told him, but he'd not listened. They were quarantining Manhattan. You couldn't do that without destroying the bridges and tunnels.

They ran past the first set of skeletal steel supporting columns. Halfway across, they passed a pair of maintenance trucks, abandoned on the road. In the back were… he wasn't sure. Folding tables, perhaps, or partitions from some office building. Did they originally have a proper evacuation plan for Manhattan that was abandoned in favor of cutting the island off from the rest of the world? And why civilian vehicles? He didn't have the breath to think. He barely had it to run.

Two-thirds of the way across the bridge, cars and trucks had been shunted to the side of the road, not pushed down into the Hudson. He ignored them, his eyes fixed on the skyline of Fort Lee, growing more distinct as the sun rose behind them.

"Look!" Helena yelled, waving to the south. He'd already heard it approach. A fighter jet buzzed the bridge, flying scant feet above the supporting wires.

"It's coming," Tom tried to yell, but he didn't have the breath. He knew what was going to happen. There was a sound in the background, almost like people, yelling. And there, horns. A siren. The sound was coming from ahead. At the far end of the bridge was a solitary military vehicle. An APC with a mounted machine gun that was pointed straight at them. Tom raised a hand, trying to wave and show that he was still human.

The road shifted beneath his feet. It rose like a wave, and he fell. A sea of noise washed over him. All sound was replaced by a buzzing drone. He could taste iron in his mouth. He tried to stand, but his legs were unsteady. No, it was the bridge itself, shaking and undulating and tearing itself apart. A hand grabbed his arm. Helena hauled him to his feet, and it was her turn to drag him along the shifting, cracking asphalt, through a storm of dust and dirt that was followed by a rain of concrete and steel. Her mouth was open, but he couldn't hear her scream. Couldn't hear anything except that high-pitched tone that grew louder and lower into a wall of white noise that became a metallic wail as the bridge collapsed behind them. And then, just as quickly, they stumbled out of the cloud of dust, and into a rifle barrel.

"Say something!" a soldier barked. "Say something!"

Tom opened his mouth, managing nothing more than a rasping wheeze. The soldier's eyes went wide, and the barrel moved forward, to point at Tom's forehead.

"Wait!" Helena said. "What do you want us to say?"

"Say something!" the soldier screamed the words at Tom.

"Trying. Trying to," he managed. The words were more cough than coherent, but it was enough for the soldier. He moved on, past them. Tom turned to watch. There were other figures stumbling out of the cloud of dust, but not nearly as many as had been on the bridge.

Gloved hands gripped Tom's arms.

"Move! This way!"

Half pushed, half dragged, he staggered off the ruined bridge.

Chapter 7 - Searched
February 21ˢᵗ, Fort Lee, New Jersey

"What the hell were you thinking?" a woman asked. Her uniform had no badges of rank, but from her tone and demeanor, she was in charge. "Didn't you hear the warnings?"

Tom tried to reply, but all that came out was a coughing fit.

"There were no warnings," Helena said.

The officer shook her head, her expression one of irritated disbelief. "Line up," she said. "Follow the fences until you reach processing." She waved a hand toward a mass of metal fencing that snaked back and forth across the interstate.

"Here," a soldier said, holding out a canteen to Tom. "Rinse and spit."

Tom did, spewing a gobbet of grey dirt onto the filthy roadway. He offered the canteen back to the soldier.

"No," the woman said. "Keep it. Your need's greater than mine." The tone was kindly, but the words were portentous. So were the fences. They ran north to south on a road that traveled east to west, and stretched for at least a mile. How many people could they contain? Thousands? Tens of thousands?

Helena took the water bottle from his hand. "Look at that," she said.

He looked around and wished he hadn't. Smoke poured upward from the island of Manhattan. The plumes weren't big, just narrow columns. Caught by the Atlantic breeze, they drifted southward.

"Do you think the other bridges are gone?" Helena asked. Her expression was unreadable beneath a thick coating of dust, but her tone was anxious.

"Probably," he said.

"Then no help will get there," Helena said. "No fire trucks. No ambulances."

"No."

"That's…" She turned around. "They've killed them all. No food. No help. No electricity. No water. I can't believe the president would do that."

"He wouldn't," Tom said.

"But he has. He's killed them all."

Tom didn't argue. The fences, clearing the bridge of stalled traffic, even the military presence suggested the original plan had been for an evacuation of Manhattan. At some point during the night, that had been abandoned in favor of quarantine.

"And quarantine isn't going to work. The zombies are already ahead of us."

"You said that before. Are you sure?" she asked.

He hadn't meant to speak aloud. "I am," he said.

"Maybe they're dead, and the outbreak's under control," she said. There was little confidence in her voice.

Though the barriers had been set up to form a snaking corridor for at least half a mile, a gap had been cleared down the middle. In the narrow alleyways that remained, and across the clear stretch of road, the ground was littered with the detritus of the refugees who'd passed this way before.

There was a sad mathematics about the scarves, hats, bags, mementos, and trinkets that lay among the empty water bottles, food wrappers, baby carriages, and broken bicycles. They were the items deemed important enough for the refugees to bring from their homes, but discarded when speed outweighed sentimental value. From the way those once-cherished keepsakes often bore the tread marks of heavy vehicles, he guessed that the barriers had been pushed aside by the soldiers who'd been on that checkpoint. Somehow that made it worse. It emphasized that they'd abandoned all hope of halting the outbreak.

He found his hands going to his pockets. The revolver, sat-phone, and tablet were still there. However, the bag with its candy and water was not. He must have dropped it on the bridge. It felt like a great loss. He could almost imagine a clock counting down until thirst and hunger would become all-consuming.

"Right now, we're alive."

"What?" Helena asked.

"Oh. Nothing."

Tom counted twenty-three other refugees on the interstate. In an effort not to think of the fate of the hundreds who'd been on the bridge or the millions still in Manhattan, he turned his attention back to the roadway. He stepped over a bicycle with a buckled wheel and broken chain.

"Where did the barriers come from?" Helena asked.

"Dunno. A stadium?"

"When? Yesterday afternoon? The evening?"

Tom couldn't answer, but he guessed the direction her questions were leading. "You're wondering how many people passed this way?"

"Yes, before they changed their minds and decided to destroy the bridge. It can't have been many."

"No." And it didn't matter. There was smoke over Fort Lee. Three plumes close enough together that the smoke merged into a single cloud as it drifted up to the sky.

Just before the New Jersey Turnpike, they came to group of a hundred soldiers dismantling what he first thought was a checkpoint. They were supported by ten military Humvees parked across the road with their machine guns pointing east. Only one had an operator, and his attention was fixed on the skyline to the north. On second inspection, Tom realized it wasn't a checkpoint. The white screens looked like they'd come from a hospital. They'd been set up behind folding desks in a line across the highway. Adding to that medical feel, the soldier walking toward them wore a white coat over her uniform.

"Men over here, women over there," the soldier said, waving her hand left and right. "Quickly now. Men to the left, women to the right."

Helena gave a shrug and what was either a grimace or a smile, and went to the right. Tom fell in with the other men. There were twelve of them, in all.

"Through there," a soldier said, gesturing toward the thin row of screens that offered only the illusion of privacy. Behind the screens were more tables, suggesting there had been a lot more people working there than the three soldiers currently on duty. One of these also wore a white coat. From the insignia on his uniform, Tom didn't think he was a nurse.

"Please strip," the white-coat said with brusque indifference. "Place your clothes and belongings on the table. The quicker you do this, the quicker you'll get to the reception center in Overpeck Park. Please. Take your clothes off."

Conscious of the two soldiers standing behind the white-coat, both of whom had fingers resting on the trigger guards of their rifles, Tom did as he was ordered.

"You can't be serious," a man to his left said. "It's freezing out here."

"No one passes this checkpoint unless they've been confirmed as having no bites or cuts on them," the white-coated soldier said.

"And what's your legal authority for that?" the man protested. "I'd say this constitutes an illegal search."

"You want to call your lawyer?" the white-coat asked. One of the soldiers behind him smirked.

"I don't need to," the man said. "I *am* a lawyer."

The white-coat gave a weary sigh. "Of course you are. If you don't want to strip, please go with the corporal." His tone that suggested this was far from the first time this had happened. "You'll be taken to the local police station, where your rights will be explained. You can place a formal complaint. And then you'll be asked to strip, or be charged. That'll take about a day, I think. Maybe two, because there were a lot of people here yesterday, and you'd be surprised how many of them were lawyers. By the time you've been processed, everyone else here will be in a nice warm house, eating hot food. So, it's up to you."

Tom was already down to his shorts, and shivering in the cool morning air. At least the skies were clear. The soldier had seen him take out the revolver and place it on top of the jacket, but he'd not said anything. In fact, Tom was far from the only one to be armed.

"You want us to take off our boots, too?" Tom asked.

"No. Raise your arms. Now turn around. Thank you. Put your clothes back on, and then continue past the trucks and down the interstate. There'll be signs to the reception center."

Tom guessed the brief inspection was more for the benefit of the objecting lawyer, in the hope that would mean these three soldiers could finish their duty all the quicker. It worked. Still grumbling, the lawyer pulled off his jacket as Tom was pulling his back on.

"You had a lot of people through here last night?" he asked as he picked up his bag.

"About five thousand," the white-coat said. It sounded like a lot until you compared it to the number of people in Manhattan. "Through there," the soldier added.

Tom made his way past the vehicles. Helena was waiting. She looked cold and numb. Her face and hands were clean.

"They didn't make you wash?" she asked.

"No. They wanted us to get us through as quickly as possible."

"Huh!" she snorted. "I got one of the most thorough medical exams of my life."

A few of the other men fell in with the woman with whom they'd been traveling.

One of the men looked around, somewhat confused. "Diane," he called.

"Come on," Helena said. She started walking.

"Diane?" the man called again, this time louder. A female soldier walked up to him, and spoke in a low voice.

"You coming?" Helena called, from a dozen paces down the road.

"You know what happened to Diane?" Tom asked, when he'd caught up.

"There was a woman with cuts on her legs," Helena said. "She was separated from the rest of us."

Tom glanced back. He shrugged. The whole thing was a nightmare. One from which there would be no waking. The walls of reality had come crumbling down. They might be rebuilt, but they'd never be the same.

Chapter 8 - Resettlement
Overpeck County Park, New Jersey

"Were you on your way to a meeting?" Helena asked.

"What?" Tom had been thinking about the events of the night, breaking them down, trying to extract the meaning behind them. Helena had almost been forgotten.

"Your suit," she said. "It's not exactly practical for a trip like this."

"I… uh…" For once, the lies that usually came so easily eluded him.

"Or was it a job interview?" she asked. He sensed she didn't really care about the answer, but was seeking the normality of conversation as a defense against an abnormal situation.

"I'm an analyst," he said. "I crunch numbers and try to find the hidden meanings." That seemed safe enough.

"Oh." She sounded a little disappointed. "I'm a teacher," she said.

"You mentioned it."

"I like kids. Hate the bureaucracy, but I like kids, and they like me. I think that's the trick to being a good teacher. Trent didn't get that."

"He's the guy who took your boat?" Tom asked.

"Tammy's boat," Helena corrected. "It was her husband's. He was a trader. Bought it when he retired. Got cancer a month later. Died a year after that. Never took it out of the marina. Tammy didn't want to sell it because it was his dream, you see. Hers and his, to take it and sail off to the Caribbean. Said I could live on the boat, but it was her way of stopping me from quitting. She knew I was thinking about it. I mean, I liked the children, but there are nice kids everywhere. Schools, too."

"You didn't want to be a teacher?" he asked.

"Who gets to be what they want? Trent thought the kids had to be scared. That was his strategy. Fear. I didn't like him, but… I warned him. You heard me, right?" There was desperation in her voice.

"Yeah. I heard you."

She lapsed into silence, and he didn't try to fill it.

A few minutes later, a truck overtook them. The back was closed, and Tom wondered if it contained soldiers, or those who'd failed the cursory medical exam. He flexed his hand. He'd not noticed until he was pulling his jacket back on, but there was a jagged cut along his forearm caused by flying debris on the bridge. The blood had mixed with the dust to form a paste over the wound, obscuring it from view. The white-coated soldier had missed it. How many other wounds had been missed, and how many of the injured were infected?

A path had been cleared down the interstate, but like in Manhattan, it was full of abandoned vehicles. A few had their windows smashed. In most of those, there was a corpse, the head blown apart. Maybe they *had* controlled the outbreak. It was possible, wasn't it?

"There's people," Helena said, pointing to a building overlooking the highway. Tom didn't care. He focused on the road, following it as the route took them off the interstate and down into the suburbs. Here the side roads were blocked. More faces were visible, these blank and expressionless.

A helicopter buzzed overhead. It looked like a civilian model. Did it belong to a news agency? Was the image of this last, desperate band of refugees being broadcast across the nation? He turned his head down until the chopper had gone away.

Step after weary step, he walked. One foot in front of the other, each step getting shorter, each breath more ragged, until the yards became miles and they reached the reception center.

He'd been expecting the hasty order of a FEMA camp, but this was distinctly civilian. It was clear there had been a plan, but also that too many people had arrived for it to be properly deployed. Tents had collapsed or been dismantled. The only activity was outside those marked with a bright red cross. Military vehicles dotted the park, usually with soldiers nearby. Their bored expressions were the only reassurance amidst the chaotic disorder.

A man in a heavy black coat broke off from a slightly larger group of soldiers and came to greet them.

"Welcome," he said. "I'm Rabbi David Cohen. You are the last, and you are just in time. Does anyone require immediate medical attention?"

No one moved.

"Good," the rabbi said, "because we are about to leave."

"To go where?" Helena asked.

"Home," the rabbi said. "A curfew is being established. Everyone is to go home and stay there. You'll do the same."

"Our homes are over there," a woman said, gesturing to the east.

"We have coaches that will take you to somewhere nearby," the rabbi said with a weary but disarming smile. "Think of someone you know who lives within twenty miles of here. Family, friends, co-workers, anyone who might be willing to share their roof. The destinations of the buses are taped to their windows. Find the one going closest, give the driver the address, and you'll be taken there."

"And if we don't know the address?" a man asked. "It's my secretary. She lives in Fort Lee, but I don't know where."

"There are police officers by the buses, they can find the addresses for you," the rabbi said.

"And if we don't know anyone nearby?" Helena asked.

"No one?" the rabbi asked. "No friends, no co-workers, no family?"

"I have a sister," Helena said. "But she's in Canada."

"Canada? There's a bus leaving for the border. If you hurry, you can catch it. Be quick."

"Oh. Right. Thanks. Um…" She turned to Tom. "Bye, I guess."

"Good luck."

Tom watched her go. She ran a few steps, then walked, then sped up as the prospect of missing the bus added urgency, then slowed again as exhaustion overtook her. Others followed until only Tom and the rabbi were left.

"You don't know of anyone nearby?" the rabbi asked.

"Nowhere a bus can reach. Did many people come through here?"

"I'm not sure," the rabbi said. "The colonel was establishing order when we arrived, separating out the infected from the sick, and telling others to find shelter."

"Infected? You mean bitten?" he asked.

"Sadly, yes. There were a lot. I'm glad for the colonel's presence. I don't think I could have done what was needed."

"Which colonel?" Tom asked.

"LeGrande. He's…" The rabbi turned toward the group of soldiers he'd been talking with. The group had begun to disperse. "Well, he was over there somewhere."

"This wasn't organized by the governor or a general?" Tom asked.

"No one has been able to reach the governor," the rabbi said. "At least as far as I know, but honestly, I don't know very much. I was in the synagogue, trying to think of some way I could help when the colonel came in. He is in my congregation, you see. He asked that I organize the evacuation and resettlement of all these refugees. It had to be done quickly, and so it has been. He requisitioned the school buses, then the civic ones, and then the coaches. I don't know how, except that a rifle usually carries an argument when the uniform can't."

"He's not regular army?" Tom asked.

"Retired. Forty years in the Marine Corps. The soldiers you see – and sailors and Air Force – they're National Guard, or on leave. The colonel lives over there." The rabbi waved to the east.

"Where's the official response?" Tom asked. "Where are the police? They pulled them out of Manhattan, so where are they?"

The rabbi gave a weak smile. "That's what I want to know. The news says the Army has been deployed. I don't know where."

"What about the bridge? The naval blockade? Who ordered that?"

"An admiral. I don't know which. The colonel informed me that it was going to happen. His words were that we were doing all we could, and it wasn't going to be enough. He was right, of course."

"So you destroyed the bridge."

"Look around you," the rabbi said. "We threw this together expecting the full weight of the government to take over. Even if they had…" He sighed. "It is a miserable truth that sometimes you have to cut out the infection. Yet, it is equally true that amputation doesn't always stop the disease. We have done what we can. Now we must get off the streets. This

73

is the only way the infection will be stopped. You should think of someone who lives nearby. If you can't, there's a shelter at the synagogue. It's the blue bus. It'll be the last to leave, but we will be leaving in three hours. No later."

"I have an old friend who lives a couple of miles from here. He'll put me up," Tom lied. "Is there somewhere I can sit down for a bit? I've been on my feet all night."

"There are cots in some of the tents, if you can find one still standing," the rabbi said. "But don't stay here long. It truly isn't safe."

Tom nodded his thanks and went to look for somewhere more secluded. His body was tired, but his brain was leaping. Someone else might have put his suspicions down to shock and paranoia, but he knew a conspiracy *did* exist. There were plans to deal with a viral outbreak in New York. They'd not been put into place. The removal of police, the lack of any military or federal deployment; it all suggested that someone had actively sabotaged the relief effort.

As to whom, it had to be Farley and his cabal. They'd seen this chaos and decided to take advantage of it. They would let the virus spread and… what? Try to seize power?

He looked around, made sure he was alone, and then took out the tablet and plugged in the sat-phone. He stared at the screen and hesitated, unsure what to do first. Find out whether the infection was spreading unchecked, he decided. That was done quickly, and with depressing results. He found the recording of a man calling home. He'd been on a sales trip to New York, and visited a mall to pick up some gifts for his kids. It was the same mall that had been featured in the news. The man had been bitten, but he'd reached his car, and been able to drive away. Somehow, it had taken five hours before he'd died. All that time, he'd been speaking to his wife on the phone. The conversation ended in a choking cough. The traffic cameras told the rest of the story. He'd reached Hagerstown in Maryland, crashing at an intersection. He died. As the first responders arrived to help, he came back. The zombie attacked and…

"And so it spreads."

Who the man was, and why his calls were being monitored, didn't matter. The key detail was five hours. Tom had seen footage of people who'd been bitten and then turned almost immediately. But five hours? He glanced at the jagged cut running down his arm.

"There's enough to worry about without *that*," he muttered, and that footage didn't confirm how far the virus had spread. The algorithm trawling through social media was proving unreliable. Everyone in the world was talking about zombies, and a lot were claiming to have seen them in places it surely wasn't possible. Germany, Korea, India, France… and then he saw the video and knew that the algorithm *was* reliable. A gendarme had been attacked on the Champs-Élysées. From the look of it, the whole world had seen. The virus was everywhere.

"How did it spread so far and so fast?" The answer was obvious, and took only a few minutes to confirm. The airports had remained open until mid-afternoon. It looked like any plane with fuel had departed. He suspected it was the diplomatic flights that were to blame. Dozens of them had taken off around the time those images of the zombies attacking people were spreading across social media. Two had been heading to Britain.

"Bill…"

Tom tapped out a message to Bill Wright. There was no response from him, nor had there been any reply to the messages he'd sent the previous day.

"Find those passengers. Isolate the planes," he muttered as he tapped in a number he knew by heart. His finger hovered over the dial-button, but he hesitated in pressing it. The only times he'd ever spoken to Bill, he'd disguised his voice. It wasn't that there was any way the man might recognize it, but Tom had needed that artificial separation as a barrier against saying something he knew he'd regret. The time for subterfuge had long since passed, and he had to know that Bill was alive. He pressed the screen. The number dialed. The phone rang. And rang.

"Yes?" a woman finally answered.

"Hi," Tom said. "I'm trying to reach Bill Wright."

"I… I'm sorry, who is this?"

"It's an old friend. To whom am I speaking?"

"This is Jenny Knight. I'm a nurse at St Thomas's Hospital."

"Is Bill okay?" Tom asked, unable to keep the concern from his voice.

"He's broken his leg. It's a compound fracture. He's sedated, but he'll be fine. You're American, aren't you? Are you calling from the States? What's going on over there?"

"Is it on the news?"

"A terrorist attack, that's what they're saying. It doesn't look—" The woman stopped. "Who shall I say called?"

Tom hung up, frustrated. If Bill was sedated, then there was no way of getting a warning to the British prime minister. Nor did he have someone who had access to the computing power needed to sort through all the information being gathered. There was another reason for his flush of concern, one he didn't want to think of, and nothing that he could do anything about here, on the wrong side of the Atlantic.

The rabbi and colonel were correct. Isolation was key. They needed to copy that strategy across the nation. No, across the world. Get everyone inside, clear the streets, then the houses, the towns, the cities, the countries. Every last one. It would be a Herculean task, and the death toll was inconceivable. However, the apocalyptic alternative was too easily imagined. He had to speak to Max.

He called Charles Addison first. The chief of staff's private line was busy. He tried the other number. Busy. He called the presidential switchboard. Busy. Almost in desperation he dialed the number used by the public. Busy. He tried Addison again. Still engaged. There was no other choice. He called Nate.

Nate Cooper was his backup plan, a way of getting word to the president without having to go through anyone else. Through the office of the First Lady, Tom had arranged for Nate and three other students from Notre Dame to be tasked with recording footage for a documentary on Max's first hundred days in office. Ostensibly to be used as part of a campaign to encourage the youth vote during the re-election, he was really there because Tom had wanted a camera crew inside the White House. That had been before he had been framed for murder, back when he

76

thought the honest reactions to the conspiracy's exposure would help persuade the world of Max's innocence. Giving Nate the phone had been an afterthought. He'd put it down to a paranoid desire to have a fallback to his backup plan in case the impossible happened. On this day, when the impossible had become real, it was his last chance. He dialed the number.

"Yes?" a voice at the other end asked, quietly and with an edge of confusion.

"Nate, this is Professor Finn," Tom said, giving the name he'd used on the three occasions he'd met the kid.

"Professor? How did you… how are you calling me? My cell phone won't work. I… I forgot I even had this one."

"Are you still in the White House?" Tom asked.

"Yeah. Trying not to get in anyone's way. How *did* this call get through? I've been trying to reach my parents all night, but the landlines have been engaged."

"All of them? All night?"

"Most of them. Or the ones here in the West Wing. No one's been able to call anyone. Someone said the lines are overloaded. I… well, everyone's busy."

"What about the president? Is he still there?"

"I… I think so. I saw him last night, at about three. He was in the mess."

"Not in the bunker?"

"No. His motorcade's still in the drive, and Marine One is on the lawn. I think he's still here. There are soldiers everywhere. You know there are tanks out front? There's a huge cordon around the White House."

"Nate, listen. Is Charles Addison there?"

"I… I don't know. Mr Gregson is."

"Gregson? Good." The communications director would do. "I need to get a message to him."

"Right. Sure. Why? Where are you?"

"That's why I'm calling. I was in Manhattan, I've—"

"They said the city's been cut off," Nate interrupted. "I saw it on the news, well, until the TV stopped working. They said it was quarantined. No one knew who'd ordered that."

"There's no television signal? What about the internet?"

"It's really slow. Anna said that it was probably the military tying up the bandwidth."

Tom didn't know much about the White House communication systems, but he knew that wasn't how it worked. "Listen, Nate. I need you to speak to Gregson. Tell him I was in New York. In Manhattan. I got out before they destroyed the George Washington Bridge."

"They did *what*?"

"There are National Guard units here, off-duty soldiers, civilians, people doing what they can, but there's no sign of the police, the CDC, or FEMA. There's no military or federal support. Everyone here is pulling back to their homes, and that's what's got to happen nationwide. Everyone should stay in their homes."

"Yeah, I guess."

"No, I need you tell to that to Gregson, and tell him to tell the president. The police were pulled out of Manhattan. They were taken off the island. I don't know where they are, or who ordered it, but someone is either—" He stopped. Nate was just a kid, and though the White House might be safe from the zombies, that didn't mean he was safe from the conspirators. "Nate, tell Gregson that Max needs to know that the police were withdrawn from Manhattan. Whatever orders he's giving, there's no sign of them here on the ground. Okay?"

"Okay. Sure."

"And tell him that it was Tom Clemens who told you that."

"Tom Clemens? Who's that?"

"Remember the name. I'll call back in a couple of hours."

He hung up and closed his eyes. Farley. It had to be. Somehow, the man had interfered with the White House communication's network. He'd jammed the phone lines, and the internet. Or was that paranoia? No. It was the only way that—

"Who's Nate?"

Tom jumped. He'd not heard Helena approach. She was standing behind him.

"I thought you were getting a bus," he said.

"It had gone," she said with a shrug. "The only ones left were all local. I don't know anyone. I…" She gave another shrug. "The rabbi says he's taking people in. He said there's a space for me. The bus will leave in two hours. And he said if you were still here, I was to make sure you came with me. Nate works in the White House?"

How much had she heard? "He's a student at Notre Dame. There's a group of them there, recording a documentary on the first hundred days in office. It's going to be used for the next election. Or it was. Our latest attempt to increase the youth vote."

"Oh." She gave another of those little shrugs, as if whatever momentary interest she'd had in the call was now gone. "What's going on, Tom? Where are the military? Where are the helicopters? Where are the fighter planes?"

"I was wondering that myself."

"But they should be here, right? Flying overhead? We should be in some cage right now. You know, quarantine, not free to roam around like this."

"Yeah. That's what I thought would happen."

"So what's going on? You know people at the White House. You're with the CIA or something, aren't you? I mean, you said you were an analyst. That's what you meant, right?"

"Something like that."

"So what's happening?"

"I don't know. I really don't."

"Oh." She sighed. "What are you going to do now? Do you have to report in or something?"

"Not really. I think I'm going to sleep for a few hours. It's been a long night."

"Right. Okay." She looked as if she was going to say something more, but changed her mind. "I'm going to… going to…" She shook her head and walked off.

Tom didn't try to stop her. He knew what he had to do; find Dr Ayers and get some answers for Max. Put like that, it seemed straightforward. He tried not to think of all that might go wrong. It was three hundred and fifty miles to her house on the edge of the Allegheny National Forest. Considering how long it had taken them to get a few miles into New Jersey, there was no telling when he might get there.

He walked over to a discarded backpack near the tent's entrance. It was full of children's clothes. He emptied them, carefully, into a neat pile. Then he crossed to an almost empty pallet of water bottles. Eight bottles fitted into the pack.

Was there an alternative? Yes, he could disappear. Now was the perfect time. Wherever he went, he would have to steal a car, so why not drive straight to the airfield? Or, if Julio had already departed, why not the coast? He could call Sophia, and press her into taking him away, just as he'd planned. Except anywhere that was safe now wouldn't be for long. When he'd renounced revenge, he'd set out to save the world. Over the years since, it had seemed almost like a game, and that was often how he'd treated it. Now that the stakes were terrifyingly real, he couldn't give up.

Whatever had crippled the White House communications system, he knew who was behind it. Farley wouldn't give up, and that meant he couldn't either.

"Find Dr Ayers." He spoke out loud in the hope that would reinforce the decision. Instead, it brought up another question. Someone was behind the virus. He'd thought it was Russia or China, but that was a guess. He could be wrong. All of this could be Ayers's revenge for being cut off from the work that had become her life. Maybe. Or maybe it was just another theory born from the need to make sense of this nightmare.

He grabbed a discarded coat, shook off the mud, and made his way to a cot in one of the partially collapsed tents. He'd sleep for a few hours, call Nate, hopefully speak to Max, and then find Dr Ayers. He'd get some answers, and then…

And then he fell asleep.

Chapter 9 - Collapse
Overpeck County Park, New Jersey

Screams tore Tom awake. Reflexively, he rolled over. The cot folded up on itself, and he collapsed to the floor. He scrabbled to his feet, trying to remember where he was and what was happening. A tent. The ramshackle refugee center in Overpeck Park. Zombies. There was a rhythmic rat-a-tat from a heavy machine gun that was over too quickly. Another scream. The gunfire returned, but this time it was the sharper retort of small arms.

Tom dragged himself out of the tent's open doors. The sun was high, the sky clear, and the park was full of blood and death.

"What's going on?" Helena asked. Tom turned around. He'd not noticed her in the tent. A scream answered her question.

"Zombies," Tom said. "I thought you were going to the synagogue."

"The rabbi said he'd come and get me when it was time."

There was a triumphant yell, more primal than anything that had come before, abruptly cut short in a gargling rasp.

"It's coming from where those buses are," Tom said. "No one's getting out that way." He ran back to the collapsed cot and grabbed the rucksack. He checked to be sure the sat-phone and tablet were in his pocket and took out the revolver. There were only three rounds. He ran outside. The gunfire was most frequent from the vehicle park to the east. Between him and it was the hospital tent, and it was from there the screaming was loudest.

A soldier ran toward the tent. She slowed and fired a burst from the hip. Stopped, raised the rifle, and fired off two single shots. She took a step back, fired, took another step, and half-turned as if she was going to run. Tom could see the effort it took for the soldier to force herself to stand her ground, firing shot after shot into the tent, pausing only when she had to reload. That was when the zombie staggered out of the tent. The soldier fumbled the magazine. The zombie got nearer. Tom raised the revolver. Fired. Missed, but the shot passed close enough that its passage caused the zombie to pivot as if it was trying to catch sight of the bullet. That gave the soldier time to slide the magazine home, and open fire.

The soldier's training had taken over. She was aiming at the center mass. Bullets riddled the creature's chest. The zombie staggered back, righted itself, and lurched forward again. More creatures tumbled out of the tent. Some were bandaged. Some wore uniforms. All were now undead, pouring from the tent as if the very gates of Hell lay inside.

The soldier emptied the magazine, and then she ran. The zombies stumbled after her, tripping on each other, their clothing, and the detritus littering the park. Two of the fallen creatures staggered to their feet and were looking toward their tent. The soldier would escape, and now they had to do the same. Helena had already reached that conclusion and was sprinting across the park. Tom followed.

"Slow down," he said. He had to pull her to a halt before she heard.

"We have to get out of here!" she screamed.

"Yes. But they can't run. Have you seen one run? I haven't. They don't run. That's our advantage. That's what'll keep us alive. We have to save our energy until we need it. Over there." He pointed at the buildings jutting up above the park to the west. "Get out of the park, find a car, drive."

"That's it? That's the extent of your plan? Can't you call for an extraction or something?"

For a moment, he couldn't think what to say. "No."

They weren't the only ones fleeing the camp, but they were the only ones walking. He tried to steer a path away from the thick clusters of people sprinting this way and that. He'd not realized so many were still in the park. There were hundreds. To his left, a group of twenty were running toward a stand of trees. A person at the back collapsed. The others didn't notice. They didn't stop.

Helena changed direction, angling toward the fallen figure.

"No." Tom grabbed her arm.

"We're not going to help?" she asked.

"We can't, and we can't help everyone. We'll be lucky to get out of here alive." Before he could say any more, the prone figure pushed itself to its feet. Hunched over, its left arm pin-wheeled forward, and then its right. The head jerked from side to side as it clawed at the air between it and the fleeing group. As those people reached the trees, there was a scream. They turned round, sprinting back the way they'd come. They saw their former friend, slouching toward them. The group splintered, each of them sprinting off in a different direction.

Helena started running again. This time, Tom didn't stop her. They steered a path across the muddy grass, keeping as far from the zombies as they could, but those staggering, lurching figures were everywhere. When they reached the fence marking the edge of the park, they were nowhere near the point Tom had planned.

The road beyond was empty, though he could hear the sound of doors slamming and vehicles disappearing off into the distance. People were taking shelter. The hair salon on the corner was a case in point.

"Over there," Tom said, pointing to the road heading away from the park. The people in the salon watched them walk past. Their expressions were mostly blank, tempered with relief that they were safely ensconced inside. The glass didn't look thick, and the store didn't look well-provisioned. Safety was relative, and theirs would seem a flimsy refuge when the undead started pushing their way out of the park.

"This way," he said, pointing at the first turning they came to.

"Why? You know somewhere?"

"No. But I don't reckon zombies can think. They'll head in a straight line, so we shouldn't."

With a grid system of roads, they'd meet zombies coming from elsewhere, but he felt better acting rather than just reacting.

Two stores from the next junction was a pizza delivery joint. Outside was a car painted in the chain's colors, with a logo and website on the side, and sign on the roof. Next to it were three motorized dirt bikes and two people.

"Do you see the bikes?" Helena asked.

"Do you see the gun in that guy's hand?" Tom replied. As they drew nearer, he could see the figure more clearly. He was young, late teens, and his head moved nervously back and forth. The automatic pistol, clutched awkwardly in both hands, moved with him, though the barrel stayed pointing at the ground. The girl standing next to him was about the same age, but looked unarmed.

"Two of them," Helena said. "Three bikes."

"Yeah." Tom said. He slowed again, moving the revolver behind his back. Whether the engines were powered by gasoline or electricity, the bikes *were* the answer. They'd be able to ride away, put some distance between them and the park. He raised his left hand in greeting and hoped he looked friendly. From the way the two teenagers stepped back, Tom guessed he didn't.

Before he took another step, the door to the pizza parlor opened. A young man came out, a sack under one arm. He carried it to the car, opened the trunk, and dumped it in. Another figure came out as the man ran back into the store. This one carried a cardboard box. It went into the car.

"They must work there," Tom said. "They're taking the flour and whatever else they can eat."

"Maybe we can get a ride," Helena said.

"Maybe."

He took another step toward them. The young man came out, a trio of bags in his hands. He saw them, hissed something to the sentry who'd been watching them with terrified curiosity. The kid raised a shaking hand, pointing the pistol at them.

"Keep walking," Tom said.

"And then what?" Helena asked.

Tom wasn't sure. Unless they were going to take a couple of the dirt bikes by force, their only hope of getting a ride was for the zombies to appear, and that a common foe might create a sense of camaraderie. That notion was dispelled two paces later when there was a booming gunshot from inside the restaurant. Three people tumbled out through the door.

The young man carried bags. Another had his hands free. The last, a woman, held a shotgun, pointing straight at the closing door.

"In. Go. Get in! Go!" the woman said. She looked a little older than the others. The two young men with her jumped in the car. It drove off as the woman waved her shotgun in Tom and Helena's direction. Tom stopped. The kid with the automatic pistol was trembling so much he'd probably shoot the ground if he aimed in the air. The woman was different. There was a stern resolve in her stance. She'd done a lot and was prepared to do more to keep herself and these others alive. They backed toward the motorized dirt bikes. The shotgun tracked between Tom and the restaurant door. They got on. They drove off.

"Do something," Helena said.

"Like what? Shoot them? There're only two rounds left."

"We need those bikes," Helena said. "We need to get out of here."

"So do they," Tom said. It was academic. The car was turning right at the next junction, the dirt bikes close behind. From inside the restaurant came the sound of bolts being slid home. The people inside would have food. They had electricity. Tom looked again at the door.

"No, it wouldn't be safe," he said. "We need to get away from the zombies."

"If we'd gotten the bikes—" Helena began. Her irate reply was cut short by an almighty crash from the west. There was a shot. Another.

Tom wasn't sure whether he ran to help or to steal the bikes. The decision was made when they reached the junction. There was no sign of the car. Two of the bikes had crashed thirty yards from the junction. In front of each was a cluster of the undead. The woman with the shotgun still sat on her bike, the weapon raised. She fired. Tom couldn't see the other two. They must have run… no. They'd fallen from their bikes. The zombies were crouched over the bodies, ripping and tearing at flesh.

The woman fired again. She missed, swore, and dismounted. She fired again. A zombie flew back. The others slowly stood and turned toward the woman.

He had two shots, and that was all. He should have found another weapon earlier. It was too late now. He raised the revolver, trying to get a bead on one of the zombies. The woman was in the way.

"Get to that bike," Tom said to Helena. "And ride away."

"No."

"They'll follow you," Tom said. "That'll give me and her enough time to get those other bikes." He wasn't sure if that was true, but you couldn't fight these creatures with fist and foot.

The woman fired again. A zombie folded in on itself, but that still left seven snarling apparitions slouching toward them.

"Get that bike," Tom repeated. He sidestepped away from her, crossing to the edge of the road, measuring his aim. The woman fired. Another zombie collapsed. There was something wrong about the shots. She was aiming at the chests. The impact was knocking the zombies down. It wasn't killing them.

He had a clear shot. He fired. The bullet smacked into the creature's temple just as it turned its head. It fell. The woman stopped. She looked back. She saw them. Her expression of grim anger froze, turning into confused recognition.

"Watch out!" Tom yelled. The woman turned back to the creatures. They were only ten feet away. She fired again. The shot was hasty. The slug hit a zombie in the side. It spun across the street, but managed to keep its feet. She racked another round. Fired. Hit a zombie in the head. Raised the gun. Nothing happened. She was out of ammo. Tom fired. A zombie collapsed, but there were still three left, and one of those on the ground was slowly pulling itself to its feet.

"Run!" Tom yelled at the woman. And she did, but not away. Swinging the shotgun like a club she charged at the zombies. The first blow knocked one from its feet, but that took the impetus out of her swing. The next staggered back a pace, its arms flailing erratically. The woman stepped forward, and into the clawing arms of a third. Its hands caught in her clothing. Her demonic yell turned to a scream of fear. Tom ran, but he was already too late. A jet of arterial blood sprayed from her throat as the zombie bit down.

He clubbed the butt of the revolver onto the zombie's head. It released its grip on the dying woman and turned its bloody mouth toward him. Tom smashed the revolver into its face again, and then lashed out, kicking at its knee. The zombie stumbled as its leg gave way. Hands pawed at Tom's jacket. Cloth tore. He punched. He kicked. A snarling, snapping mouth got closer. From nowhere, the butt of the shotgun slammed into the zombie's face. It fell sideways.

Helena screamed as she swung the shotgun at the other creature's legs. It fell.

"Get that bike," Tom yelled, pushing her toward it. He ran to the other, nearest bike, pulling it to its wheels.

Helena was on hers, fumbling with the ignition. She got the engine started, wheeled it around, and drove off, the bike wobbling across the road. Tom started his. He glanced behind. He saw two things: the woman to whose aid they'd come slowly sitting up, and in a house across the street two faces were watching them, just as they must have watched the entire bloody fight. He drove away.

His clothing was torn, his hands were bruised, and one still clutched the revolver. He thrust the gun into his pocket, almost losing his balance. He was mobile and heading west. That was something, but there was no sense of victory in it.

Helena was already accelerating away from him. He didn't try to catch up. They'd fallen into traveling together by accident, and though there was safety in numbers, he didn't know if he wanted companionship. Then Helena slowed and came to a stop. Tom came to a halt next to her.

She was shaking. The shotgun, which had been balanced across the handlebars, fell from her grip. Her expression was one of abject misery.

"Why?" she asked. "All this… it's… why?" There was no real question in the words. Or perhaps there were so many that none could be answered, certainly not by Tom.

"How much fuel do you have in the tank?" he asked instead.

Slowly her head turned to the gauge. "A quarter. You?"

"About the same."

In the distance, there was the sound of a helicopter. A moment later it was drowned out by the roar of an explosion.

"Will anywhere be safe?" Helena asked.

"I don't know." He wiped his hands against his coat. Automatically, he searched for cuts, and wished he hadn't. He saw none, but knew there was nothing he could have done had he found any. He picked up the shotgun and stuck it in the straps behind Helena's seat.

"We need to find better weapons," he said.

"Or more ammunition. Or a world where—" She stopped, took a breath. "We need to get out of here."

"Let's keep moving, as far as we can get, and hope safety finds us if we don't find it first."

"Hope?" She shook her head. "What good is that?"

Chapter 10 - Grand Theft Auto
Fair Lawn, New Jersey

West End Avenue, Essex Street, Berkshire Road: the British names made him think of Bill Wright. He rocked his head from side to side, trying to shake those thoughts away. It was shock, he supposed, calling to mind all the things he'd left undone and unsaid, but it was a distraction he couldn't afford.

The fuel gauge bounced erratically between empty and full. He had no idea what that meant other than it was time to find a better vehicle. The further west they rode, the more streets they found barricaded. Some of the barriers were hasty constructs of vehicles and junk. Others were of wood, concrete, and steel, made with an impressive professionalism matched by the armed figures standing sentry at windows and on rooftops. They passed a turning blocked by two police cruisers. A pair of uniformed officers stood nearby, and the people with them all wore vests marked 'police', but Tom didn't think any of them carried a badge. At least, from all that he could see, people were staying at home. Whatever warnings had been given, and whoever had given them, they were being heeded.

There was a bang from Helena's bike, a rattle, a high-pitched whine, and it came to a sudden stop, billowing smoke from the exhaust. He brought his own bike to a halt. Wordlessly, she climbed on the back. When he tried the throttle, the engine wouldn't start.

"On foot, then," he said.

"There's a car over there," she said, pointing toward a drive.

"Look at the window above. People are watching."

She grabbed the shotgun from the back of her stalled bike. "So?"

"So they're probably armed, and with ammunition for their guns. What have we got? A few bottles of water." Automatically, he checked his pockets. He still had the money he'd brought with him from the apartment. He doubted that would buy them anything any more. He started walking. "Besides, do you know how to steal a car?"

"I sort of assumed you would," she said. "Isn't that the sort of tradecraft they teach you in the CIA?"

"I'm not CIA," he said. "I'm not a spy. I analyze data."

"Yeah, sure. So are you saying you don't know how to hot-wire a car?"

"Well…. yes, I do, but not one that's made of more silicon than steel. I need something at least a decade old."

"Ah." She gave a self-satisfied smile as if he'd just confirmed her suspicions. He let it go.

The next street was guarded, but there were no barriers. Vehicles were lined up on the curb, with people scurrying back and forth, loading their possessions. From the irate yells of the bearded man who seemed to be in charge, they were putting together a convoy.

"Keep moving," the sentry yelled at them. Tom did.

"Remember the road," Tom said.

"Why?" Helena asked.

"If we can't find anywhere else, we'll double back. They won't have taken every vehicle with them. We'll find an empty house with a car in the drive, break into the house, and find the keys. That'd be far easier than trying to hot-wire it."

"They might leave some cars, but they won't leave the fuel in the tanks, will they?"

"We won't know until we check," he said, but she had a point. Surrounded by armed people, even when those guns were being pointed at them, he felt safe again. Not relaxed, but able to think more clearly about the next stage of the journey.

"We could look for a vehicle rental place," she suggested. "Or a hospital parking lot, or—"

There was an explosion behind them. They both turned around. Smoke billowed up from the east. The moment of calm was gone.

"The next turning," Tom said. "And we'll take the next likely-looking car we see."

It was a slightly smaller road, filled with slightly smaller houses.

"Do you see the people at the windows?" he said. "They're protecting their own properties, not each other's."

"So?"

"So, do you see the pickup truck, four houses down?"

"The one with 'Mr Wu does the gardening for you' on the side. Sure."

"The house is empty," he said.

"How can you tell?"

"The leaves haven't been cleared from the lawn in a week. If the guy's a gardener, he'd keep his lawn pristine as an advertisement. The only explanation: the house is empty. Stay on the curb, hold the shotgun like you're prepared to use it, and hope no one realizes it's empty."

"Hope? Huh!" she muttered, raising the gun.

Tom darted ahead, down the drive, and to the truck. There was no time to pick the lock, so he smashed the window with the butt of the revolver. Making a point of waving the gun above his head, he ducked inside, and pulled the panel away from under the dash. It was a long time since he'd done this. He'd learned the knack during his childhood, and had been surprised to find that cars across the world were wired more or less the same. The only problem now was remembering which one to—

"Tom!" Helena called.

"Ten seconds," he said.

"Not sure we have that long!"

The engine bucked, stopped, and then it roared. He pulled off the handbrake, slid it into reverse, and slammed a foot down on the gas. Only then did he look behind. He saw Helena dive out of the way. There was a shot. Another. Helena jumped into the truck bed. Tom shunted the car into first. There was another shot. He glanced in the mirror. People had come out of the houses. One held a rifle, and Tom saw him lower it without firing again. He took the next turn, and they were all lost from sight.

Chapter 11 - Syphon
February 22nd, NY, NJ, or PA

Tom woke, but didn't open his eyes. As long as they were closed he could pretend it had all been a bad dream. The pain in his neck told him that wasn't the case. A bird trilled nearby, echoed by another in the distance. At least there was no screaming. He opened his eyes. They were surrounded by trees, though they were not as densely overgrown as he'd thought when they had stopped.

They'd driven, sometimes south, sometimes north, but more west than east until it was dark, pulling in to what he'd thought was a campground. They'd slept in the cab, covered by a muddy tarpaulin from the back of the truck. He'd tried telling himself that he'd slept in worse places. Trying to come up with an example had kept him awake long after Helena had begun snoring.

They weren't in a campground, just a cleared patch of woodland at the side of a farmed forest. Helena was by the tailgate, arms folded, her eyes on the trees.

"Morning," he said.

"Hey. It's so quiet, isn't it? It's wonderful. Peaceful. Listen. No traffic. No planes. Nothing."

He found himself looking up. He'd no idea precisely where they were. They'd kept driving until they'd left the suburbs and exurbs behind. He wasn't even sure if they were in New York, New Jersey, or Pennsylvania.

"The airports were shut down," he said. "I checked, but it was done too late. The virus had already reached Paris."

"Oh, I wish you hadn't said that," Helena said, turning away from the trees. "I was trying to enjoy the moment. I know it's stupid, but I've spent most of my life in cities. I mean, sure, I've been away on holidays, but I don't think I've been anywhere that seemed as remote as this road."

As far as he could tell, it was no different to any other country road he'd ever traveled.

"I was enjoying the dream," Helena continued. "Imagining that I'd left New York and was finally beginning the next chapter of my life. But I have to wake up, now, and face reality."

"Yeah. And I wouldn't mind it if this reality included some breakfast."

Helena gave an exasperated growl.

Tom took out the sat-phone, plugged in the tablet, and waited for a signal. Waited. Waited. There. "Hmm."

"What?"

"I can give you our longitude and latitude, but the map's not loading."

"What does that mean?"

"That particular part of the internet is overloaded. The only maps I downloaded were of New York and Washington D.C. I've got nothing for here." He glanced up again. "Wherever that is."

"Oh. So…" There was a pause. "Where do we go now?"

He glanced up and down the road, hoping for a sign he'd previously missed. There wasn't one. Dr Ayers's home was around three hundred and fifty miles from New York. Precisely how far it was from where they were now, he wasn't sure, but if he could find the gas, he could be there before evening. *He* or *they*, that was the real question.

"You said you had a sister in Canada?" he asked.

"Yeah. Why?"

"I'm heading west, almost as far as Lake Erie. You might be able to catch a ferry across the lake from there. Where in Canada does she live?"

"She had a place in Toronto," Helena said. "But she moved a couple of years ago. She's not there anymore."

"So where is she?"

"I don't know," she said.

He recognized the tone. With a little prompting she'd confess to some secret. He didn't have time for that. An idea came to him. He sent a brief message to Bill. If the man was out of surgery and back at a computer, he could find a map.

"Who's Bill?" Helena asked.

"What?" He put it down to tiredness, but he'd not realized she'd been reading over his shoulder. "A friend. In London. He works in the government."

"Oh. Right." She looked at the tablet, the sat-phone, and then at Tom, this time with greater scrutiny than since they'd met.

"And there's no reply from him," Tom said hurriedly putting the sat-phone and tablet away. "Well, there's no point standing here. Maybe there'll be a diner open in the next town."

"Maybe," she said thoughtfully.

Tom's policy the evening before had been to avoid the interstate. He still thought that a prudent decision, but it meant they were now on a two-lane road absent of any useful signs.

"We're traveling south," Helena said. "Don't we want to go west?"

"There's not much I can do about it." He was missing his morning coffee. He was missing his bed, his house, even his life – as far from normal as that had been. "Sorry," he added. "Didn't mean to snap."

Helena made a noncommittal noise. "Who's Bill? I mean, really."

"Like I said, he works in the British government."

"He's a spy, too?"

"No. And neither am I," he said.

"That's what you're meant to say, right? I mean, you have a contact in the White House, and then first thing this morning, you try to reach someone in the British government? That's not what normal people do."

"Show me a normal person, I'll show you someone putting on a very good act."

"Hmm. So who is he, really?"

Tom sighed. She wasn't going to be fobbed off. He'd long ago learned that it was easier to tell a version of the truth missing some facts than to lie outright. "He really does work in the British government. He's a professional political operative. A strategist for hire. I tried calling him yesterday, a nurse answered. He was in a hospital with a broken leg. I thought that if he was conscious, he might have been able to help."

"If he was *conscious*? Don't you have any other contacts?"

This time, the truth was far too complicated to explain. "It's all down to what phone numbers I can remember. His is one of them." He checked the tablet. "And there's no reply. He's probably still sedated. Which means he can't find us a map, and can't tell us where we are."

"Oh. Okay," she said. "So who's out west?"

He glanced over at her. Yesterday, she'd seemed... normal wasn't the right word. Quiet, subdued. Had that been shock? Was this inquisitive questioning her true nature, or was it the product of all they'd experienced?

He reset the odometer. "About a fifth of a tank left," he said. "Do you want to take a guess at what the most fuel-efficient speed would be?"

"Thirty-five? Who's out west?" she asked again.

He thought of lying, but there was little point. "A scientist. Someone who might know how these... well, who might be able to give them a more useful name than zombies."

"You know him?"

"Her. And we've never met."

"Okay. And so you go to this scientist, and she says... what?"

"I don't know. She might know how to stop them."

"You mean she might have an anti-virus in a fridge or something?" she asked, skepticism returning to her voice.

"No. Maybe it would be more accurate to say that she might know where we start in coming up with a plan to stop these things."

"If she did, wouldn't she already have told someone at the CDC or somewhere?"

"Maybe. Maybe not. There's no way of knowing until I ask her."

"There's more to it than that, isn't there," she said. "I'm a teacher, believe me, I'm used to subterfuge and evasion. Do you think she created it or something?"

He didn't answer immediately. "Possibly. I don't know. I mean, I have no reason to suspect her over anyone else, but at the same time, I can't think of anyone else who could come up with something so horrific. Maybe she didn't create it, but the scientific world is small, she might know who did. Yeah, it's not much of a lead, and maybe you're right. I'll get there and find she's already working with the CDC, but what's the alternative? Wait this out in some well-stocked bunker? I don't know where one is." That wasn't strictly true. "But even if I did, this isn't going away overnight. How long do we hide? Months? Years? No bunker will have enough supplies. You saw what Manhattan was like. It'll only get worse. People might stay in their homes and barricade their streets, but the power grid will collapse. The water will stop running. The food will run out, and people will turn on one another. Neighbor against neighbor, friend against friend. They'll fight. They'll kill. Some will run, straight into the arms of the undead. They'll be infected, and we'll—"

"Stop!"

He slammed a foot on the brake, looking around for the threat. He saw none.

Helena swore. "I meant stop talking like that," she said. "I get it. This is bad. I… I don't need you to spell it out. I was there. I saw it, too."

"Okay. Sorry. Sorry." He sighed. "Seriously, do you know of anywhere between here and the Great Lakes we can go?"

"Everyone I know is in New York."

"There's a place in Maine, I—" He stopped, remembering himself in time. "It's too far." He glanced down at the fuel gauge. There was Julio and the airfield. Depending on precisely where they were, that was due south, and perhaps a little to the east. It was probably closer, but he wasn't going to run and hide. He couldn't. "I don't know of anywhere we can reach without stopping for gas. We might make it to the Allegheny only having to stop once. Right now, that's as good a destination as anywhere."

"The Allegheny? That's remote, isn't it? Okay. Fewer people means fewer zombies. Okay." She sounded mollified. "But we're going to run out of gas in seventy-five miles."

"You sure?"

She tapped the odometer. "Teacher, remember."

He started the engine, driving more slowly. Perhaps he could leave her in a town, or find someone heading to Canada. He wasn't going to take her into more danger, but nor was he going to tell her that. Not yet, at least. To forestall any further questions, he turned on the radio.

"I know this is a tragedy," a woman said. "And maybe it's because of that. Seeing all those videos of deaths yesterday, but there's something... I dunno... reassuring in the way they blew that bridge up."

"Reassuring? Yeah, I know what you mean," a man replied. "With Manhattan isolated, it does seem like they're getting a handle on things."

"The military are," the woman said. "I don't think Washington has a clue."

"When does it ever?" the man said, adding a nervous laugh. "But let's leave the party politics alone for a while. This has to be the time for us to put aside our differences and come together as—"

"No, I think this is exactly the time to talk about politics," the woman cut in. "Maxwell won the popular vote with fifty-five percent, and he's claimed that as a mandate. That means that nearly half the voters chose someone else. Now, look at the turnout. Look at the people who couldn't even be bothered to turn out. He's only got the support of thirty-two percent of the population eligible to vote. That's not a mandate."

"I really don't think this is the time to discuss the election," the man said.

"And I agree," Tom said, and changed the station.

"I'm going to repeat the information we have... um... the news, I suppose," a woman said. She spoke with uncertainty, in a voice that wasn't right for radio. There was the sound of paper shuffling. "Um... according to the major news networks, the outbreak has been mostly contained to Manhattan. The island has been cut off. The bridges have been destroyed. Shipping has been... has been sunk. There are isolated cases in the United States and overseas. Yesterday, they broadcast an... well, an attack, I suppose, in Paris. There was video footage, recorded on the Champs-Élysées. Two of the networks are reporting incidents in Sydney and in Moscow. Um... look, I've seen the footage they're talking about and I couldn't say where those where. They could have come from anywhere. Um..." There was a pause. "That's what the major networks are saying. I... I'm not saying they're lying. I mean..." She took a breath. "Look, there's a huge contradiction in what they're saying. They can't have contained the virus on Manhattan while saying there are outbreaks in

Australia, Russia, and France. What? Oh. Um… Brad says… My producer, Brad, he said that it could be possible, if the outbreak began simultaneously in multiple locations. I hadn't thought of that. Is there a way of confirming it?"

From the pause, Tom thought the question was asked of the unheard producer.

"Good point. Okay, people. Listeners, um… I suppose it doesn't matter whether this began in New York or not, or if they've got zombies on the moon. They're here, in America. So what do you do? What should we do? The official line is that you should stay inside. Do not travel. Isolate anyone who gets infected. That's it. That's all we've been told. Or I assume it is. It's just me and Brad here. Maybe FEMA's sent us a message we're meant to broadcast, but we've not found it. Everyone who was here yesterday has gone. No one else has come in. Hey, maybe you guys are listening." Her voice rose to a yell. "If so, come to work!" There was a pause. "Yeah. Right. Okay. Well, that official line seems to be the best advice. What else do we know? The schools are closed, at least that's the case for the ones around. No trains are meant to be running although I saw freight trains moving on the railroad when I went up to the roof a few hours ago. The hospital isn't accepting any new admissions. Patients are being sent home. They've said that you shouldn't come in to collect any family members; they're moving them by ambulance. That's for the Mother of Mercy hospital, and direct from their chief administrator. What else? Do we have anything else? Okay, well there's no point me repeating the same thing over and over. I'm going to see if we can find something new to tell you. We'll be back. As long as there's electricity, we'll keep broadcasting. Stay inside. Stay safe." There was a moment of silence. "Do I press the red button? The green—" Her voice was cut short by a guitar riff that led into an old protest song Tom hadn't heard in a decade.

"Do you think they can contain it?" Helena asked.

"Possibly. If it's really only spread through blood and saliva, then it's easy to avoid infection."

"As long as you have the supplies to stay inside. You were right. They'll run out. The power will go, and then…" She shivered and turned the music up.

At about the same time that song ended and another began, they turned onto a wide, four-lane road that ran roughly east to west. A blue hatchback had been driven into the ditch, a hundred yards from the turning.

"Must have crashed," Helena said. "Hey, you're going too fast."

"There's someone in the front seat." Or something. "It's moving."

"Then stop. Stop! We have to stop!" She grabbed at the steering wheel.

"Okay, okay." He slowed, and pulled in, fifty feet from the crashed car. "You know what it is, right? It's a zombie."

"It might not be," Helena said, getting out. "You shouldn't assume. It might be someone hurt, someone like us, someone… oh."

He followed her out and saw what she'd seen. He'd been right. It was a zombie, sitting in the driver seat, and now trapped inside by the seatbelt.

"Do you… do you think he put the seatbelt on so he couldn't get out and infect other people?" she asked.

"Maybe." He took a step closer. The person the zombie had been was on the younger side of thirty, with a face that looked oddly familiar. "Do you recognize him?"

"Me?" Helena asked.

"I think he was on TV."

"We should do something," she said firmly.

"Kill it, you mean?"

"No, I… well, yes. I suppose."

"There's no ammo for the guns," Tom said walking back to the truck. "It's trapped in there, so we should leave it alone. There's no point putting ourselves in more danger than we have to." Other than the tarpaulin there was little in the truck beyond an electric lawnmower and a thin layer of soil. He heaved the lawnmower out of the back. The casing was cracked, and the wire had been cut through, six feet from the handle.

"What are you doing?" Helena asked.

He grabbed the cord and pulled it free. "Should be long enough."

"What for?"

"You're right; we have to do something. We need fuel, yes? Maybe that car crashed when he turned, maybe not, but there might be some gas in the tank. If there is, he doesn't need it anymore, but that gasoline might mean the difference between life and death for us."

"You can't be serious," Helena said, still twenty feet away. "You're going to syphon fuel from the car while… while that thing is in the front?"

"Yep." He walked back to the car. The zombie, which had been rocking back and forth in its seat, began moving more violently. Its hands beat at the dash, the door, the window. No, he thought, not beating. Its arms were moving, and the hands were hitting objects, but there was no aim behind the blows. Only when he was satisfied that the seatbelt would trap the zombie inside did Tom pull the fuel cap free.

The zombie slammed his head into the window. The door rocked.

Tom slid the wire inside.

An elbow slammed into the door. Then its head. Elbow. Arm. Head.

Tom pulled the wire free. The bottom eight inches were damp. It wasn't a rigid cord, and he didn't know the size of the tank, but there was gasoline in there.

Metal creaked. The car door shook.

Tom took a step back, and another.

"We should go," Helena said.

"There's fuel there. Not sure how much, but it might be more than we'll find anywhere else."

"Anywhere except a gas station," Helena said, "but, okay, fine. We need some hose and a container, right?" She headed back to the truck.

"Other than the water bottles," Tom began, "I don't think—" There was a sudden, sharp snap from inside the car. The seatbelt had broken. The zombie was free. It slapped its face against the window, and then its hands. The car rocked, the door shook, and Tom knew the lock wouldn't hold for much longer.

100

Panic replaced the calm of a moment before, and he looked around for a weapon. Upending the lawnmower, he peered at the blade. It was sharp, but firmly attached and so deeply recessed within the casing that the only way it would do any damage was if it were dropped on the creature's head. The handle, however, was made of two connected sections. One folded back on the other for storage, and could be extended when in use. Two small clasps connected each section. He pulled, trying to jerk the top half of the metal frame clear.

"Tom!" Helena ran back toward the truck. He kept his eyes on the car, tugging and twisting the metal frame free.

The zombie slammed its head into the window, and this time it broke. Fragments of glass lacerated the zombie's face and tore at its scalp. Hair and skin were torn off, leaving a red-brown fluid, darker and thicker than blood, to ooze down the car's paintwork. The creature didn't notice. It didn't stop moving. Only the uncoordinated way it pushed its shoulder through the window before its hands slowed its progress.

Helena was back at his side, carrying the empty shotgun as if it were a club. Tom hefted the lawnmower's handle. The hollow, U-shaped piece of steel felt absurdly light.

The zombie kept squirming free. They could drive away, but they *needed* that fuel. He ran forward, raising the handle above his head, stabbing it down, but had to jump back as the creature's arm came through the broken window. It swiped a hand through the air, missing his legs by a hair's breadth. Then, with its torso outside the car and only its legs still inside, it sagged forward. Tom stabbed down with the hollow-handled piece of steel. There was a crack of bone, and the handle stuck, but with less than an inch inside the creature's skull. He tried pushing, but the zombie still thrashed. Its hand reached out and caught around Tom's leg.

"Like a nail!" Tom yelled. "The shotgun. Like a hammer. Quick!"

Helena ran up, and Tom leaned back as she swung. The stock hit the metal at the point where it bent at a right angle. The metal went in another inch. The creature spasmed.

"Again!"

But Helena was already swinging. The stock hit the handle. It went in another eight inches. The zombie sagged, motionless.

"Thanks," Tom said, taking a step back. Helena did the same.

"I.." She dropped the shotgun. "I..." She doubled over, and threw up.

"I found this in the back," Tom said, holding out the bag. Inside were twenty packs of pecan and peanut butter cookies. "There was a photo I.D. for a grocery store. He worked there." He threw a glance back at the car. The zombie still sagged half in, half out of the window. Brown-red fluid dripped to the ground through the hollow metal rod embedded in its skull. "He wasn't on television. Must have had one of those faces. The kind you easily mistake for someone else. Here. Eat something."

"I don't think so," she said as she took the bag. "Was there much gasoline?"

"A couple of gallons."

"Enough to get us thirty miles?" She gave a hollow laugh. "This is my new life, is it? This is the fruition of all my dreams?"

The only replies that came to mind were either trite or a lie. He said nothing, letting the radio fill the silence as they continued driving west.

That morning's first sign of life came twenty minutes later when a two-seater vanity-mobile shot past them on the outside lane. As the fuel needle resumed its inexorable descent toward the red, more vehicles filled the road.

"They don't look like refugees," Helena said. "It's like they're trying to get somewhere."

"They probably are. Out of the city to their country homes, or to relatives or somewhere. Yesterday they couldn't believe what had happened. Today, they're worried they've left it too late."

Tom slowed the truck, pulling into the side of the road.

"Are we out of gas?" Helena asked.

"Not yet," Tom said.

Ahead lay hills covered in a light dusting of snow. His attention was on the interstate, visible slightly below them and two miles to the north. A trio of helicopters buzzed over a hive of military activity. Trucks, tanks, and other equipment were being set up on the highway.

"Are they setting up a checkpoint?" Helena asked. "That's good, right?"

"Is it? What are they going to do with the people they stop? I think... yeah, I think those are tents, aren't they? Is that what they're going to do? Hold them there? They won't be able to send them home."

"Maybe. And maybe it'll be terrible for the people who end up trapped out here, but it'll stop the infection. Except it won't, will it," she added, her tone changing. "The infection's ahead of them. Behind them. They're concentrating people in places with no walls to protect them, no food to eat, and no water to drink."

"And then there's this road we're on," he said. "People will get around the interstate. All they've done is moved the troops from their bases in towns that they could otherwise have protected. Moving them back to somewhere they can do some good will take time. Too much time. The infection will spread. This wasn't the plan."

"There can't have been a plan for this," she said.

"Ironically, there was. Well, not exactly this. There were plans for pandemics, and for outbreaks that began in Manhattan. The military was meant to support the civil power on a local basis. Command was meant to be decentralized to secure towns, cities, and... hell." He walked back to the truck.

"I don't suppose we could beg some gas from the military?" she asked. By way of reply, he started the engine. "No," she said. "I suppose not. Maybe we'll find more zombies in crashed cars." She gave a short, brittle laugh. "No, this is not how my life was meant to be."

There were no more crashed cars. Twice, they pulled over next to vehicles abandoned by the side of the road. On both occasions the tanks were dry. Once they saw a zombie drifting down the road. Tom sped up, swerving around the creature.

"If those cars were abandoned," Helena said, turning in her seat to watch the zombie disappear, "then we should have seen the passengers, right? Hitching along the road."

"And if we see them, we'll stop," Tom said. "For all the good we can offer."

"I meant that… I mean, someone might have stopped, right? Picked them up? But if they didn't… I mean, where did that zombie come from."

He knew what she was saying. "Try not to think about it," he said.

Chapter 12 - Gas
Pennsylvania

They were running on fumes when they saw the sign for a gas station. The relief of seeing it was open was tempered by the presence of the police. The filling station was at a T-junction. A police cruiser was parked across the left-hand lane, effectively blocking it from traffic. Two other police cars were parked on the edge of the lot, facing in opposite directions. He couldn't tell if those vehicles had police officers inside, but he counted six in the gas station with another ten civilians carrying long guns and wearing high-viz vests. Tom had given little thought to Powell since they'd left the apartment behind, but he was now all too consciously aware they were driving a stolen vehicle. They had no choice; they had to stop.

"If they ask, say the truck was abandoned on an empty street," Tom said. "There was no sign of the driver. No one answered the doors in the nearby houses. We knocked. We shouted. There were people there, but no one wanted to help."

"You mean we shouldn't tell the cops that we stole the truck at gunpoint?" In a less sarcastic tone, she added, "They look like they're expecting trouble."

"Wouldn't you be?"

Ahead, a hybrid they'd been tailing for the last four miles turned into the gas station. The driver was waved down by one of the civilians and directed to a pump. Tom slowed and came to a stop next to a pump. He wound down the window as a cop approached.

"We just need some gas," Tom said, pre-empting the officer's first question.

"Where are you from?" the cop replied.

"Fort Lee," Tom said.

The officer gave a thoughtful nod. "And where are you heading?"

"To my mother's," Helena said. "In Erie, near the lake."

The cop gave another nod. "Just the two of you?"

"That's right," Tom said.

The cop clicked his teeth and looked at the car ahead. The driver had opened the door and stepped out. She was arguing in hushed tones with the civilian who was taking a step back with each vigorous gesticulation of the woman's arms. The cop reached a decision.

"Four gallons," he said. "That's all you get. You pay cash. I need to see it now."

"How much is it?" Tom asked.

The cop gestured to the sign by the road. It displayed prices that hadn't changed from the week before.

"You're not charging more?" Tom said.

"Nope. You get the fuel, you keep going."

Tom understood. "We need more than four gallons to make it to Erie."

"Maybe so, but you'll have to find the rest elsewhere. Four gallons is all you'll get. Can you pay?"

Tom pulled out the stack of bills from his pocket. The cop's eyes widened at the sight of them.

"My life savings," Tom said.

"And not worth a fraction of what it was yesterday," the cop said. From his tone, he wasn't talking about the money.

"Jack?" the cop called to one of the civilians, before heading toward the arguing woman.

"I'll fill her up," Jack said. "You pay inside."

"Can we get food and water?" Tom asked.

"The diner's closed. There might be some supplies left. But when the tank's full, you've got to leave."

Tom took that as his prompt and got out. Helena followed him into the store. If the digital bleep of the opening door was a reminder of normality, the rows of empty shelves were an indication of how much had changed.

"Do you have a restroom?" Helena asked the couple behind the counter.

"Through the back, hon," the woman said.

"Anything for sale?" Tom asked, as Helena made her way to the back of the store.

"In the cabinet," the man said. His voice was as cold as his eyes. His hands were hidden behind the high counter.

"Thanks."

The cabinet contained a motley assortment of wilting pre-packaged sandwiches, stale doughnuts, and milk.

"One doughnut, one sandwich, one quart of milk each," the man called.

"No fruit?" Tom asked.

"Nope," the man said.

"You started rationing?" Tom asked, picking through the meager selection.

"Nope."

"We've got to share it out equally," the woman said. "As to their needs, and as to our ability. It's little enough, but it's what we can spare."

"Fair enough." Tom carried the food over to the counter. "You had many people coming through here?" he asked.

"Enough," the man said.

"You're the ninety-third this morning," the woman said, she held up her hand. In it was a click-button counter.

"Is that a lot?"

"Nope," the man said.

"There've been no truckers," the woman said. "Not today."

There was something off-putting about the woman's civility. The man's near-mute suspicion was closer to a normal reaction, as much as anything could be called normal.

"How much do I owe you?" Tom asked.

"There's the gas, and let's see," the woman said. She ran a finger down a long list before methodically ringing up each item on the register.

"That's all?" Tom asked, looking at the total.

"You can pay more if you want," the man said.

"It'll go off if we don't sell it," the woman said.

"Fair enough," Tom replied, wanting the encounter to be over so he could get back in the truck. "Do you have any maps?"

"Local?" the man asked.

"No. We're heading west."

"Here." The man finally detached a hand from whatever firearm he was holding, grabbed a pair of maps from somewhere below the register, and dropped them on the counter. "No charge."

"Thanks," Tom said. Before he had to come up with any more small talk, Helena returned.

"Thank you," she said.

"Your truck's waiting," the man said. "It's time to leave."

Helena raised an eyebrow. Tom said nothing as they went back outside. The woman who'd arrived before them was still arguing with the police officer.

"You need to leave," the attendant, Jack, prompted. Tom didn't need the encouragement.

"Strange place," Tom said, as they drove away. "Like civility is barely holding on at the surface."

Helena picked at a doughnut before placing it back in the bag uneaten. She reached for one of the packs of cookies. "Did he give us four gallons of gas?"

"Almost exactly."

"And how far do we need to go?"

"About a hundred and forty miles."

"Hm. Then we'll be on foot for the last eighty of them. That's a week of walking."

"Probably. I doubt we'll find anywhere selling more gas. Nor do I think that place will be selling it for much longer. There was something… weird about it. Did you sense that?"

"Who cares? We're not going back."

Silence settled for a mile, at least within the truck. Outside, an increasingly regular stream of traffic overtook them.

"Where are they going?" Helena muttered. She turned the radio back on.

"That's confirmed." It was the same woman they'd been listening to before. "There are widespread outbreaks throughout Chicago and New Orleans. The details are different, but the stories are the same. The roads out of the cities are flooded with people. Help can't get in, and stranded motorists can't get to safety. People... okay, this isn't confirmed, but I've got six different video clips that show the same thing. People are putting their infected loved ones into anything with four wheels and are trying to take them somewhere. I don't know where. Hospital? Who knows? The internet's creaking under the strain, but I've seen rumors flying around that there are safe places out there. I don't know how they start, but there aren't! Think about it, people. Why would Salem be safer than San Francisco? As for Greenland, how would you get there? You can't drive!" She took a very loud breath. "So... yeah, I have to give you the official message. Stay at home. Don't go looking for your loved ones. The interstates are now closed. The military, at least the ones who came here yesterday, they said that they're going to close the local roads soon. They didn't say when, but seriously, wherever you are, you're safer there than trapped on some highway. If you haven't got any supplies, ask your neighbors for help. We've got to work together. These days, a good fence is only going to help if your neighbor is behind it with you. What? Oh. Yeah. Brad's saying I need to tell you about the CDC guidelines. I don't know why, I mean, you could work these out for yourself. Don't get bitten. If you are, isolate yourself. The virus is transmitted through blood and saliva. If you get it on your skin, wash it off with bleach or other high-strength detergent. Destroy— What? We are? Okay, we're back online, and we've got some information coming in. I'll put some music on while we sort through it."

A song came on, one of those upbeat, instantly forgettable tunes. Helena tapped her fingers on the window in time with the beat. Tom watched the road, viewing each passing car with a new, deep suspicion.

Chapter 13 - Locked Up, Locked Down
Carthage, Pennsylvania

They crossed I-81, twenty miles from Scranton. Below them, two military convoys trundled along the interstate, one heading north, the other south.

"It makes no sense," Helena muttered. "If one lot is going north, the other south, why didn't they both stay where they were? It's like they're being moved for the sake of it."

The signal for the radio station came and went. A quick flick of the dial had found other stations, clearly broadcasting, but they were filled with religious gloom and political recriminations. After a minute of nothing but static, they turned the radio off.

Traffic was overtaking them at a rate of one vehicle a minute, with about the same in the eastbound lane. Increasingly, the backs, and often the roofs, were laden with belongings.

"It's hopeful terror," Helena said.

"What?"

"Or terrified hope. The expressions on the people in those cars. They all look the same. It's as if they can't believe what they've seen and hope that where they're going will be different. Hope's dangerous."

"It is?"

"It's like a wish or a prayer. It doesn't change your circumstances. Only you can do that, and sometimes you have to accept that things won't change."

He glanced over at her. Her tone had that familiar edge to it, suggesting that she was on the verge of some confession. He didn't prompt her.

"Gas station ahead," he said instead.

"Something's wrong. Do you see that car?"

The grey sedan in front of them had slowed as it neared the filling station, then accelerated away. There were two possible explanations, and the worst of the two was confirmed when they drew nearer. A figure staggered out onto the road. He or she wore a red quilted jacket and an almost matching hat so bulky it was impossible to tell whether this was a man or a woman. Except it was neither. The zombie raised its arms, clawing at the closing space between it and the truck. Tom turned the wheel, pulling into the other lane. The zombie staggered across the asphalt. Thirty yards. Twenty. It was heading straight for them.

"You're going to hit it!" Helena yelled.

Tom swerved again. The zombie lurched toward the truck, not quite diving, not quite falling. It hit the ground, and there was no time to steer around it. There was a wet, sodden thump as the truck drove over it. When he forced himself to look in the rear-view mirror, the zombie's arm was still twitching.

It was almost a relief when they saw the police car ahead. Next to it were three police motorbikes and a large collection of civilian vehicles, parked end to end, neatly sealing all but one lane of the road.

"Looks like a checkpoint," Helena said.

"It's a detour, I think," Tom said. "They're trying to keep people away from somewhere."

Though the RV ahead of them slowed as it reached the checkpoint, it didn't stop. When they came level with the lead police vehicle, Tom did.

"You can't stop here," the cop said.

"We need some gas or we'll be on foot," Tom said.

The cop leaned in and looked at the fuel gauge. "Where're you headed?"

"Lake Erie," Tom said.

The cop gave a thoughtful nod, took a step back, and gave the truck an equally thoughtful inspection. "There's a filling station a quarter-mile down the road," he said, gesturing toward a side road. "Pull in there."

"Thank you," Tom said, uncertain he meant it. He took the turning. Behind them, the cop got into the police cruiser and followed.

"I don't like this," Helena whispered.

Neither did Tom. It might mean nothing, of course, but paranoia had reared its head once more. He ran through their options and found there weren't any. If he tried driving away, they would run out of gas before the pursuit got anywhere near a high speed. That did little to quell his desire to stamp on the gas pedal.

There was a filling station, just where the cop had said it would be. On the far side of the pumps were two minivans, an SUV with blacked-out windows, and a silver pickup so new it still had the dealership shine. However, the only people were a pair of sentries on the gas station's flat roof. Both wore hunting gear and carried rifles, and were watching their approach.

Tom pulled in, next to a pump.

"I guess it's self-service," Helena said, with a nervous laugh. They got out. Tom tried the pump. It didn't work. The police cruiser pulled in behind them. The cop got out. A civilian climbed out of the passenger side. The officer had a hand on his holster. The civilian grabbed a shotgun from the rack behind seats. No, it hadn't been paranoia.

"The pump doesn't work," Tom said.

The cop shrugged. "Which one of you is Mr Wu?" he asked.

Tom frowned, momentarily confused. He followed the line of the officer's gaze to the sign painted on the side of the truck. The officer would have seen the New Jersey plates, and the exposed wires under the dash. The question, then, was why had they been stopped? Was it because they came from the east, or for grand theft auto? Before he could formulate a calculated lie, Helena spoke up.

"We were in New York," she said. "We got out before they destroyed the George Washington Bridge. The car was like this, abandoned outside a house. We knocked... I mean, there were zombies around. People, infected, you know? We knocked on the door, and... they wouldn't let us in. We took the car. It was that or die. My mother has a place on Lake Erie. We're just trying to get there."

"They said they had New York quarantined," the cop said.

"No," Tom said. "They destroyed the bridges, but it was already too late. I don't know about you, but the first footage of the outbreak I saw was of a mall in upstate New York."

"That's as may be," the civilian said, "but we have a quarantine here. Anyone who might have been exposed has to be quarantined for twenty-four hours."

"We left the city over thirty-six hours ago," Tom said.

"And we've only got your word for it," the cop said. "The rules are the rules. Twenty-four hours, then you'll be allowed to go on your way." His hand curled around the butt of his holstered sidearm. Tom didn't need to look up to know the two sentries on the roof were aiming weapons right at them. There was no point arguing.

"I don't suppose this quarantine would involve a hot shower?" he asked.

The town was called Carthage, but they weren't taken there, nor to a police station, but to a warehouse to the south. On the other side of the road, a small mall was dwarfed by the large grocery store next to it. From the activity, the whole town had come together to strip the stores bare.

They were hustled out of the back of the cop car and into the warehouse. They weren't quite under arrest, the cop even opened the door for them, but there was no opportunity to run. Inside the warehouse, behind a folding table, sat a grey-haired older woman. Ruining the material of an absurdly smart suit was an FBI badge. Behind her were four men and two women, none older than twenty. All carried matching, holstered sidearms.

"Did you search them?" the agent asked the cop.

He blinked, then shrugged.

"You're meant to search them," the agent said. The cop gave another shrug, and left.

"Empty your pockets," the agent said. "Tyler, get me some boxes."

One of the teenagers grabbed a pair of empty plastic storage boxes from a stack by the wall and placed them on the folding table.

"I have a revolver," Tom said. "It's unloaded."

There was a general shifting among the group of youngsters.

"If he was going to use it," the agent said, "he wouldn't have warned us. Take it out, put it in the box."

Tom did. More reluctantly, he added the sat-phone, tablet, and the last of the money.

"That's it?" the agent asked.

"Aside from some lint? Yes."

"Your turn," the agent held out a box for Helena. She had even less than he did.

"Names?"

"Thomas Dennis," Tom said, hoping that Helena wouldn't remember his surname. If she did, she didn't say anything. The agent wrote the name on a piece of paper, and then again on the lid of the box. "And you?"

"Helena Diomedes."

"I need your home address."

Helena gave the boat, and that caused a few eyebrows to be raised. "It was sunk," she said. "It's why I'm on foot."

Tom gave an address a few blocks from the apartment.

"I need you to sign this," the agent said, turning the sheet of paper around. "Next to your names."

"What is it?" Tom asked.

"You're confirming your name and address," the agent said. "Nothing more. You're not under arrest, but you are being detained for the safety of everyone in the community. After twenty-four hours, you'll be released, and returned to your vehicle."

That wasn't an answer to his question, but he recognized he'd lost his right to any legal recourse long before the events of New York. He picked up the pen.

"How did you get those?" the woman asked.

As he'd reached for the pen, he'd exposed his forearm and the jagged cut running halfway to his elbow.

"It was a couple of days ago. A piece of rubble," Tom said.

"I see. Fine," the agent said. "Ryan, go and get some bandages. We'll see if we can get you some new clothes, too. Those things aren't fit to be rags."

There was something about her tone that belied the conciliatory nature of the words.

"Men and women are being housed separately," the agent said. "Madison, please show Ms Diomedes to the lounge."

"And me?" Tom asked.

He was taken to a storage room near the rear of the warehouse. It was full of wire cages, eight feet high, six feet square. The room was partially illuminated by harsh strip lights dangling from the ceiling, but mostly from the narrow windows high up on the far wall. They added shadows to the shapes of two figures in separate cages on either side of the room, but not enough depth to make out their features.

"What is this place?" Tom asked.

"Isolation," the agent said. "You'll be here for the night. You'll get some food, some rest. Tomorrow you'll get some clothes, and then you can be on your way."

"But what was it before?" Tom asked.

"It was for compartmentalized shipping," the agent said. "And if you can tell me what that means, I'd consider myself grateful. Inside. We'll get you something to clean your arm."

Tom stepped into the open cage. The door was closed. He was locked in. The agent left, and he took a closer look at his surroundings. His first thought was that it was a black site; some secret facility for temporarily holding detainees that the judicial system didn't know existed. The lock was wrong and would be too easily broken. Yes, he decided, two or three good kicks, and it would give. The question was whether he should try. If he were to escape, that would mean leaving Helena behind, but she'd be safe here. This town was organized, and large enough that another mouth wouldn't be too great a burden.

So he'd break the door, but then what? The FBI agent was old enough to be retired, though he knew appearances could be deceptive and age wasn't a determinant of strength. The teenagers could be easily dealt with, but then what? He'd have to steal a vehicle, hope that the roads in whatever direction he traveled weren't barricaded, and that there was enough fuel to outdistance the pursuit. Or, since he had to sleep somewhere, he could take advantage of the relative safety, and hope the new day brought some better prospects than this one had.

"Hope," he muttered. "It seems like that's all that's left."

Chapter 14 - Cellmates
Carthage, Pennsylvania

He wasn't sure how long it was before the wide doors opened and one of the young guards came in. Tom stood as the man approached.

"I brought a bucket," he said. "You have to sit down with your legs spread in front and your hands on your head."

Tom sat. "My name's Tom. What's yours?"

"Ryan," he said, opening the door. A bucket was placed inside.

"Hi, Ryan. Do you live in the town?"

"The bucket's clean. There's some soap and three bottles of water inside. And a bandage for your arm. We'll bring food later."

"Thank you."

Ryan locked the door again. When it was closed, he seemed to relax. "You were in New York when it happened?"

"More or less."

"Is it as bad as they say?"

"I don't know what they're saying," Tom said, "except what's been on the radio, and I'd say it was worse. The police were pulled out of Manhattan. There was no federal response. The National Guard did what they could, but there was little coordination."

"Oh. Um... they said Manhattan was quarantined."

"Who's they?"

"The mayor. There was a meeting. She told everyone the infection was being controlled, but that there might be a few infected people who got out before the cordon could be set up."

"Who told her that?"

"Dunno."

"Well, it isn't true," Tom said. "Manhattan was cut off, but it was done too late. The people were left to fend for themselves after the police were withdrawn. Boats were sunk, the bridges blown up. God knows what it's like for anyone still there. Did you hear about Paris?"

"The virus is in Texas?"

"Paris, France. But I heard a report on the radio saying it was in New Orleans and in Chicago. It's all over the world. You're stripping the grocery store?"

"What? Oh, yeah. Pooling our resources. The mayor says that it's going to take months before it's safe to leave the town."

"She's probably right. Do you have enough supplies for that?"

"Absolutely. I mean, I think so," he said. "It's really everywhere?"

"It is."

Ryan left, lost in his own thoughts. He wasn't a soldier on leave, or even a cop straight out of the academy. He was a kid barely out of high school, handed a gun that he carried without knowing how to use it. Tom took a bottle of water out of the bucket and began to wash and bandage his arm.

The interstates were the nation's arteries, pumping truckloads of food from depots to stores to homes. Every part of the supply chain had been shut down. Assuming that grocery store was the principal supplier of food for the town and the surrounding area then, regardless of how large the town was, it wouldn't stock more than a week's worth of supplies. Of course, that was at a normal rate of consumption. If that was scaled back to a calorie-controlled diet, with communal meals to reduce wastage, it would stretch further. Two weeks? Factor in however much food people had in their homes. Around here, some would have a lot, but just as many couldn't afford to store anything more than for their immediate needs. Hunting and foraging might stretch that a little further, but it was the tail end of winter. So how long would they last? Three weeks? A month? Sooner, not later, their supplies would run out. They would turn on one another, and a leader capable of organizing the systematic looting of their town would know that. The only course of action open to them was to look for other supplies.

"Raiding, not looking. Taking them by force from people as desperate as themselves." People who'd made the terrible choice of turning refugees away, and then survived the onslaught of the undead. They wouldn't be strangers, either, but neighbors and friends. Many would die. Those who survived might have the supplies to last a little longer, but until when?

Would anyone, anywhere, plant a crop this year? Would there be enough people left to plant one in a year's time?

He finished wrapping the bandage around his arm.

The worst part was that there was only a small chance this town would survive a month. He'd made the right choice getting out of the city, but selfish self-preservation wouldn't keep the rest of the world alive. There had to be a plan. He eyed the lock again. Yes, it would be easily broken, but then what? He could call Nate and tell him to pass the phone to Max. He thought the president would take his call. But then what? What would he say? What advice would he offer?

He'd always viewed politics as a game. Even with Max, and with all that was riding on that campaign, electoral victory had been the prize. The actual business of governing had never interested him. Yet he'd spent enough time talking policy that surely, taking what he'd seen, what he knew, there had to be a solution. The harsh truth was that millions would die, but billions could still survive. There had to be a way for towns like this to become beacons in the chaotic wasteland, the hubs from which the nation, and then the world, could be rebuilt. He sat back and tried to work out what it was.

The next time the door opened, it didn't herald the arrival of food, but of another inmate. The FBI agent had her weapon drawn, the barrel pointed at the man's back. Ryan followed a pace behind, his own weapon drawn, but it was aimed more at the ground than the prisoner.

"Inside," the FBI agent said, gesturing at a cage opposite Tom's.

"You can't do this. It's detention without trial," the man said.

"I look forward to your lawsuit," the agent replied. "Now get in."

Still protesting, the man was pushed into the cell. "I have rights!"

"Simmer down," the agent said, as Ryan locked the door. "You'll be out tomorrow."

"I'll have your badge!" the man said. The agent shook her head and left. Ryan stopped. He looked at Tom as if there was something he wanted to say.

"And you," the new prisoner yelled at Ryan. "I'll have you arrested. You'll be an old man before you're eligible for parole."

Ryan hurried from the room.

"They can't do this," the man muttered. "They can't."

Tom was too slow in sinking back to the rear of the cage. The man spotted him.

"What are you in here for?" the man called.

"A cut on my arm," Tom replied. "You?"

"For telling them they have no right to do this," the man said.

There was no point arguing. "Where did you come from?" Tom asked instead.

"Boston. You?"

"New Jersey. What was Boston like?"

"A nightmare," the man said. "The police set up roadblocks and told us to stay inside. Then the Army drove through them and told us to leave. The whole place was a mess. Disorganized. Like no one was talking to each other. I don't think anyone has a clue what's going on. And this bunch? I'll sue the lot of them. All I want to do is get to the cabin. It's my property, isn't it? What right do they have to detain me?"

"Your cabin, is it remote?" Tom asked. He wasn't particularly interested, but if the man was going to insist on talking, Tom would rather it was more than a litany of complaints.

"Yeah, it's—" And then, as if realizing that giving away the address of his secret hideaway wasn't a wise course of action, the man finally stopped talking. "It's remote, yeah," he finished. Silence descended.

Beyond knowing that the world outside the high-fitted windows was dark, there was no way to track the passage of time. At least the warehouse was warm. In fact, he thought it was temperature-controlled. Forcing himself to ignore the mystery of what the warehouse had been built for, and the memory of the pointlessly old-fashioned watches he'd once owned, he turned back to the problem of how the nation could drag itself out of this apocalyptic mire. He'd got as far as realizing the closed interstates could be used to bring supplies to towns like this one when the new prisoner started talking once more.

120

"Hey! Did you see any zombies?"

There was an irritated grunt from the occupied cage in the far corner of the room, but neither of the other two detainees replied. Tom copied their example.

"Hey! Hey you! I'm talking to you!" the man called, without qualifying which 'you' he was addressing. "You seen any zombies?"

The man clearly wasn't going to shut up, so, in the hope he might stop shouting, Tom replied. "A few, yeah," he said. "In the city. In a refugee camp. A few more about fifty miles from here. What about you?"

"No. That's what I mean. I've not seen any, so why are they locking me up? How could I be infected? You see what I mean? It's pointless."

Tom silently vowed to say no more.

"They said it was terrorists," the man continued, oblivious to the indifference of his audience. "But terrorists can't do this. I mean, they can't! How long would it take to create a zombie? Decades, right?"

"They're not zombies!" The words were shouted from the dark recesses in the far corner of the room."

"Really?" the man opposite said, his tone brighter now he had a responsive listener. "So what are they?"

"Victims? I don't know, but we can't hide in a fantasy world."

"It's not a fantasy." This came from the room's other detainee, a gruffer, wilder voice than the other two. "These are the end times. I have seen the pale horse! This is the last plague, the final revelation before the ultimate judgment!"

"Right? Really?" the Bostonian said. There was an edge of glee to his voice. "Because I saw a priest try to stop them. He had a cross and a Bible, and they ripped him apart. Precisely how is your religion going to save you?"

"It is not religion, but faith," the gruff man began. "A test placed before us…"

Tom sighed as the pointless debate raged. They were all filling time, none listening to the others, no one sharing any real information about what they'd seen. They were talking as a way of covering their own fear. That wouldn't have been a problem if they'd done it quietly. The argument droned on until the door opened. The room went silent as Ryan came in, pushing a small metal trolley.

"Dinner," he said, self-conscious embarrassment muting the half-hearted shout.

"What is it," the man opposite asked.

"Fish stew," Ryan said.

"I don't eat fish," the man said.

"Oh, I am sorry, sir," Ryan replied, frustrated anger giving him confidence. "Would you like to see a menu? Sit down, hands on your head, or you can go hungry."

"Thank you," Tom said when it was his turn.

"It's what we're eating," Ryan said. "It's what everyone's eating tonight."

"Using up what won't keep?" Tom asked.

"Yeah. And then what's frozen. The mayor's worried about the power grid. She says it won't last much longer and we need to prepare for when it stops."

"Wise." He looked at the bowl. "Thanks."

The stew wasn't bad. It wasn't good, but it was hot and the spices overwhelmed the contrasting flavors. When the bowl was empty, he stretched out on the floor, and tried to sleep.

A cage door rattled. It wasn't his. He opened his eyes, guessing the cause. The man opposite wasn't prepared to use the bucket as a bathroom and wanted to share his discomfort. The lights had been dimmed, but not extinguished. The rattle came again. He was tempted to tell the man to stop, that no one was going to come, but if he knew Tom was awake, he was likely to start complaining once more.

Then there was a hiss. A groan. A gasping moan. Tom leaped to his feet, curling his fingers around the wire as he peered into the darkness. All he could see was an indistinct shape. There was an atonal plinking as of a hand being dragged down the side of a cage. And again. And again. Then a banging, metallic creak as if a figure was trying to walk through the door.

He opened his mouth, about to shout for help. He closed it again. If there was no one there, if the sentries were all asleep, all he'd do was tell the zombie where he was. Zombie. That's what it was, and that cage door wasn't going to hold.

The dragging of fingers down the cage grew quicker. The butting, beating of flesh against the wire frame grew stronger. The creaking of the metal gate grew louder. Tom looked around for a weapon. There wasn't one, and he wasn't safe inside the cage. He kicked at the door. Once. Twice. The sound from opposite grew louder. He kicked again. The lock broke. The door swung open. He stepped outside, keeping his eyes on the cage opposite. The door was bulging. It wouldn't hold for much longer. He backed away until his elbow hit the warehouse door. He tried pushing and pulling the handles. The doors were firmly locked. He slammed a fist against them.

"Hey!" he yelled. "Help! Someone!"

There was a sharp crack of metal. He spun around. The thin welding around the cage door's topmost hinge had broken. The door sagged, and the zombie moved with it, adding its weight to the door. The lower hinge broke. The door fell outward. The zombie, its fingers still caught in the wire mesh, went with it, adding a meaty thump to the metallic clang as the door hit the floor.

"What's going on?" The yell came from one of the other detainees. Tom ignored him.

The zombie tried to stand. It pushed upward with its knees, and then its legs, but its fingers were still trapped in the mesh. There was a sucking pop, and another, and a third, as one by one, its fingers were torn from its hands.

The creature straightened. It raised the gory stubby hands toward Tom. Its mouth opened, and an inhuman sigh escaped its lips.

Aim for the legs, immobilize it, he thought as the creature lurched toward him. Behind him came the sound of a key in a lock, and then a chain being pulled back. The warehouse door opened. Ryan came in, pistol drawn. He saw the zombie and froze.

"Shoot it!" Tom yelled.

The zombie staggered another step, a dark pus oozing from its fingerless hands.

"Shoot it!"

But Ryan didn't fire. Tom stepped forward as the zombie threw out an arm toward him. Ducking under the ill-aimed roundhouse blow, he swept out his leg, hooking his foot behind the creature's knee, pulling it up. The zombie toppled over, landing on its back. Almost immediately, it pushed those bloody nubs of hands against the concrete as it tried to stand.

"Now! Shoot!" Tom yelled. Ryan was immobile, staring in shock at the creature. Tom swore, ran over to him, and snatched the gun from the young man's trembling hands. The zombie was on its knees. Tom flicked off the safety, braced himself, and fired a shot straight into the zombie's head. He fired a second round, just to be sure.

Everything was quiet, but only for a second. From deeper in the warehouse came another rattle of hands being drawn down a wire cage. Tom stalked toward the sound.

"Not me! Not me!" a bearded man cried, as Tom neared. "It's him! Over there!"

The figure was dressed in clothes as ragged as Tom's own. He was older, though, nearing sixty, at least. Tom raised the gun, aiming carefully between the wire grille that was bulging under the pressure of the zombie struggling to escape. He fired. The zombie collapsed.

"Ryan? Ryan?"

The kid was still frozen to the spot near the warehouse door. Tom looked down at the gun, then at the warehouse's remaining occupant.

"Lock us in, Ryan. If you hear a shot, you know what's happened."

He waited until the teenager had left, then walked over to the occupied cage.

"My name's Tom. What's yours?"

"Phil."

Tom sat down with his back against the cage next to Phil's.

"Try to get some sleep, Phil. Whatever tomorrow brings, we're both going to need it."

Chapter 15 - Another Miserable Day
February 23rd, Carthage, Pennsylvania

Dawn had barely arrived when he heard the chain being drawn back on the other side of the warehouse door. Ryan came in. He wasn't alone, but with a middle-aged man Tom hadn't seen the previous day. The man held a shotgun, raised to his shoulder. Tom still held Ryan's sidearm, but kept the barrel pointing at the floor.

"We're both human," he said, trying to force some jocularity into his voice. "Here. Safety's on." Holding the gun by the barrel, he passed it to Ryan.

"Thanks," Ryan said.

"You, get up," the older man barked at the man in the cage. "Unlock it."

Ryan unlocked the cage.

"Now get out," the man said.

"You're letting us go? It's not been twenty-four hours," Tom said.

The shotgun swung toward him, the barrel not six inches from his face. "You want me to tell you again?"

Tom raised his hands, took a step to the side, and headed for the door. Ryan fell into step next to him. "What's going on?" he asked the young man.

"It all went wrong last night," Ryan said. "A convoy arrived. Some were military, some weren't. Said they came from Lexington. It was a general leading them. Or he said he was a general. Said he was taking over the town. He said he had orders. I... The zombies were following them. I think. Or maybe they had infected people with them. I don't know. The mayor's dead. The general drove off. It's all chaos."

He pushed open the door and led Tom outside. "Here." He grabbed the plastic crate with Tom's name on it. The sat-phone and tablet were inside. The adaptor, money, and the unloaded revolver were not. "Take them and go. Go quickly."

"What aren't you telling me?" Tom asked.

"They're saying we should kill the outsiders. Anyone who might be infected. You have to go. Please."

Tom grabbed the sat-phone and tablet, and went outside. The parking lot was filled with men, women, and children. He guessed these were the other detainees.

"That was hellish," Helena said, coming over to join him. "I don't know about you, but that was one of the worst night's sleep of my life."

Tom started walking, out of the lot, and down the road leading away from the town.

"Hey!" Helena called, running to catch up. "I need to get my stuff."

"Leave it."

"But—"

"Look behind."

"What— oh." Three plumes of smoke rose up from the town.

"A kid told me that people arrived last night, brought the infection with them. Said others were going to come and kill the lot of us," he said.

"They… what?"

He didn't repeat himself. They had no water, no weapons, no food. He had the sat-phone and tablet, and on a whim he took them out. The battery was drained. It looked like someone had tried to use it the previous night. A barrage of gunfire came from behind them.

"Are they shooting them?" Helena asked.

"It's not from the warehouse. Not yet." He started to jog. They had to stay ahead of the rest of the detainees, and far ahead of whoever, and whatever, was in the town.

Tom remembered the lightning-struck oak from their journey to the warehouse. It meant they were less than half a mile from the gas station. There was a single shot, and then another, but it wasn't coming from behind. Tom stopped. The shooting kept on. Four shots. Five. Then silence.

"They're ahead of us," Helena said.

"We can't go back," Tom said. There was no safety there. No safety anywhere. His fists bunched as he started walking. Fury slowly took hold.

"Tom! Tom!"

He ignored her. A burning anger had gripped him. It was an old, familiar companion. He'd suppressed it in recent years, but it had always been there, lurking beneath the surface. He almost welcomed the prospect of the fight that would come, and gave no heed to the almost certain death that would follow.

"Tom! Stop!"

She grabbed his arm. He saw the abject fear in her eyes and realized he'd seen the same thing in Ryan, the man who'd let them out of the warehouse, and almost everyone else he'd come in contact with in the last three days.

"We can't go back, so we go on," he said, forcing the rage back down. "But we'll do it carefully," he added.

Outside the gas station was a police cruiser. Its doors hung wide open. A large truck had crashed into the filling station, knocking down the struts supporting the roof. There was no sign of the two sentries who'd been on guard, though on the ground were two clusters of zombies. Four in one, five in another. The truck must have breached the barricade. The cops had chased it. The truck had crashed. The zombies... he didn't know from where they'd come, except that now they truly were everywhere.

"That cop car. That's how we get out of here," he said. "When I say run, do it. Get inside. Start the engine. Don't argue."

He kept his eyes on the zombies. They were milling around aimlessly. Some heading up the road, some toward the filling station. And then one turned around. Its head cricked to the right. It took a lurching step toward them.

"Not yet."

It managed four paces before another creature noticed the movement. Then a third. A fourth. Then the rest of that small pack, turned as one toward them.

"Now!"

Helena ran. So did Tom, keeping a step behind.

127

They were going to make it. They were going to make it. A zombie lurched across the road, slightly quicker than the others. They weren't going to make it. Tom changed direction, putting on a burst of speed, bringing up his elbow, smashing it into the zombie's face. The creature went flying, and Tom kept running.

Helena reached the car and jumped inside. The engine roared. Tom's heart sang. The vehicle began to move. His heart skipped a beat as he thought Helena was about to drive off without him. The car jerked to a halt.

"Come on!" she yelled.

He threw himself through the open door. Helena slammed a foot on the pedal. The car rocketed forward before Tom had even closed the door.

Chapter 16 - It's Not a Virus
Allegheny National Forest, Pennsylvania

"There's no spare ammo in the trunk," Tom said. "Just what's in the magazine."

"I'll take the pistol," Helena said.

Tom picked up the shotgun. Its eight shells and the pistol's fifteen were of little reassurance when he thought of the fate of the officer at the gas station. The rest of the trunk's contents were useless: a couple of bulletproof vests, some high-viz tabards, and an assortment of tools that suggested Carthage's police force spent as much time dealing with breakdowns as they did break-ins. He picked up a tire iron, long enough to be called a crowbar. It was reassuringly sturdy.

"What about the bulletproof vests?" Helena asked. "It might help us if people think we're police."

It wasn't an idle suggestion. They'd come across roadblocks twice during their journey west, and got through both by turning on the siren.

"No," he said, after considered deliberation. "People who'd believe we're cops would expect us to help them, or they'd shoot at us. Against zombies, it would only be extra weight."

Helena took a swig from the gallon-jug of water. It was already half empty. She passed it to Tom. They'd found that in a minivan, abandoned twenty miles from the town. The only trace of the occupants had been a bloody stain on the asphalt, and another on the passenger-side door.

"You sure it's this road?" Helena asked. "It's more gravel than asphalt, and more mud than both."

"I'm as sure as I can be." And if he was wrong, they were stuck in the middle of nowhere, with no fuel for a car that was barely road-worthy. They had half a gallon of water, no shelter, and the undead were no more than two days' lurch to the east. Not counting however many might be ahead of them. He slung the shotgun, but kept the crowbar in his hand.

"So who is this scientist?" Helena said, as they walked along the rutted track. "How do you know her?"

Tom tried to recall what he'd told Helena, but so much had happened that he couldn't remember.

"I've not met her," he said. "At least, I don't think I have. She's one of those brilliant scientists completely lacking in a moral compass. Because of that, she was involved in some questionable research, disregarding most of the basic safety considerations."

"What do you mean, questionable?"

"She smuggled infected tissue samples back from West Africa, developed a cure, and tested it on her grad students."

"Wow. And she didn't get locked up?"

"Odd, right? It was over ten years ago, and she was working at the CDC at the time. There was an investigation. It concluded her findings were useful. They couldn't announce that she'd been acting without any kind of oversight, so a compromise was reached. She was sent into internal exile, never to go near a lab again. In return, she stayed out of prison, and there was no embarrassing court case."

"Hmm." Helena was quiet for a long while. When she spoke, the question wasn't one Tom expected. "Do you think she created the zombie virus?"

"If you'd asked me a year ago, I'd have said that no one could. Since someone clearly has, the next question is whether she's technically able."

"And is she?"

"I think so." He mulled it over. "In fact, I'd go one step further. Out of all the people in the U.S., I'd say she was one of the few who could."

"But did she, do you think?"

"I suppose we'll find out when we get there."

After another mile, and just as Tom began to think they'd come the wrong way, they turned a bend and saw a timber-framed house. A mud-splattered Jeep was parked out front.

"No dogs. No smoke. No smell of cooking," Tom murmured. There was no sign of life more recent than the wide-wheeled ruts dug deep into the mud either side of the road.

Helena reached for the door.

"Wait." Tom pointed at the alarm. About the size of a cereal box, it was ridiculously large for such a remote house. The bell might scare deer, but it wouldn't have much effect on anyone who'd come all this way to break in. A more effective system would be a silent alarm linked to the county police or, considering the woman's identity, the Feds.

"Try knocking," he suggested. She did. There was no answer.

"Hello!" she called. There was no response.

Tom pulled a plant pot across the decked veranda, climbed up, and looked at the alarm. He nudged the box, and then lifted it clear. All that was inside was a small battery attached to a blinking red LED.

"Anything else you want to try?" Helena asked.

Tom shrugged. Then he realized. "The tire marks don't match the Jeep," he said. "Look at them. Someone drove in, turned around, and drove off again."

"Okay, but is that a reason we should stay out here in the cold?"

Somehow, he thought it was.

Helena opened the door. No alarm sounded. That wasn't reassuring. Nor was the organized chaos they found inside. Whiteboards were positioned around the room. Each was covered in overlapping scrawls. Where there wasn't room, the writing continued on the windows and walls, sometimes onto the once-polished floor – at least in the places not obscured by a drift of paper, each covered in their own incomprehensible collection of hieroglyphs.

It was a small house, and it didn't take long to confirm it was deserted. On returning to the living room, he found Helena staring at the whiteboards. She pointed at one of the few phrases written in non-mathematical English.

"It's not a virus," she read aloud. "It doesn't say what it is. At least not in any language I understand."

"But it explains what she was working on," Tom said.

"And probably means that she wasn't the one who created it," Helena said.

Did it? Tom stared at the phrase. Maybe she'd written it in frustration at the descriptions given by the hysterical media. He traced a finger along the equation that had led to the scientist's conclusion. He couldn't make sense of it, but the calculation had begun on the adjacent whiteboard.

"I think you're right," he said. "She had no idea someone was working on this until it happened. But she might know who was. See if you can find any names there."

Discounting the recent mess, the house had the sparse, battered furnishings of an owner who'd had few visitors. There was a television in a corner. Near it, and looking more frequently used, was a desk, down the back of which the cables for the keyboard and display dangled uselessly. The computer tower was missing. He knelt down. Under the desk was a multi-plug power-strip filled with adaptors. One was for a laptop, though that was missing as well. Another was the right size for the sat-phone. He plugged that in, and the tablet into that, leaving both devices to recharge.

"There's electricity," he said, only realizing as the power button on the sat-phone blinked red.

"Shouldn't there be?" Helena asked.

"No. I mean, it's a relief to know that's still working." For good measure, he checked the light switches, and then that water still ran from the faucet. He walked back into the main room, stood in the middle, and slowly turned on the spot. Three-sixty degrees, seven-twenty...

"What is it?" Helena asked, staring at him.

"Something's off."

"What do you mean?"

"Someone came here and took her away. A heavy vehicle with wider tires than you'd find on a car or domestic truck."

"So?"

"And she was working on zombies," he said, now talking to himself. He was trying to get a sense of the woman who'd lived in the house. The television had a thin layer of dust on it, suggesting it was used infrequently enough to be forgotten. The couch didn't quite face it, and wasn't as worn as the chair by the window. Yet there were few books on the half-empty shelf, and enough dust to suggest there hadn't been more that were taken away with her. Other than the desk, the only other furniture was a table with four chairs, each pushed in. The table had been shoved against the wall suggesting it was rarely used.

"Maybe it was the CDC," Helena suggested. "Someone there remembered her name and thought she could help. That's the obvious answer, isn't it? I mean, why look for a conspiracy?"

"Because conspiracies exist," Tom muttered. There was only one ornament in the room: an iron statue of a horse on a thick steel base.

"Why have the alarm outside? It's not going to scare anyone away," he said, and picked up the statue. "The only reason is so people don't look for the real alarm system. When you can't deter theft, the best you can do is make sure you'll get your stuff back." The statue's base was hollow, but sealed shut. He smiled. There was a thin line around the animal's neck. The head unscrewed, revealing a small camera inside.

"A nanny-cam?" Helena asked.

"Looks like it. A camera, a battery, a memory card, and a USB port." He plugged it into the tablet. "Let's see. Yes. The footage is low quality, but it looks like it'll record for forty-eight hours without being recharged."

He pressed play. The first twenty hours showed a woman with wild, grey hair stalking back and forth across her living room, a pen in each hand. She scrawled notes on the whiteboard, occasionally crossing to the computer, and sometimes to the laptop. Sometimes she would wipe the boards clean, other times simply write over whatever had been there before. At the end of twenty hours she seemed to reach some conclusion, tapping her pen repeatedly on the whiteboard nearest the door. She put the pens down and disappeared. The recording wasn't of a high-enough definition to make out what she'd written.

"She's gone to sleep," Helena suggested.

Tom skipped forward. The woman was only gone for two hours. When she returned, she wiped the boards clean and ripped down the sheets of paper she'd pinned to the walls. She began writing again.

"It has a forty-eight hour battery," Helena said. "So it kept recording after she left. Skip forward to then."

The writing and erasing continued for another eight hours. Dr Ayers stopped.

"There!" Helena said. "Is there sound?"

"No."

There didn't need to be. Ayers looked out the window, and then at the door. Her expression was confused. She smiled at the camera. It wasn't a happy expression, but one of resignation. She turned to face the door and raised her hands as if she was shouting at someone. Two figures came into view. Both wore Army fatigues and carried assault rifles. A third man came into the room. Like the others, he was dressed as a soldier, but Tom knew he wasn't military. Even before the camera caught the man's face, Tom knew from the shock of white hair whom it was. Powell.

Ayers was escorted outside. Powell lingered in the room. One of the soldiers came back in. Tom paused the video.

"What are you doing?" Helena asked.

He skipped back a few minutes. "There. That soldier. He's one of the two who took her outside."

"So?"

"So there are only three of them. If there were more people, they'd leave more to guard her."

"So?" Helena repeated.

Tom didn't answer. He let the video play. The soldier collected the computer tower. Powell picked up the laptop. They left. The video continued playing, but there was nothing more to see until it recorded the door opening once more, and Helena and Tom walked into the room.

"She was taken away seventeen and a half hours ago," Helena said. "Maybe eighteen since we arrived, give or take."

Tom stood up.

"Where are you going?"

"To find the other cameras."

There was one, at least he only found one. It was outside, on the opposite side of the door to the decoy alarm box, hidden within a bird feeder.

"Attached to a motion sensor," he said. Helena shrugged and walked over to the whiteboards. Tom plugged in the camera, and skipped through the footage of deer, of Dr Ayers arriving, leaving, arriving, more deer, and then he saw it.

"It's a BearCat," he said staring at the four-wheeled armored car on the screen. "Painted green, but it has no markings." He watched as the doors opened. Three people got out. He watched Ayers being brought out of the house. The vehicle drove off. He skipped forward again, until he found the footage of himself and Helena arriving, and then went back to the footage of Powell.

"There were three of them," he said. "Only three. And in a vehicle with no markings."

"It's a military vehicle, though?" Helena asked, half turning around.

"What? No. I mean, yes, the military use it, but so do law enforcement. This one has no markings that I can see. It means wherever they went has to be within driving distance." Maybe it was nearby. Maybe he could find Powell, and perhaps he would find the other conspirators. It was a beguiling idea that filled his mind with fantasies of revenge.

"So what's the range on one of those?" she asked.

"I don't know." The fantasy was popped. It would be hundreds of miles.

"Oh. I've read books," Helena said. He looked up. She was standing by a whiteboard, running a finger down the mathematical inscriptions. "Popular science, I mean. You know, the kind that always comes out before Christmas. I'm not a scientist, but I'm not stupid. I don't think I could differentiate an equation, but I know what the symbols look like. These? They're not even Greek. Is there a scientific equivalent of shorthand?"

"I don't know," Tom said, turning back to the screen. He replayed the video, looking for some clue he'd missed.

"Not even Greek," Helena repeated. She sighed loudly enough for Tom to look up again. She headed into the kitchen.

If Powell had arrived here eighteen hours before, so at about the same time that they'd arrived at the filling station, then when did he leave New York?

"There's food here," Helena said, looking in the fridge. "Mostly salad. All of it fresh. None have plastic wrappers. She must have gotten it from somewhere nearby. Somewhere with a hot-house."

Tom was about to start the video from the beginning, but forced his hand away from the screen. Watching the same clip over and over wouldn't help unravel the meaning within all these disparate threads. He put the tablet down, walked over to the armchair, and collapsed into it.

Powell had been dressed as a soldier. So had the two men with him. He'd had time to change, and presumably catch a few hours sleep. Tom envied the man.

"There are steaks in the freezer," Helena said. "Nothing else, just steak. I don't think she had a varied diet. We might as well eat. I... I guess I'll be cooking?"

"Hmm? Oh, yes. Thanks." Ignoring her exasperated sigh, he returned his attention to Powell. Give or take a few stops, he'd come here straight from New York. He would have flown out on a helicopter to the location where they'd collected that BearCat. It meant Powell's orders had changed. He wasn't looking for Tom anymore. And that meant—

"How did you know Dr Ayers?" Helena asked.

"What? Oh. I didn't. I thought I said."

"You said you came across her. You didn't say what you were looking for."

"Suspicious activity among scientists," he said, almost automatically. "Money had gone missing from a few budgets. I was chasing it, and got caught up in a bit of a rabbit hole."

There was the sound of a cupboard opening, water running. It stopped.

"Let me ask you something else," she said. "Who's that man with the white hair?"

"A soldier."

"No. Really, who is he?" Her tone had changed. It was calm, measured, though with a dangerous edge. He turned to look at her. Her teeth were gritted, her jaw clenched. "He was outside that block you said you lived in," she said. "I saw him. He was there. Now he's here. Who is he? Who are you? And what the hell is really going on?"

After he'd confirmed the house was empty, he'd left the shotgun by the couch, some ten feet from where he now sat. It wasn't there. Helena's hands were hidden below the counter of the island workstation, but it wasn't a stretch to imagine the pistol held in one of them.

"His name's Powell," he said.

"And who is he?"

"I don't know. Not exactly. Over the last month, he's passed himself off as a cop, a Fed, and now as a soldier. I doubt he's any of those, not any more. And it's unlikely Powell is his real name."

"Like how Tom Clemens isn't yours?" she asked. "You called yourself Thomas Dennis when they asked for your name in that town. You said you were an analyst, but you act like you're on the run. You've got contacts in the White House, but can't call anyone to help us. You know things, and have access to the kind of data that no ordinary person would. And now we're here, in the home of some scientist who's been working on God knows what, and who was taken away by three soldiers, one of whom was obviously looking for you a couple of days ago, and would have caught you if there hadn't been zombies in the streets!" Her voice rose to a scream. "The country's being torn apart! What the hell's going on?"

Could he trust her? Probably, and what was the alternative? He could disarm her easily enough, but then what? Wasn't the whole point of his original plan to expose the conspiracy to the entire world? So maybe he should start with that, one person at a time.

"It's a long story," he said, "and it begins years ago. The short version is that there's a conspiracy aimed at seizing control not just of our government, but also of nations across the world. I tried to stop it. Powell is the triggerman, but he works for Farley."

"Farley? The secretary of state?"

"There are others. He's not running this alone, but he's one of those at the top. Farley ran for president to secure the cabal's grip on power. To stop him, I persuaded Grant Maxwell to stand. I… I made sure he won. He's a friend, but he's also an honest man, and I thought that if he defeated Farley, it would mean an end to the conspiracy. I was wrong."

"And this… this cabal, are they behind the zombies?"

"No. I don't think so." He looked around Dr Ayers's home. "It probably wasn't created in the U.S, but by Russia or China, or someone else. They learned what this group was planning, and pre-empted it with something truly horrific."

"What do you mean? What were they planning?"

"It began in Britain with research into biological warfare during the early days of the Cold War. Someone realized that they needed a defense against the virological weapons that were being developed in the Soviet Union. Research began into a universal anti-viral."

"Did it work?"

"Not really, but it used up a lot of funding. When the Soviet Union collapsed, the research was put on hold. A few years ago, the cabal resurrected it. As I say, I still don't know the names of all those involved. There are Brits and Americans involved, all with their eyes on the highest —"

"Yes, yes," she said dismissively, "but this anti-virus, did it work? I mean, can we use it against the zombies?"

"I don't know. But it did work. At least, I found proof of trials that show it was effective against HIV, Ebola, Marb—"

"So it won't?"

"No. Not without being modified."

"Well, maybe that's why they came for Dr Ayers."

Tom stared at her. He'd been so consumed with Powell's presence, he'd not really considered why the man had come here. "Probably. Almost certainly."

"So that's more proof they weren't involved in making it," Helena said. "I say 'more', but you've not actually given me any yet. All you've said is that a group of politicians planned to take over the world through a scheme that would see all diseases being cured. To be honest, that doesn't sound… well, it doesn't sound all that bad."

"Firstly, the election was rigged. I might have helped Max win it, but they'd moved the finishing line before we'd even entered the race. That speaks to their character; they're consumed by a self-righteous belief in their right to rule the world. Democracy means nothing to them. And," he added, seeing Helena was about to interrupt, "they've killed to keep their conspiracy secret. The real villainy isn't in what they've done, but in what they intend. They aren't going to give the vaccine away. And they're not going to sell it, not for money at least. They want favored nation status, special economic trading zones, and the imposition of Western democracy anywhere they give the vaccine. And that might not sound too bad until you consider that your idea of democracy is markedly different from theirs."

"Fine. But that would be better than millions of people dying from disease, wouldn't it?"

"That would depend on how they got sick." He leaned back and closed his eyes. "There's a lot I don't know, and too much I can't prove. I suspected they were putting a plan into place whereby they would infect the populace of recalcitrant nations with resistant strains, and that was why I began investigating Dr Ayers. What I do know is that there are some nations who will not be cowed. The kind with their own labs, who would take this vaccine, synthesize their own version, and thus negate the conspiracy's scheme. They called this part of their plan Prometheus. It's a pre-emptive tactical nuclear strike on any nation that would never sit back and let them win."

"You're not serious? Nuclear war?"

"They're insane. Didn't I mention that? I have the targeting data. The problem is that so do the Russians and the Chinese. Well, why wouldn't they? If I was able to discover all this with my meager resources, is it any wonder that they did, too?"

"Then why didn't the FBI or the NSA discover this?"

"Because someone high up in those organizations is working with the cabal. There was a demonstration in New York on the twentieth. I think that was when Farley was due to make his final threat. Russia or China or someone guessed what was going to happen, so they released the virus. That's what I think happened. I know that the cabal had people working in foreign governments, but... but like I said, there's a lot of gaps. Because of that demonstration, I was in New York. I thought I could get proof of all of this, and release it to the world before Farley had a chance to begin the apocalyptic part of his plan. Unfortunately, it looks like someone else beat him to it."

"That doesn't explain Powell," she said.

"I decided to wait until after the inauguration to tell Max what I'd discovered. As president, he'd have the power to do something about it. As president-elect, he might have felt duty-bound to refuse the oath. Before I could tell him, I was framed for murder and... do you remember the bombings on the day of the inauguration?"

"Of course."

"I was blamed for them. There was evidence found on a journalist's computer. The journalist was murdered in my house. Shot with my gun, by Powell. I didn't get to speak to Max, and I've been on the run ever since."

"That's some story."

"I have the video." He walked over to the tablet and found the footage of Powell shooting Imogen Fenster. He pressed play and placed the tablet on the counter. Helena watched it.

"That's the man with the white hair. It doesn't prove anything else you've said."

"I've some files I can show you."

"Well, go on, then."

He pulled them up. He didn't store many on the tablet, just enough to remind him of what he was doing and why.

"I... I see," she finally said. "I have no way of knowing if any of this is real."

"True. I could have faked it. This is one of those times where you'll have to decide whether to believe me or not."

"I don't know if I entirely believe you," she said. "And I don't think what you believe is the entire truth. You've admitted as much, even if you won't admit it to yourself. But you seem like a decent guy, Tom Clemens." She raised her arm. Sure enough, the pistol was in her hand. She placed it on the counter. "Is that even your name?"

He relaxed. "Names are complicated, but for the last thirty years or so, I've called myself some variation of Thomas more often than anything else."

"And before that?"

"Thaddeus. That's what my mother named me."

She nodded to herself, seemingly satisfied, and sparked the stove. "You mind if the meat's tough? I'm too hungry to wait for them to defrost. Right, so if the Russians are behind the zombies, there's no reason to think there won't be another attack? Something worse?"

"It's possible, but not likely. The zombies are already everywhere. I doubt that was planned, but no one will have the resources to launch any more attacks."

"That's another theory, right?"

"An educated one."

She opened the drawers until she found a knife. She savaged the steak's packaging. A gust of smoke and steam erupted from the pan as she threw them in. "Okay, let's say you're right. That means we've just got the zombies to worry about."

"No. There's still Powell, Farley, and the conspirators. You're right; kidnapping Dr Ayers has to be part of a plan to adapt the vaccine."

"Good."

"What?"

"Well, someone has to do something to stop the zombies. It seems like that might work."

"You saw how the police were called back from Manhattan, but how there was no federal support in New Jersey. They had a quarantine and they destroyed your boat, but they didn't stop us crossing the bridge. You saw the military on the interstate. All of that is evidence of conflicting orders being given, all so the official response is slowed down. It can't be stopped, but they don't need it to be. They don't want it to be. They just need enough time to get the vaccine ready. Farley will take the credit. That's what he wanted all along. It's what Archangel was all about. These are petty men who want history to remember them."

"But you don't know their names?"

"Not all of them, no. I knew some. They died. Killed by their comrades to protect the conspiracy. I have my suspicions about the director of the FBI. In fact, suspicion isn't a strong enough word."

"Okay, but do you know anything? I mean, is it all just suspicions and hunches?"

"I'm certain that there aren't more than a hundred and fifty of them. I suspect it's around seventy. That's people who actively know what the cabal's ultimate goals are. That Powell came here with only two goons confirms it. Of course, when you have the secretary of state, and the director of the FBI as part of the inner circle, they can call on a lot of resources without ever having to explain why those orders are being given."

She flipped the steaks. "It's not a virus. That's what she wrote."

"I wish she'd said what it was."

"Well, she's not here. Any idea where they took her?"

"Not a clue."

"The steaks are done," she said, slapping them onto plates. She carried hers over to the table and sat down. He went to collect his plate.

"There's one other thing," she said as he stared down at the charred meat. "What did you mean, the elections were rigged? The *really* short version," she added.

"The candidates the cabal picked for the primary were so unelectable that Farley was the only choice until Max entered the race. In part, and by comparison, he was a breath of fresh air. I hacked Farley's email account and sent some messages from him to people I knew would leak them to the press. That did most of it. I set up a Super-PAC ostensibly supporting Farley, and which made such an outrageous attack on Max that the media jumped onto it, using it as an example of how dangerous those ads were. Farley had to come out and disavow it, and from then on, despite the money behind him, he was on the defensive."

"And in the general election?"

"There were some dirty tricks, sure, but to be honest, that was the cabal's work, funding candidates they thought would lose when facing Farley. Against Max, they didn't stand a chance."

"But you helped them along, anyway?"

"Sure. The fate of the world was at risk."

"Hmm. There's more to it, right? I mean, things that would be thought of as criminal?"

"Serious jail time, yes, but compared to what we're dealing with now, it doesn't seem so important."

"Not to you, and maybe that's your problem. Eat your steak. It's getting cold."

Chapter 17 - Air Force Two
Allegheny National Forest, Pennsylvania

"What are you going to do now?" Helena asked. He finished his last mouthful. She was watching him expectantly.

"That was nice, thank you." He placed his knife and fork together with geometric precision. "A last meal." He crossed to the alcove and picked up the sat-phone. "I'm going to call Nate, get him to hand the phone to the communications director, Gregson, and I'll ask him to give the phone to Max. I'll tell him everything I know, and precisely where I am. If it's Powell who comes here, I'll kill him. If it's not, I'll let them take me in and hope…" He smiled. "Hope they believe me. You should take the car, the rest of the food, and head north. Look for your sister. Family's important."

Helena chewed her lip, but said nothing as Tom dialed a number. Nate answered on the second ring.

"Prof?" Nate whispered.

"Nate? Are you okay?" Tom put the call on speaker.

"It's… it's… it's a nightmare."

Tom frowned. "Nate, I need you to listen. I need to speak to Gregson."

"You can't. He's not here."

"He's not? Where is he?"

"I don't know," Nate said. "He didn't come back."

"What do you mean? Where did he go?"

"I told him you called. I told him what you said. He went outside to see if he could get a proper connection. He didn't come back."

"Who else is there?"

"I don't know. I mean, I don't recognize anyone!"

"What about the other students from the university?"

"They all left," he hissed. "People go outside, and they don't come back."

"Is Max still there? Is the president in the White House?"

144

"He's here. Yeah. He's going to give a talk to the nation."

"When?"

"I'm not sure."

"What about Claire? Is the First Lady there?"

"No. She's in Vermont."

"Okay. What about Addison?" Tom asked.

"I haven't seen him."

Tom frowned. "Who else is there? What about the VP? The speaker? The—"

"Carpenter's dead," Nate interrupted. "The vice president is dead!"

"How? When?"

"This morning. Air Force Two went down. There were no survivors."

Tom allowed himself a moment of grief. General Carpenter was a strange man, but a good friend to Max, and the very definition of an honorable soldier.

"Professor?" Nate whispered. "Are you there?"

Grief was replaced with a wave of guilty responsibility for the student he'd placed in the White House. "Listen, Nate. You need to get out of Washington. Get out, and get far away. Do you remember me telling you about fishing, in Maine?"

"Yeah, I think so."

"Crossfields Landing. It's a small village. My place is a mile to the north, overlooking the bay. There are supplies there. Find a car, make sure you have enough gas to get there without having to stop."

"I'm going to stay," Nate said. "Something's going on. I'm recording it. All of it. I've tried to upload it to that server, but the internet's still not working. I'm going to record everything. That's important."

"No, Nate, it's not. I want—"

"I have to go. Call back if you can."

The line went dead.

Tom put the phone down. "Did you hear that?"

"The vice president's dead," Helena said.

"General Carpenter was an old friend of Max's," Tom said. "A good soldier. A good man. He was the obvious choice for VP. Farley's making his move."

"You think he can arrange for Air Force Two to crash?"

"Zombies couldn't. You'd need to plant a bomb on board. At any other time the security detail would discover it and an investigation after the fact would certainly uncover the truth, but now? It's possible he might get away with it. More than possible."

"You have no proof. It could be a—"

"A coincidence? There's something wrong with the communication system at the White House. Nate's been unable to get online. He says the phone network is overloaded. The national security system is separate from the administrative one, but what if they've both been compromised?" He held up a hand. "Don't ask me how, but that's what's happened. They're trying to control the flow of information... and did you hear about Gregson, the communications director? Disappeared. So has everyone else Nate knew. They're keeping Max in the dark. Whatever he thinks is going on, whatever orders he's giving, they're not being followed."

"But... No. I don't believe it. That wouldn't work."

"Maybe it would, for a few days. Long enough for Farley to make his move, and he has. He's killed the VP."

"But how does that help him? He's only the secretary of state. Next in line are the speaker and the president pro tempore. He'd have to kill them both."

"No he doesn't. The president will require a VP, and he'll have to nominate someone immediately. His choice will be limited to who's in the bunker with him. As for confirmation, I imagine that whatever members of the House and Senate are still in Washington would rubber-stamp the nominee."

"That would be illegal, wouldn't it?"

"Who's going to care until long after the event? Or maybe Farley has a plan to kill the speaker. Or the speaker is in on it."

"Or Air Force Two's crash had nothing to do with the conspiracy."

"Maybe." Tom picked up the phone. He tried calling Nate again. There was no answer. "Whatever the truth, it doesn't change anything. I'm going to Washington."

"Isn't there someone else you can call? The FBI or the CIA or someone?"

"Not without knowing who is involved in the conspiracy. The list of people I know can be trusted is small: the president, the First Lady, and Chuck Addison, none of whom I can reach; General Carpenter, who's dead; Gregson, who's disappeared; Bill Wright, who's on the other side of the Atlantic and he's… that's complicated. I trust Nate, but I'm surprised they haven't kicked him out of there. I guess they've become so used to him and his camera that they don't notice him. There's not much he can do to help. No, I need to get to Washington. As soon as Farley's been sworn in as VP, he'll kill the president. It'll be a heart attack or something. Some poison in a drink, something slow acting—"

"But that's insane," Helena said, and he wasn't sure if she was talking about his plan, or his theory.

"What's the alternative?" he asked. "Look for Powell? He could be ten miles from here or two hundred, or he drove Ayers to a helicopter and is now in Alaska." He walked to the front door. On the wall, hanging on a hook next to a battered leather hat, and another with a ragged scarf, was a set of keys. He grabbed them.

"Wait, you're going now?"

"I want to check the car."

"Let's say you're right," Helena said. "And Farley murders his way to the presidency. What will he actually do next?"

"Gloat."

"Seriously!"

"Hold a press conference," Tom said, stepping outside. "Announce the existence of a vaccine, but that time will be needed to manufacture enough for the entire nation. He'll hope that the mere prospect of salvation will be enough to quell the chaos. It won't. People will descend on military bases and hospitals, desperate for this vaccine, hoping it's a cure. The chaos will get worse, and he won't care."

"Right. Right. But what if it did work?" Helena asked. "What if people listened and didn't panic? What would they do next?"

Tom considered it. "He'd probably decide that not everyone could be saved, so he'd pull the military resources back to a few agricultural areas close to the coast. Use the Navy to secure them and let the rest of the nation fall apart."

"That's what you'd advise the president?" Helena asked.

Tom opened the door, stuck the key in the ignition, and watched the needle bounce up the fuel gauge. "Nearly full. No," he said. "It's not what I'd do. No situation ever comes down to an either-or. There's always another way. I don't know what it is, but I have a long drive to work it out."

Helena reached in, turned the key, and took it out of the ignition. "I voted for Maxwell," she said. "You remember the election slogan? Of course you do. *Here we stand.* I didn't think much of it, and wasn't going to vote for him, not after what he said about food stamps, but then I saw the debate. That thing he said—"

"Here we stand, a nation divided," Tom said, reciting the lines he'd written himself. "Anger and fear have filled our lives for too long. No longer. United we stand, and we shall not fall. We shall not fail, nor shirk from the task ahead. It will be a long road, a hard road, but if we stand together, as one nation, we will triumph."

"No," she said, "not that bit. That was way too jingoistic. It was what he said about thinking what the world would be like for our grandchildren's grandchildren, and comparing it to the world our grandparent's grandparents had known. That was what got me. How far we'd come, and how far we've got to go." She shrugged. "I guess I agreed with him. We each have to do what we can, all that we can, all of the time. I'm going with you. You said the fuel tank was full?"

"Almost full."

"How's that possible? I don't see a filling station out here."

They found the fuel cans in a small shed, almost lost among the trees.

"How far to D.C.?" Helena asked. "Two hundred and fifty miles, due south?"

"Closer to three-fifty, south-southeast," Tom said.

"Then we've more than enough, because I'm guessing this is a one-way trip."

"I'll get some water. I don't suppose we need food, and—"

"We should leave tomorrow. We won't make it before nightfall."

"I don't think we need to worry about the speed limit."

"We're both exhausted," she said. "We need a night's proper sleep. A wash, maybe some clean clothes. Whatever happens tomorrow, we'll face it better if we're rested."

He glanced at the sky. Sunset was still a long way off, but the clouds were gathering. The idea of a proper night's sleep was beguiling.

"At first light."

Helena found clean clothes that almost fit. Except for the hat and scarf, Tom didn't. He settled into the seat by the window with the sat-phone and tablet.

"What are you looking at?" Helena asked, emerging from the shower.

"Clouds, mostly," he said. "On satellite images."

"Of here?"

"No. But it's nearby. I was hoping I might find Powell."

"You've hacked into a satellite?"

"No. I have the access codes. I did a favor for a member of the programming team before the satellites were sent into orbit. Right now, all I can do is see what they've been tasked to take pictures of. I could probably alter their orbit, but only if you don't mind a ninety-percent chance that they'd crash into the atmosphere. What I was really doing was working out a reply to this message from Bill."

"The guy in London?"

"With the broken leg. He's out of hospital, and back at a computer."

"Great. Can he help us?"

"Judging by the content of his message he's so dosed up on painkillers I'm surprised he could find the keyboard. There's an intriguing line at the end. He says he's thinking of recommending an evacuation of London and all the other major cities. Move the populace to the coast, where they can build up fortifications closer to the food supply. I assume he means fishing."

"An evacuation? Could that work?"

"In Britain? Maybe." He tapped at the screen, adding a few lines to his message.

"What are you writing?" Helena stepped closer, peering over his shoulder. His first instinct was to shield the screen, but there was no point.

"They need to protect the farmland and get crops planted. Fish will only keep them alive for so long."

"Would it work here?"

"Now? No. They're reporting no outbreaks in Britain and Ireland. I know for a fact that's a lie, but maybe they've got a handle on it. Small islands like that are more easily defended. Small boats might land, but larger craft and planes can easily be destroyed. The question becomes whether they can protect enough of the coastline long enough for defenses to be put into place. But that's on the other side of the Atlantic. It's not our problem." He finished the message. When he tried to send it, an error message came up. The connection had been lost.

"I'll try it outside," he said, picking up the tablet. "As for here," he continued as Helena followed him to the door. "I don't think so. It's too late to move people. We need to move the food to them. I'm not sure..." He pressed send again. The progress meter jerked across the screen, stalled, and finally the bar filled. The message was sent. "Done. I think we need to start in one corner of the country. Maybe Washington State. Clear the state, town by town, and then move south and east. Redistribute the grain, wheat, and rice that was in storage for shipment overseas, airlifting it into the places that we want people to remain. Recruit every able-bodied person into either helping clear the roads, or plant in the fields. I suppose we'd have to deal with Canada as—"

"Tom!"

A figure was moving down the dirt road toward them.

"Is… is that…?"

"I don't know." He walked back to the porch and picked up the crowbar from where he'd left it when they'd arrived at the house. When he got back to where Helena was standing, the figure had managed another four steps.

"Hello!" Helena called and then clamped a hand over her mouth. The figure staggered another pace and then collapsed.

Helena was already sprinting toward the figure before Tom had started running. A hundred yards, and halfway there, he knew it was too late. The figure began to rise, the arms moving with that uncoordinated erraticism of the undead. Helena staggered to a halt. Tom did the same.

"I'll… I'll get the gun," she said, turning around.

"No. We have to save the ammunition." He hefted the crowbar. It wasn't the first time he'd used one in a fight, and that other time, not long after he'd arrived in America, came back to him. A dark alley, a large gang, a soul full of justified rage. He didn't remember the fight itself, just the emotions ripping through him beforehand, and the bleeding, moaning bodies afterward. This time was different, and in so many ways. The zombie, a woman, wore a police uniform that was ragged, torn, and covered in too many stains for all that blood to have been hers. How had she gotten so far, been infected, yet stayed alive long enough to reach here?

Her head tilted to one side, her mouth opened. A ragged hiss escaped perfect teeth. She swung an arm out. He raised the crowbar and took a step back. She swung again. With each swing, her leg came forward, and she took a step, almost as if the arms were attached to her feet by strings.

"Tom!" Helena called, anxiety clear in her voice.

The officer clawed at the air again. As her arm came down, her head was exposed. Tom swung. The iron bar slammed into the side of her head. Bone cracked, seemingly louder than a gunshot. The zombie collapsed. He stared at the body, and then bent down.

"What are you doing?" Helena asked, coming up to join him.

"I want to know who she was. Where she came from."

Gingerly, he prodded her pockets, until he found a wallet. "Officer Shawna Williams, from Indianapolis." He stood. "Sidearm's gone. No ammunition left."

"Is that all you care about?" Helena asked.

Tom looked down the road. "No. But she's dead. There's nothing we can do to help her."

"We can bury her."

Tom said nothing. He was listening to the sounds of the forest, trying to tell if there were more zombies coming.

"I said we should bury her," she said.

"Load up the car first. If there are more, I'd like to be able to get out of here."

They dug the grave at the side of the road. By the time it was four feet deep, two hours had passed, and no more zombies had appeared.

"That's it," Tom said. "The ground's too cold, and the roots of these trees are too thick for us to get it any deeper. Unless you want to try again?"

"No."

With crowbar and shovel, they rolled the body into the grave. To Tom, that destroyed any solemnity in the occasion.

"We can't bury everyone," Helena said. "But this… this will have to do for all the others."

Tom could understand her emotion. He didn't agree with it. Dead was dead, and they'd done nothing more than waste two hours digging a grave that was shallow enough that the body would be dug up by any scavenging carnivore. Assuming that animals ate the undead. He decided not to voice that question out loud. They filled the grave.

Helena went inside, and back into the shower, staying there long after she would have washed off the dirt. Tom stripped his muddy, dirty, ragged, stained suit and bundled it into the washing machine. He locked the front door and moved the chair close to the window with a view of the road. With the shotgun beside him, he tapped away at the refresh button, trying to find a signal. When he did, he went through the other messages he'd received. There was no reply from Bill, but there was one from someone else in Britain. A submarine commander to whom Tom had sent that first message about Prometheus, back before he knew about the zombies. The message contained two words. "Prove it." Tom formulated a reply, attaching a few files that he thought might. Then he turned back to the track, watching as the sun set, and thinking about evacuations, about Britain, and the past.

Chapter 18 - The Road to Washington
February 24th, Pennsylvania

"You ready?" Tom asked. Dawn was still an hour away.

"Let me finish the coffee," Helena said.

"You want to savor your last cup?" he asked.

"No, it's not that. It's Officer Williams. The other zombies didn't seem like people. Abstractly, I knew they were, but not in the sense that I could see the living person in that un-living face. Maybe it's because I know her name, I don't know. It's… well, now I can see that happening to me. Infection, death, coming back, you know?"

"Not necessarily. It doesn't have to be like that."

"I'm not being a defeatist, and I don't want it to happen, but it could, and I'm trying to be rational about it. I mean… I've never really thought about my own death. It's never seemed imminent before. I guess you have?"

"Yeah. Since I was a kid."

"Some traumatic incident?"

"I saw my family die," he said. "I ended up running with a gang, being a gopher for drugs and guns. I came to America to start a new life… Well, no. I walked into a bloodbath, and walked out of it carrying a bag of fake passports, and laundered cash. Half of the money was in dollars, and the passport with a picture that looked most like me was from the U.S. That's why I came here."

"Oh. I guess that explains a lot. Me, I…" She downed the coffee. "I expected that the world would keep turning, and that though tomorrow would be more or less the same as yesterday, next week would be much better than the last." She put the cup in the sink. "We should go."

"You don't have to come with me," he said.

"We've been through that. What's the alternative? Stay here? There's enough food for a week. Less, if the power is cut, but the food *will* run out, the power *will* be cut. Unless you left the car, it's not like I could drive to the store. If we don't get to Washington, there's a good chance there never will be any stores, not anymore. No, I'm coming. I've packed all the food that'll keep. It's mostly canned peaches and some crackers."

"Can opener?"

"And spoons. We need anything else?"

"Weapons. Here," he placed a hatchet on the table. "It came from the tool shed."

She picked it up uncertainly.

"Bullets run out," he said.

With a sigh, she slid it into the belt of her borrowed clothes. "Did you find a flashlight?" she asked.

"No. I've got some matches, and a couple of candles, but no flashlight."

"And the route?"

"Stay off the interstate, and head south, east, then south again until we hit Gettysburg. Then keep going until we can't." He pulled on the hat.

"You look ridiculous," she said with forced cheerfulness and a brittle smile.

"Thanks." He glanced at her jeans. She'd had to trim six inches off the legs, but despite her inexpert tailoring, she looked far closer to respectable than him. The washing machine hadn't been kind to his suit's silk and wool blend. Blotchy white patches from where he'd doused the more suspicious stains with bleach added an ugly contrast to the original dark grey. "Maybe we'll start a new trend."

As they drove past Officer Williams's shallow grave, he tried not to look. Helena turned in her seat, watching until the road curved and it was out of sight. The track ended at the road they'd walked down the day before. A hundred yards to the east was an abandoned van. Tom put his foot on the brake.

"I think that's how Officer Williams got this far," Tom said. "We better check it."

"What for?" Helena asked.

Tom didn't answer because he wasn't really sure. For other people? Other zombies? He was still uncertain of his motivation when he threw the doors open and found the van was empty.

"You think we should see if she left a note, or letter, or something?" Helena asked.

"She drove this far, ran out of gas, got out, and stumbled toward the only turning she'd seen, hoping she'd find people, and safety with them," he said. "She died. Knowing any more won't change anything, or make it better."

"What if she left a letter to her family?"

"And if we took it, and if we ever found them, what would we say? That Shawna Williams is dead? How would that help them? As long as they don't know, they have hope. Contrary to what you might think, that's often all we have."

They drove east until they reached another, equally ill-maintained road that led south, curving in and out of the forest. It was almost peaceful until a yellow sports car appeared from nowhere and sped past at over a hundred miles an hour.

"Wonder where they're going," Helena muttered.

"I wonder why they're heading south," Tom said. A minute later, a car traveling almost as fast overtook them. As dawn properly arrived, more vehicles passed them. A few were heading north, but most were going south. At first, one would disappear around a bend before another appeared. Then there were two in sight at all times, then three, four, and, after forty miles, they were part of a long stream of traffic.

Helena tried the radio, twisting the dial, muttering, "Nothing. Nothing. Nothing," until they found the woman they'd heard a few days before. The signal was faint, but her words were clear.

"For those of you keeping track, add Hawaii and Alaska to the places where the outbreak has spread. I've seen messages saying that there's no virus in Greenland. I don't know how that rumor started, but don't believe it. Why should they be different from everywhere else on the planet? The British news is reporting that there are no outbreaks there, but that's for domestic consumption, people! They're saying that to keep order. Besides, Britain, Greenland, you can't drive there, so stop trying. And stop trying to drive to the coast. What do you think's going to happen, that there are boats there, waiting to take you out to sea? Any ship's captain with an ounce of sense would already have set out. The rest, well, I bet the crew would already have mutinied and done what the captain should have. Stay inside. Seriously, look at these creatures, these zombies. They can't last forever. If we can hold out for another few days they'll start dying. If you go out, you're going to get killed, and come back to attack us." She took a breath, and when she continued desperation had been replaced with weariness. "The ports are closed. The airports are closed. The interstates are shut. Just stay inside. We've got a message here that says that the president is going to make an announcement… Brad, you've not written when. What? Oh, okay, so we don't know when. They said they wanted us to keep broadcasting, but they don't give us anything to tell you, let alone…" The voice descended into muttering. "Some music now, we'll be back in ten."

Helena turned the radio down but not off. "Doesn't sound good. Have you noticed the traffic's all heading south? No one's going north."

"I had." The other lane was empty, and for the most part, the traffic was still staying in the correct lane. Even so, they were managing fifty miles an hour, and the traffic was moving freely.

"They have to be heading somewhere. What's due south of here?" Helena asked.

"I don't know. Maybe a—"

"Hey, did you hear that?" Helena turned the radio back up.

"The FEMA camp at Winchester has been closed. They don't say which Winchester but they want me to say this: refugees coming to this camp weren't being flown out. They want me to stress that. It was a rumor. A myth. It wasn't true. A cargo plane crashed into the runway in the early hours of this morning, killing hundreds of people who'd run on to the tarmac in the hope of catching a flight. Dozens were infected due to a passenger on the—"

"Look out!" Helena yelled.

Tom's attention had been on the radio. He'd not noticed the RV weaving across the road toward them. The cars in front had, and had swerved around the coach. Tom spun the wheel. The RV slammed into the side of the car, and they were pushed off the road. The wheels bit into gravel and mud. The car spun, skidded, and slammed into a pine tree. The airbag exploded. Tom was stunned.

"Are you okay?" Helena asked, pushing her airbag out of the way.

"I think so."

"You sure? You're bleeding."

He raised a hand to his forehead. It was only a small cut. "I'm fine," he said, rubbing his neck. "I'm fine. What's a little whiplash between friends?"

"Yeah, well next time, I'm driving."

His arms worked, so did his legs. His hand was sore, and so was his neck, but that was all. He tried the door. The handle wouldn't move. He saw the reason and should have realized it before. The door was dented inward and jammed shut.

Clambering across the passenger seat, he followed Helena outside, and then had to catch hold of the roof to steady himself.

"You okay?" Helena asked.

"Just dizzy. It's fine. It'll pass."

Helena, seemingly unscathed by the accident, began a methodical examination of the vehicle. "Front tire's gone, but we've got a spare. Bumper's gone, but we don't need that. The— oh."

"What?"

"We need a new engine. The tree's buried in this one."

He blinked away the spots from in front of his eyes. "How far did we get? Sixty miles? Probably less, and not all of it was due south." A thought came to him. He looked north. There was no sign of the RV, just a red sedan, heading toward them. He raised a hand, waving at the driver. The car didn't stop.

"I guess we're walking," he said.

"You could try calling for a tow-truck," she suggested.

He opened his mouth to tell her what an idiotic idea that was, but why not? He took out the sat-phone and paused. "I don't know a number."

"911?" she suggested.

"Right. Yeah, of course." He dialed. There was a brief busy tone before the line disconnected.

"It was worth a try," Helena said. "We could try hitching. I mean, there's all this fuel. That's got to be worth a ride."

"Try it."

Helena walked closer to the road. As a car drew nearer, she waved her arms. It moved into the other lane, accelerating past.

"See?" Tom said.

"No," Helena replied. She tried it again. This time, the driver aimed the car straight at her, and she had to dive out of the way.

"On foot, then," she said. She grabbed the bags. He picked up the shotgun and slung it over his back, keeping the crowbar in his hand. He held out a hand for one of the bags.

"Can you manage?" she asked.

"I'll be fine."

She clearly didn't believe him, but reluctantly handed him the bag.

"No first responders. No police. No phones, even," Helena said as they walked. "Maybe when things do come back, it'll be different. There'll be blood tests before you can board a flight. Or maybe people won't fly any more. Maybe the kids will all be homeschooled, never going outside from one year to the next."

"Maybe." He wasn't listening. His attention was divided between the traffic and the woodland surrounding them. His thoughts were on where the people were heading. That woman on the radio had said something about a FEMA camp near an airport. In itself it meant nothing, unless there was some rumor going around the creaking internet that you could fly out of the danger zone. Was that where these people were going? It wouldn't be long before there were more crashes. Not long after that, this road would blocked. So would all the others. The entire nation would grind to a halt. Helena's fears about a changed world would seem like a glorious fantasy. It was too late. Certainly by the time they got to

Washington, it would be far too late. They couldn't walk there. He pulled out the sat-phone.

"Who are you calling?"

"Nate." There was no answer. "There's a trail over there, you see it?"

"Shouldn't we stick to the road?"

"No one's going to stop, so we'll be walking all day, and at the end of it, we'll be on a stretch of road, not dissimilar to this. Except, by then, we'll be surrounded by other refugees. All of whom will want food, water, and shelter that probably won't be there. But the zombies will be. No, we need to get away from people. Maybe find another remote house where we can steal a car." He tried the sat-phone again. Still nothing. "Or a clearing where a helicopter can land."

"Or bicycles," Helena said, following him into the woodland.

The sound of traffic vanished, replaced by creaking branches, and the rustling of rotten leaves.

"Or dirt bikes," Helena muttered, but a lot quieter than before.

Tom was dialing the number for the ninth time, and the third time he'd told himself that the next time would be the last, when a mechanical thudding of rotor blades broke the silence.

"Did you get through?" Helena asked.

"No," he said, looking up, back, around, searching for the helicopter. Wherever it came from, it disappeared to wherever it was going without them catching sight of it. Silence returned, more complete than before. He took that as a signal to put the sat-phone away.

The trail thinned, widened into a clearing, and then disappeared.

"I read somewhere," Helena said, "that if you blindfold people and tell them to walk in a straight line, they'll walk in a circle, almost always returning to where they began."

"That doesn't sound right," Tom said. Did moss grow on the north side of trees, or the south?

"My point is: do we know which way we're going?"

"I was thinking of that myself," he said. "This way, I think."

"That's north."

"You sure?"

"The sun sets in the west, rises in the east. Come on."

He let her take the lead.

In his mind, the rustle of leaves became the shuffle of undead feet, the creak of branches became that of breaking bone. The sigh of wind became the hiss of air escaping through necrotic lungs.

"I think it's funny," Helena said. Her voice was such a welcome relief against his dark thoughts that he laughed. "Not that funny," she added.

"Sorry. What were you going to say?"

"That for all we achieved, all we've built, people are inherently incapable of walking in a straight line."

The day wore on. Sometimes they stopped. They saw no one, heard no one. Tom was a city boy, through and through. He'd grown up in a world of alleys and roads, concrete and steel. Trees belonged in parks, and never in such profusion as this. There was no escaping the truth. They were lost.

By mid-afternoon, the sky was overcast. They stopped at a stream to fill their water bottles. With no better direction to travel, they followed it, even though it was taking them down a hill Tom was sure they'd just walked up. But streams led to rivers, and those to lakes. People fished in those, and that meant roads. That reasoning kept him going until the stream grew so wide they had to make a decision as to which side of it they should walk on. They decided to cross. Helena managed it safely. Tom slipped halfway over. He lost his footing on the slick rocks. His leg plunged into the ice-cold water. The chill seeped up his leg and drained away the remaining heat.

"Keep going," he said, brushing away Helena's concern. There was nothing else they could do.

An hour later, they spotted their first sight of civilization since that morning.

"We have to stop," Helena said.

"Not yet. Not here."

"No," she said. "You need to rest."

He was too embarrassed to admit that was true and too cold to argue. The two-floor building was about four weeks away from being a house.

The roof was in place, and the two walls he could see looked finished, though not painted. Plastic sheeting covered the windows. The yard was nothing but mud, ruts, and congealed concrete.

"Do you think that pit is meant to be a swimming pool?" Helena asked.

"Or where they were going to put the septic tank."

Leading from the house, and disappearing into the woodland beyond, was an unpaved track. Even from fifty yards away, he could make out the heavy tread of construction vehicles, but there were none on the site.

"Hello?" Helena called out.

There was no answer. The back door was locked and secured with a padlock. So was the front, but it only took one twist of the crowbar to break it. The house was empty and sparsely furnished. There was a black leather couch and matching armchair in the living room, and a mattress in the master bedroom, all still in their plastic wrapping. Next to the mattress was a pile of broken wood, discarded screws and an instruction leaflet, torn up in frustration, then taped back together during the owner's attempt to construct the self-assembly bed. Throughout the house, the floors were bare wood, still covered in sawdust. Rolled carpets had been stacked in one of the smaller bedrooms. The kitchen cabinets had been fitted. The stovetop lay on the floor, waiting to be installed.

The protective plastic sheet rustled loudly as he collapsed into the armchair. A half-finished house? At least they'd be dry. He kicked off his boots and peeled off the socks.

"You can dry those in another room. Or throw them out," Helena said, collapsing on the couch. "No water's coming out of the faucet. There's a chimney for a wood-burning stove, but that hasn't been delivered."

"Right." He had a strong desire to close his eyes and sleep. "Can you start a fire?"

"Of course," Helena snapped.

"Great. Do that. Boil up that water we got from the stream."

"How? Because you know what we didn't bring with us from Dr Ayers's house? Pots, and there aren't any here."

"Oh."

"It's fine. I'll figure something out. We can use the cans the peaches are in. Boil those up first, I suppose. I mean, hot food is hot, right? Warm peaches. It'll be a new delicacy. What are you going to do?"

"Walk down the track, find out if it leads to a road. Maybe there's a city on the other side of those trees."

The track took a meandering path through the wood. When building the house, they'd chosen the route that would be easiest to clear. After half an hour, it ended at a two-lane road. A hundred yards away, a tree had fallen down, partially blocking one lane. Other than that, there was nothing to see. No signs, no mailbox, not even a conveniently addressed statement of ownership warning off trespassers. There was no clue as to where they were.

A ray of sun broke through the clouds, adding a shimmering glow to the water-filled pothole. He leaned against a tree, watching the shadows slowly encroach on that patch of light. They weren't going to make it to Washington. Not on foot. They'd not seen any zombies during the day, but that didn't fill him with hope. Quite the opposite. They'd crossed no roads, no logging tracks, and barely any hunting trails. The logical explanation was just as Helena had suggested. They'd walked in a large circle. No, they weren't going to reach Washington on foot, but was there any point trying? Max might have left the capital. If he hadn't, other than warning him of the conspiracy, what advice could he give that experts couldn't? There were people who spent their lives planning for disasters and emergencies. Wasn't it simply arrogance that made him assume his counsel had value? More likely he'd be doing nothing but wasting Max's time.

Wouldn't it be better to identify the conspirators first? He could imagine himself back in the Oval Office, pointing at one conspirator after another, presenting damning evidence against each in turn. But then what? They wouldn't go quietly. Could the secret service be trusted if he suspected the FBI had been compromised?

Powell had come from somewhere around here, so didn't it make sense to try to hunt him down? Of course, for that he needed information, weapons, and supplies, and the only place he *knew* he'd find them was hidden beneath his cottage in Maine. There was less chance of reaching there than the capital.

The clouds closed, the ray of light disappeared, and the golden water filling the pothole turned dark once more. He headed back to the house.

Chapter 19 - Trapped
February 25th, Elk County, Pennsylvania

A snuffling rustle cut through Tom's dreams. It came again, louder, rudely tearing him out of a restless sleep. He opened his eyes. It was coming from the other side of the front door. Was it a bear? Did they have those in Pennsylvania? Then came a slow, rasping scratch. Fingernails. He stood. The plastic sheet he'd been using as a blanket crackled to the floor. There was a thump from outside. Then another. He knew what it was. Zombie.

It might have been due to exhaustion, but the mistake he'd made was clear. The house was a mile from the road. The undead were people. How would they get out here? Like Officer Williams, they would have driven. Bitten, infected, thrown out or left behind, they'd turned. The zombies they'd become had followed the road, chasing one passing car after another until—

There was an almighty thump from beyond the door.

Until they saw the light from the fire Helena had lit. Or perhaps they'd smelled the smoke, or—

Another thump.

However they came here, it didn't matter. He found himself edging around the chair. It was foolish, a childish illusion of security.

Thump.

Was it they, or it? How many were out there? He concentrated, listening more carefully. There was a soft slap of flesh against wood, then a harder bang. One. There was only one. There was no comfort in the realization.

He grabbed the shotgun from the ground, raised it to his shoulder, and aimed the barrel at the door. Closer, he needed to get closer. He forced himself to take a step toward the unseen foe.

Thump. Slap. Sigh.

Another step. Another. He was eight feet from the door. Close enough. He breathed out, his finger curled around the trigger, and he realized what he was about to do. He forced his hand away from the stock. Blowing a hole through the door wasn't smart. There might be only one out there now, but what if more came?

He had to open the door. He rehearsed the scene in his mind, but there was no way he could do it while keeping the shotgun aimed at the zombie. With his eyes on the door, he backed away until his foot banged against the bottom-most step. From outside, the thumping slap of flesh against wood became more strident. Walking backward, he went upstairs, not hurrying until he reached the landing.

Helena had taken the room with the mattress, and lay on top, curled in a nest of packaging paper and plastic sheeting.

"Helena," he whispered as loudly as he dared.

"What?" she groaned.

"Helena!"

"What?"

"There's a zombie outside."

She sat up straight. "Just one?"

"I think so," he said, though the dark demons of doubt questioned whether that was the case. "I want you to open the door so I can shoot it."

It was a long minute before she replied. "You sure?"

"It's now or in the morning, and will you be able to sleep knowing it's there?"

"I could've, if you'd not woken me," she grumbled, pushing her way clear of the paper.

He went first, shotgun leveled at the door, only realizing how foolish that was when he stumbled on a stair.

"Are you sure it's a zombie?" Helena asked, slightly too loudly.

The creature answered for him, letting out a low rasping hiss before thumping a palm against the wood.

"Open the door," he said, raising the gun high. "I'll fire."

"Be careful. Of me," she added.

He breathed out, aiming the gun at where he thought the creature's head would be. "Now."

She pulled on the handle. The door opened. There, movement. He pulled the trigger. The gun roared, and the shot sailed over the diminutive creature's head. It staggered into the room as he hurriedly chambered another round.

"Shoot it! Shoot it!" Helena called.

It was too close. He swung the butt of the gun into its face. It staggered back a step. He did it again, and again, until it was level with the door. Not thinking, letting the terrified, animalistic part of his brain take over, he punched the shotgun into its chest, and then at its knee. There was a dull pop, and as the creature took another stumbling step, it collapsed onto the porch.

"Shoot it!" Helena yelled. Tom didn't hear her. He slammed the shotgun down on its skull, over and over, until the creature was still.

Slowly, he straightened.

"Back inside," Helena hissed, dragging at his arm. He stood, immobile. "There may be more," she said.

Those words cut through the fog. He looked around at the moonlit woods. All seemed still. A light snow had dusted the ground, but the sky was once again clear.

"There's nothing there," he said. His skin began to prickle in the chill.

"And no sound," she said. "No animals. Get inside."

He did, and she closed the door behind him.

She opened her mouth. Closed it. Opened it again. "I'm going back to bed."

He stood near the door, listening to the sound of her feet going up the stairs. A door closed. There was silence. His racing heart began to slow.

He shifted his grip on the shotgun, touching the bloody gore coating the butt. In the kitchen, he found the bottle of paint thinner, and doused his hands. At first by firelight, and then by the light of the tablet, he cleaned the shotgun. Where he'd found white flecks of bone on his suit, he'd doused them in the corrosive paint stripper. The room filled with the odor of the flammable liquid so he stayed away from the fire, letting the embers burn low.

Knowing he wasn't going to sleep, and not wanting to sit alone with his darkening thoughts, he turned the tablet back on. He wandered from window to window, trying to get a signal for the sat-phone. His mind began to still. The activity log showed Bill Wright had been accessing the files that the algorithm had scoured from the internet. There was a message from him, a request for advice regarding his evacuation plan. Tom didn't trust himself to reply. He would be too likely to say something that should only be said in person. Instead, he brought up the satellite feeds of North America. Even accounting for cloud cover, the sleeping continent seemed darker than before. Maybe an evacuation would work for Britain, but it was too late for it to be tried in America. Even if Farley died today, would it matter? The world had been torn apart. Whoever remained, and whatever they rebuilt, it would never, *could* never, be the same.

He went back to the files on the remote server, and began clicking on them at random. Some he deleted, others he flagged for Bill to watch, though he was no longer sure why. He came to a video of a woman standing in front of a tool bench. She was demonstrating how to make weapons from items found in an ordinary home. There was a theme of heavy weights and sharp points attached to poles and broom handles, but it was something. Certainly, it meant more than nothing that this individual was taking her time to try to help others, even in this weird twenty-first-century way.

Another video contained a call to fight, and the more he looked, the more of those he found. People talking into the camera, saying goodbye to unidentified loved ones, before signing off. Too many of them closed with a variation on the election slogan, of choosing a place to stand, and doing so together. He felt his throat tighten at the repetition of a message he'd suggested not because he'd believed it, but because it looked good on a poster and had tested well with focus groups. These people believed it. In face after desperate face, he saw that they needed to. But these were individuals with only the resources they had to hand. He wondered whether the people in the videos knew that it was unlikely anyone would see their last testaments. He might not be able to help them, and the reality was that most of them were probably already dead. But he could ensure that if or when civilization was rebuilt, these messages would become the epitaph of the old world and the moral foundation of a new one.

He brought up a subroutine he'd created himself as an academic exercise intended to improve his programming skills. It remotely turned on the electricity supply to his cottage in Maine and then booted up the servers he'd installed in the hidden room beneath the basement. Another few clicks, and the files were being transferred from the cloud. If the server farms went down, there would be a copy. A few more keystrokes, and he had it set up so the power would turn off again when the server was full.

If the server farms went down? No, when. And he was assuming that he would ever get there. There was Nate, of course. He picked up the phone, but changed his mind. He'd call the kid in the morning and make sure he was going to leave. It would be a dangerous journey, but nowhere was safe, especially not Washington. As for himself?

The tablet beeped. There was another message from Bill. Tom stared at the screen. The man was complaining about being trapped in a warm room in a city where the power still worked.

"Doesn't know how lucky he is."

Chapter 20 - Surrounded
Elk County, Pennsylvania

"Tom? Tom. Tom!"

He opened an eye. Helena stood before him, her face drawn.

"They're outside," she said.

He blinked, only half understanding until he looked at the windows. Dawn had arrived, and it had brought company. With glacial slowness, his eyes fixed on the humanoid shadows visible beyond the semi-transparent plastic covering the glass, he stood up.

"Shh!" Helena hissed. A muscle in her cheek twitched with the effort of not saying anything more.

"Upstairs," he mouthed back. She climbed the stairs with exaggerated caution, and at a speed he found frustrating.

"Stay here," he said, pushing past here when they reached the landing. Ignoring his instruction, she followed him as he went from room to room, counting the undead.

"About ten out front," he said. "Six at the back. Maybe some more in the trees. Call it twenty."

"Twenty? Twenty. Okay." Her head nodded, almost rocking back and forth. "We shoot them, right?"

Tom was still half asleep and took that as the reason he'd not noticed the pistol was clutched in her trembling hands. He took it from her. The safety was off. He slid it back on. "No. Sit. Wait."

He sat on the bare wooden boards of the landing, his feet against the unpainted pine bannisters, and his eyes on the window at the front of the house. What were they going to do? It was the wrong question. Were they safe? Clearly not. Could zombies climb stairs? There was a movie, one he'd watched only three weeks before, in which they'd pushed and tumbled their way to the top of a tower block. But in the movies they could climb, fly, run, or do whatever else the narrative required and the budget could afford.

She crouched down beside him. "We have to do something."

"The sound of the shotgun last night brought them here," he said. "If we wait, they'll go away. If we start shooting more might come. We'll be out of ammunition and we'll still be trapped."

She slid down the wall. "Are you sure it was the sound of the gunshot?" she asked.

"Yes," he said, though the answer was no.

Helena nodded. More time passed.

"What if they don't go?"

He'd been wondering that himself. The twin fogs of fear and sleep were clearing, and he was beginning to realize how precarious their situation was. He pushed himself to his feet and crept into one of the rear-facing rooms. There were nine out back now. Had those additional three come from the front of the house? Then he noticed their clothing was all the same. Beige slacks, white shirt, a high-collared maroon blazer. Only one wore a scarf, and that creature was heading toward the trees. The rest were milling about the construction site. The zombie with the scarf suddenly disappeared from view. There was a damp thump as it landed in the waterlogged pit. Two zombies turned toward the sound. The others didn't, but that gave him some hope.

He stepped away from the window. Helena stood in the doorway, her back against the frame, her head jerking back and forth between him and the front door.

"One of them fell in the pit," he whispered. "Two more are heading that way. They're dressed the same. Some kind of uniform. Maybe from a golf club or somewhere. They must have been stuck at work when the outbreak hit."

"A golf club?" she asked. "Around here?"

He realized how illogical a conclusion it was, but couldn't come up with a better one. "The clouds are getting thicker. Looks like a storm. Maybe snow."

"So? What about the zombies!" she hissed.

"They came from somewhere nearby. Somewhere they could have lurched from. That's where we have to head. They'd have driven there originally, right?"

171

"Are you asking? How would I know?"

"Right." He thought of saying that he was as terrified as she was, that he was extrapolating from the same data available to her. He didn't. Instead, he smiled. "It's going to be fine."

"You have a plan?"

"I'm working on it. Where's the food?"

"In the kitchen."

He handed her the pistol. "Safety's on. Wait here."

Rather than walking, he slid his feet across the wood, hoping that if they heard the sound, the creatures would think it was made by another of the undead. They didn't attack each other, did they? He reminded himself that just because he'd not seen it happen, didn't mean it hadn't. He reached the stairs. One step. Another. He strained every muscle in his legs to balance his weight on the far edges of the staircase, gritted his teeth against every squeak and creak, and ignored the rasping, slapping, clawing, thumping from the other side of those thin walls.

When he reached the ground floor, he first went to the table by his chair and pocketed the sat-phone and tablet. He grabbed the shotgun and crowbar, and then went to the kitchen. It took two trips, one for each bag, but he wasn't going to be unarmed, not even for a second.

He didn't immediately climb back upstairs. He watched the silhouettes beyond the windows, ruling out one plan after another. They couldn't block the doors and windows because it would make too much noise. They couldn't escape through the kitchen door, as it was still padlocked from outside. They could try to shoot their way out, but then they'd have to run. He'd not seen any evidence of these creatures running. That didn't mean they couldn't, just that they hadn't done it yet. He grabbed the bags, climbed upstairs, and felt better with his back against a wall once more.

"We could break the staircase," Helena suggested.

"They'd hear it. They'd know we're here, and we'd be trapped with..." He opened the backpacks. "A couple of boxes of crackers, five pints of water, and three cans of tinned peaches. Not as much as I thought. But it's okay," he added. "It's going to be fine."

"How is anything ever going to be fine ever again?"

"All we can do is wait." Wait and hope the zombies would go away, shoot their way out if they didn't. He closed his eyes and thought of ski resorts. He'd not enjoyed skiing, but he had liked the hotels. The warm fires, the remote locations, and looking at the snow. Of course, it was different when you had a centrally heated chalet to enjoy it from.

"Tom?"

"Hmm."

"It's been two hours. What do we do?"

He blinked. He must have drifted off to sleep. He breathed out. As he straightened he realized how stiff his muscles were. It was the cold, his age, the lack of sleep and proper food. Almost immediately, he rebuked himself for the thought. Sinking into self-pitying despair wasn't going to change the situation. He went to check the windows. There were ten zombies at the back. There was another dull splash as one fell into the pit. But there were ten out front, and weird shadows in the trees near the track suggesting that there were more, currently unseen. How many were there between here and the road? And if they followed it toward wherever these zombies had come from, wouldn't that mean they had to go through the tail of this column of creatures? And what would they find if they reached the golf club or resort or whatever it was? Cars? Perhaps, but the keys wouldn't be in the ignition. By then, they would have used up their ammunition. Helena would have to hold off the undead with that crowbar and her hatchet until he'd hot-wired a car, assuming that he could. What if the fuel tank was empty? What if he was completely wrong, that there were no cars, or no resort? They'd be on foot, and this time they'd have to follow the road, and hope that safety somehow found them. Hope. Maybe Helena was right. But what did that leave?

"Tom?" Helena prompted.

"Just a minute." He'd already come to the conclusion, but he wanted to play it out, so that in the days to come, he wouldn't second-guess his actions. There wasn't a choice. When he'd thought of doing it before, he'd felt like he'd been in control. He could have watched the helicopter arrive from a distance, waited to see who got out before revealing himself. Now? He was gambling on the identity of whoever turned up. The alternative was a hard-scrabble race from one refuge to the next, scavenging food, and hoping that dawn would follow night. Hope. Well, if that's what it came down to, then he'd place his hope in Max agreeing to speak to him.

"Damn. I'm going to call Nate. I'll tell him that he should give the phone to anyone who can pass it to the president. Even so, there's a good chance Powell will be the one to arrive. If he does, your best chance is to run for the woods."

"But we won't know who's coming until the helicopter arrives?"

"No." Assuming that they didn't simply blow the house up from a distance.

"So there won't be time to run. Well, there's no point surviving if there isn't a world left to live in," she said. "Call him."

"Okay." He moved closer to the window. He dialed the number.

"Prof?"

"Nate, I—"

"I can't talk. I'll call you back."

The line went dead.

"After all that build-up," Helena said. "Now we have to wait for him to call."

Tom shook his head. "He doesn't have the number. We'll try again later."

He did. Sometimes the phone rang. Sometimes it didn't. Clouds gathered. He worried that a storm might disrupt the signal, but then they dispersed, and Nate still didn't answer. It was beyond frustrating, but there was nothing to do but wait, listening to the banging clatter of the zombies traipsing through the building site outside and, with frustrating irregularity, collapsing into the pit.

One o'clock. Two.

"We should have left this morning. First thing," Helena said. Tom agreed. With less than four hours of daylight left, they might make twelve miles before darkness fell. If they were to wait until morning, they'd be able to travel twice that far. Maybe. Did it matter? Twenty miles or ten, they'd be venturing into the unknown.

He picked up the sat-phone. "One last time," he said.

"Prof!" Nate said answering almost immediately. "I've been trying to reach you."

"Listen. I need to speak to Max. I'm in a cabin, somewhere in Pennsylvania, there're zombies outside. We're trapped. I've information the president needs to—"

"You need to speak to him. You said. I know. Wait. Hang on." There was a moment of silence. "Okay. I know where he is."

Helena leaned in close so she could hear, but all that was coming through the speaker were muffled sounds and indistinct voices.

"I need to speak to the president," they heard Nate say.

"Who doesn't?" a tired man replied. "Go back to—"

"Mr President! Mr President!" they heard Nate call "It's important. It's about Tom Clemens! Hey, no, stop."

"You got to back up," the man said, his voice no longer tired but angry, aggressive. "Step away! Now!"

"Wait," another voice said, a familiar one that Tom hadn't heard in a month. "Did you say Clemens?" he heard Max say.

"Yes, sir. Here. He's on the phone," Nate said. "He needs to speak to —"

The line went dead.

"What happened?" Helena asked.

Tom looked at the handset. It had run out of power. He leaned back against the wall and closed his eyes.

"They could trace the call," Helena suggested.

"Nope. Can't." Tom said. "Can't trace it."

There was a splash from outside as another zombie fell in the pit. And then another sound, of something small hitting glass. It came again. Rain. The skies opened as the storm finally arrived.

It was tumultuous, filling the landscape with thunder and lightning. The house shook, and they could no longer hear the undead outside. Throughout it all, they stayed huddled on the landing, shivering against the cold, both lost in their own misery.

The storm ended as abruptly as it had begun, and in time for the last light of day to shine through the windows. The zombies were still there.

175

Chapter 21 - Escape
February 26th, Pennsylvania

During the night, the noise from outside had ceased. He'd thought the zombies had gone. When it was light enough to distinguish the windows from the frame, he nudged Helena awake, quietly stood, and made his way to the bedroom window. He'd been wrong. They were still out there, but were no longer moving. Three stood, half bent over, almost as if the weight of their arms was dragging them down. The rest - twelve at the back, fifteen at the front - were squatting on their haunches, almost completely motionless.

"Are they dead?" Helena asked.

It was a beguiling thought, but he shook his head. "I doubt it."

"I'm getting out of here," she said.

"Me too. We don't shoot our way out."

"We don't?"

"We'll save our ammunition. We walk out of here. You've got that hatchet? Right. I've got the crowbar. It'll take them a few seconds to stand. We walk straight past them."

"You walk, I'll run."

"The ground is more mud than earth. We run, we slip. We fall, we die. Walk. Swing. Save the bullets for when we need them. We follow the track to the road, and then go left or right depending on whichever direction has less of them."

He walked back to the landing, looked through their dwindling supplies, and split them equally between the two bags. "Just in case," he said.

She nodded, understanding. They went downstairs.

"Ready?"

She opened the door. A zombie squatted in the doorway, its knuckles flat against the wooden porch. Its head turned upward. Rain had washed streaks through the mud and blood covering its face. Sightless eyes bulged from dirt-encrusted sockets. Half its lower lip had been torn off. The remainder flapped loosely as it opened its mouth and slowly stood up. A grunting breath slipped from that dark maw, the smell as dark and earthy as that of the forest surrounding them.

"Tom!"

He kicked out, slamming his boot into that hideous face. The zombie flew back, tumbling off the porch and into the muddy drive beyond. Holding the crowbar across his body, Tom stepped into the doorway. He sensed the movement, and ducked under an out-thrown, broken hand. Barely thinking, he punched the crowbar up. The point smashed into the creature's chin, the chisel tip piercing through its gullet and up into its mouth. A twist, a tug that brought the flailing creature far too close, and the crowbar was free. He jabbed it forward again, this time aiming higher. The point smashed into its forehead, tearing skin from its nose, before finding the path of least resistance. The crowbar slammed through its eye, and into its brain. The zombie went limp, and for a moment he was holding it up.

"Tom! You're in the way! Move!"

Another twist and he had the crowbar free. The zombie he'd knocked into the mud was on its knees. He shifted his grip, raising the crowbar over his head, bringing it down as he jumped from the porch. His feet splashed in the muddy ground as the metal bar smashed down on the zombie's head. It fell, motionless.

"Walk!" Helena yelled. He didn't. He looked around for the next foe. That primal rage had come over him once more. He didn't see zombies surrounding him, but two faces merging into one: Powell and Farley. He shifted his stance, swinging the crowbar two-handed and low. There was a crack of bone as steel hit the zombie's leg. It fell, and he ignored it, already moving on to his next target.

He flipped the crowbar up over his head and chopped it down like an axe. Before the blow could land, the zombie slipped. The metal slammed into its shoulder. The impact pushed the creature to its knees, but one of its clawing hands caught Tom's legs. It pulled, dragging its mouth closer and closer. Its head exploded. The sound of the gunshot brought him back to reality.

"Run!" Helena screamed. "Run!" It wasn't an instruction, but an inhuman bellow as if that was the only word her terrified mind could remember.

Tom grabbed her arm, dragging her with him. There were ten more ahead of them that he could count. He didn't look behind.

He let go of her arm, skipping a step, shifting his balance, and swung the crowbar at the zombie's knee. It fell. That was the tactic. Don't waste time and effort killing them.

"Go for legs!" he yelled. Another two steps, he swung again. Another step, another swing, and he almost lost his grip on the crowbar as he sidestepped out of Helena's way. Her hatchet cut left and right, slicing into nothing but air.

He followed her and thought they might make it. There was a thin path through the undead, but it was narrowing. She started to run. She slipped. He caught her as she fell, but lost the crowbar in the process.

It was his turn to scream at her. "Move!" he bellowed, dragging her along a pace.

A zombie staggered out from their left. Tom let go of her arm and reached for the shotgun slung across his back. The sling caught in his elbow, and the zombie got closer. Closer. Helena screamed. Her arm came up. The hatchet came down onto its crown. It fell. She tried to pull the axe free.

"Leave it!" He had the shotgun in his hands. Two were near them, too near. The rest could wait a second and that was all the time he had left. He fired. The shot hit the creature in the chest. That had been the instinct to always aim for the largest target. It didn't matter. They just needed space. Time. He racked another round. There was a shot, not from him. Helena had fired. He didn't see where the bullet hit; shoulder, neck, it didn't matter. The zombie kept coming. Tom fired again. Its head exploded. The path ahead was clear.

He grabbed Helena's arm and dragged her with him. Each helping the other, they staggered through the muddy morass, up the track, away from the house.

"There!" Helena yelled. She raised the pistol, firing one-handed at the zombie twenty feet away. Once. Twice. She missed.

"Save the ammo," Tom hissed, raising the shotgun. He fired at almost point-blank range. Its head vanished in a spray of blood and gore.

They were everywhere. The trees were full of them. Of course, he realized. The track curved and kinked through the woods, but the zombies had stumbled in a straight line from the road. He was tempted to do the same, but salvation lay in getting out of the woods. They couldn't risk getting lost.

"There, I've got the one," Helena said, her voice calmer. She raised the gun with her left braced against her right. She fired. It collapsed.

"No time for aiming. No time for shooting." Tom said. The ground seemed firmer. "Run."

His heart pounded. His mouth was dry. His vision blurred. Mud caked his legs. It was like running through a bog. As he began to dread they'd gone the wrong way, the track curved, and he saw the road ahead of them. It was clear of the undead, but not empty.

"There." Tom waved a hand to the right. "There." He couldn't manage anything more coherent as he gestured toward the bus. The grey metal and white paint were coated in mud. *St Mark's Covenant* was etched in gold paint on the rear window. Two bodies, both wearing that same uniform of beige slacks and overlong blazers lay on the road near the door. He raised the shotgun, aiming at the supine figures. People died. They turned into zombies. Zombies didn't just collapse.

"Maybe the bus works," Helena said, running toward the vehicle.

"Wait! Watch out!" Tom yelled, as she jumped over one corpse, and sidestepped another. They didn't move, and she was already climbing through the half-open door.

Tom kept the shotgun's barrel fixed on the two bodies, but his eyes darted along the bus's windows. He saw no movement inside until Helena appeared in the door.

"It's empty," she said. "Except for another body. But it's definitely dead." She disappeared again. Tom turned his attention to the corpses. They were dead, their faces fixed in the rictus of a more natural death than the creatures at the house. The house. The track. The road. The zombies would follow them. There was no time to solve this particular mystery.

"Helena?" he called.

Instead of replying, there was a roar from the engine. Tom's heart leaped. He grinned at the unbelievable, impossible, serendipitous salvation. There was something wrong with the sound. He crossed quickly to the far side of the bus and saw what Helena had missed. The tires on the right-hand side had blown, and the rims were dug deep into the mud.

"Turn it off!" he yelled. He ran to the door. "Turn it off. The tires are gone. It's stuck."

Her face fell, and her hand trembled as it reached for the key. The engine died. Silence returned.

"It's that tree," he said. "The one that fell. The driver can't have seen it in the dark. They crashed. Someone on board must have been infected. The rest..." He didn't finish. He didn't need to.

"What now?" she asked.

"We walk. First, get some of those bags. Quick."

"What?"

He gestured toward the suitcases scattered along the aisle. "We need clothes. Food. Water. There has to be some, but we've got about a minute before the zombies get to the road."

He grabbed a bag. It contained clothes, nothing else. He tried another. More clothes. There had to be food. Surely there was food.

"Here!" Helena had pulled a leather bag down from the shelf above the seats. She'd opened it, and was now holding up a plastic box. "Cookies, I think. And some water."

"That'll do. Go. Go!" He grabbed two of the suitcases he'd opened which he thought had clothes that would fit, and followed her outside.

She stood by the door, her eyes on the road, the gun raised. "There. I see one."

"Then get moving!"

A mud-splattered figure lurched onto the road. Two more staggered onto the cracked asphalt. The trees behind were filled with the moving shadows of many more.

Helena began jogging up the road. Dragging the suitcases, he followed. He tried to keep up, but it was cumbersome trying to carry the shotgun and drag the suitcases along at the same time. The wheels were too small, the road too rough. The noise…

He looked behind. The zombies were following. They weren't running. The lead-most creature was now level with the front of the bus. The next was a few yards behind. He watched it trip on one of the corpses and fall to the ground.

Carrying the cases, he ran as fast as he could. Helena stopped, ran back a pace, and grabbed a case from him.

"We can't carry these *and* run," she said.

"A little further," he said. And after another hundred yards he stopped, flipping open the case. He looked down the road. The zombies were following, but the nearest was at least two hundred yards behind.

"We can run. They can't," he said. "Find the stuff that fits, put it in those bags." He opened the other case. The shoes were too small, the slacks far too large, but with a belt they'd be better than the rags he was wearing. He stuffed the clothing into his pack, and then looked down the road. The zombies kept on.

"Ready?"

"Yeah."

Jogging. Walking. Running. They kept it up long after the zombies were lost from view.

"I need a watch," Helena said as she tugged on the blazer. "How far ahead are we? An hour? It's like one of those problems I'd set the kids: if two humans run at eight miles an hour for one hour, and they are being chased by zombies who can stagger along at three miles an hour, how long will it be before they are eaten?"

"I'd say their top speed was around five miles an hour, but they can't keep it up," Tom said. "Most of the time, I'd say one mile an hour. Maybe two."

"So the question becomes how long they'll keep going before they slow," she said, kicking her soiled clothes into a pile. "Last night, the zombies which came to that house stopped. That was about a mile from the road, right? So we should be okay."

"No." They were on an incline, on a narrow road, still surrounded by trees beyond which were hills tall enough that he wondered if they were mountains. He doubted they'd managed anything close to eight miles an hour. Nor did he know for how long the zombies would follow them, and that was before thinking about any others which lay ahead. From Helena's expression, she was thinking the exact same thing, so he said none of that. Instead, he asked, "What's in those boxes?"

"The food?" She peeled back the lid. "Flapjacks, I think." She picked one up by the corner and took a tentative nibble. "Wow."

"They're good?"

"No. Terrible. No spice. No sugar. No flavor whatsoever. That's impressive."

A cool breeze whipped across his exposed ankles. The slacks were four inches too short. He tucked the ends into the socks. "Another new fashion statement."

"There have been worse," Helena said. They started walking.

"I suppose they were a church group," he said.

"Nope. Well, yes. Kind of. I think they were a cult."

"A cult? Bland food isn't enough to assume that."

"Here." She pulled a folded piece of paper out of the bag she'd taken from the bus.

"The thirteen steps to a happy marriage," he read. "So they were on a couples' retreat."

"In matching clothes? Look at the back. That upside-down pyramid."

He did, but there didn't seem anything untoward in the contents. "No address," he said. "Pity. They had to be heading somewhere."

"Wherever it is, you wouldn't want to go there, even now."

There was something in her tone. "You know them?" he asked.

"Not personally. I know their type."

"Tell me," he said.

"There are some things you don't share."

"Sure. But this is bothering you, and right now that might get us both killed. Besides, I've told you my secrets."

"Not all of them," she said. "Not even close, I bet."

"I could tell you why Farley wanted Senator Clancy Sterling to be his opponent in the general election," Tom said.

"I don't want to know."

"There was an email," Tom said. "Max didn't use it. That's how honest he was. I said I got some information from an anonymous source. He wouldn't touch it."

"Stop," she said, her actions matching her words as she turned around to face him. Her face was flushed, and not just from exertion, terror, and cold.

He smiled. "Come on, you can't tell me you're not even a little curious." His smile grew wider. "You hear that? Birdsong." He glanced at the tops of the trees in the hope of catching sight of the animal. He couldn't. "Didn't hear any of those at that house." He started walking, setting a slower pace than she had. "I can tell you want to know, and I want to know about this cult. But if you don't want to tell me, don't."

He decided to take the birds as a good sign. There was no logic to that, except that there had been so many portentous ones he thought it was time his luck changed.

"It's my sister," Helena said.

"The one in Canada?"

"Probably in Canada. At least, she was there last time I found her."

"She joined a cult?" he asked.

"Yeah. It's a long story. The really, *really* short version: she escaped. I spend all my money trying to find her. Well, no, I *spent* all my money to find out she was in Toronto. When I got there, she saw me and ran. Literally ran. Didn't even go back to her apartment. I waited outside for the rest of the weekend, but she didn't come back before I had to return to work. I went back the following Friday, but she'd moved out, and left no forwarding address. I couldn't afford to hire another detective."

He looked down at his clothes. "And this cult, did they wear maroon blazers?"

"No. And, okay, fine, maybe those people were just on some prayer retreat or something. It's just... My mother died while Jessica was... away. Cancer. It was hard. Before she died, she... Religion was important to her, but after Jessica... left, she found no comfort in prayer. All she'd say, and the last thing she said to me, was that we could only hope that Jessica would come home."

"Ah."

"I mean, yeah, I get that—" She stopped. "Do you hear that? It's an engine, isn't it?"

"More than one." He turned around, trying to place the direction, as the reverberating murmur bounced off the trees. The low rumble grew louder. "It's coming from ahead." And it was clearly heading their way. The sound resolved into the growl of dozens of engines just before the column came into view ahead of them. One, then two, then four, and then dozens of motorbikes.

"Harleys, I think," Tom said. "But not all of them. There's a racing bike or two, I think. A gang, maybe?" There was something regimented about their leather and denim.

"Doesn't matter. They're people," Helena said.

As he hurried over to the verge and debated whether to hide in the trees, she stepped into the middle of the road, waving her arms above her head.

"Hello!" she yelled, even though there was no way the bikers would be able to hear her over the roar of their engines. "Hello!"

The bikes got closer, closer, and then close enough that he could see the stocks of weapons slung across backs and jutting out of panniers. Closer, and he realized they weren't going to slow down. He ran forward, grabbed Helena's arm, and dragged her out of the way as the first of the bikes sped past.

"Wait! Stop!" she yelled. The bikers didn't, and as soon as they'd appeared, they were gone, leaving nothing but a trail of dust in their wake.

"Stupid!" Helena said, grabbing her bag. She stomped along the road, stamping her frustration out on the asphalt.

Tom waited until they were through the settling cloud of dust, and the sound of the engines had disappeared behind them. "Not that stupid," he said. "Most of them were already carrying a passenger. Maybe they figured they didn't have room for anyone else."

"Most of them," Helena said. "Not all of them. And yeah, sure, you can find a way to excuse any behavior, but that doesn't make what they did any less idiotically suicidal."

"What do you mean?"

"Don't you get it? They're riding straight toward the zombies from that bus. If they'd stopped we would have warned them, but no. They decided they couldn't stop to help someone, so they've ridden off toward their deaths." She kicked at the road. "Stupid. That's how civilization dies. The selfish stupidity of the individual."

"Hmm."

"Is that it? You don't have anything else to say? No smart retort?" she asked.

"What's the point? You're probably right. They could have stopped. Now, chances are some of them are dead. Or maybe they'll see the zombies and kill them. Who knows, and I don't care." A bird flew above the road, coming to settle on a branch nearby. He didn't care about that, either. What little comfort he'd gained from the creatures was gone.

He saw another bird, and another. "Crows?"

"What?"

"Nothing."

There were a lot of birds. They weren't quite circling the road, but flying above it, occasionally settling in the trees, and more often flying away. The road dipped, rose, and they saw why.

It was impossible to tell what had caused the car and three motorbikes to crash. Metal, plastic, and glass were strewn across the road, along with bodies.

"They're all dead," Helena said.

Technically, that was true. There were eight bodies, but he could see a leather-clad arm rising up from the ground. He unslung the shotgun. As they walked nearer to the crash site, what had taken place became clear. There were three bikes, two on the road, and one underneath the buckled wheels of a blue minivan. On the ground were seven dead people. Two wore military uniforms. Five of the others, he guessed, had been civilians. The other two bodies were bikers. One had been shot in the head. The other had not. Its legs were missing below the knees. Slowly it crawled along the asphalt toward them.

"They *were* a gang, going by the rocker on the jacket," Tom said, watching the creature raise its right arm. It came down on asphalt. The fingers curled, dragging along the stone, leaving a trail of brown viscous fluid behind. Its other arm was broken. As it came out, the jagged stump of bone caught the ground. As it shifted its weight, dragging itself forward an inch, there was a tearing sound. He couldn't tell whether that was muscle or cloth. Its arm came forward. It moved another inch.

"You going to shoot it?" Helena asked.

"His friends didn't," Tom said, but that was no excuse not to do what had to be done. He wasn't going to waste a bullet, however. He looked around the wreckage for something heavy, and picked up a twisted section of handlebar. He walked over to the zombie. The zombie's arm swept around, the stubby fingers brushed against his boots. He stabbed down, twisting the metal through bone and brain.

"They must have stopped here, got infected. The rest of the bikers stopped. Killed the others, but not this guy. Maybe they liked him too much."

"Or disliked him," Helena said. "To leave him like that, I mean. There's a couple of bags in here, but they must have taken everything with them. The people, too."

"Any food?" he asked.

186

She flashed him a recriminating look that was gone almost as soon as it had appeared. She opened a bag. "Some jerky, if you fancy risking it. And a canteen." She took a sniff. "Iced tea, I think." She took a sip. "Seriously hard," she said, spitting it out.

"No water?"

"No."

Two dead bikers, but three bikes, all of which would require a week of repairs before they could be ridden again. A hundred yards beyond the wreckage was a steeper road, leading up into the hills.

"Uphill?" Helena asked. "Maybe zombies are like people, they'll chose the path of least resistance, and won't follow us."

"Maybe." He doubted it.

Chapter 22 - A Proper Bed
Clearfield County, Pennsylvania

The motel was a welcome sight. Designed in a 'U' shape around a parking lot, it was decorated in bright red and yellow, with sharp lines and steep curves emulating an idealized vision of the 1950s. Next to it was a separate building Tom guessed was a restaurant. Beyond that was an access road that disappeared into the woods. On the far side of the motel was a gas station. It looked deserted.

"That curtain moved," Helena said.

"Where?"

"Ground floor, near the end."

No one came out, or even opened the door. Unsurprising, he supposed. Their clothing was stained, and they were armed.

"Try the reception?" he suggested.

The sign might have read *welcome*, but there was no one to greet them. The walls were covered in black and white photographs showing smiling couples and grimacing children dressed in period costume, and always in front of cars that he'd only seen in a museum. And that, he guessed was where the pictures had been taken. There was something indefinably anachronistic about the photographs. The teeth? The skin? Maybe it was how the people stood near the cars, without actually touching them. The romanticism extended to the long counter with its visitor's book and little brass bell. He ran a finger along the top.

"A week's worth of dust," he said.

"What? You'd expect them to clean the place after the news of New York?"

The faux old-world charm stopped at the door behind the counter. The manager's office was furnished in flat-pack steel and wood. A computer sat on the desk. A flat-screen TV was affixed to the wall.

"Is there power?" Tom turned on the television. There was.

Tanks rolled across the screen. He unmuted it.

"This will provide security for the Californian agricultural belt," a reporter said, "ensuring that the nation has enough to eat until the crisis is past."

Something about what the reporter was saying didn't match the image on the screen. He saw what.

"You see at the side of the road, the sign?" he asked.

"Shh!"

The sign was for I-82, and that was in Oregon, not California. The image changed to an aircraft carrier at the center of a massive fleet.

"Overseas evacuation of military assets is nearing completion," the reporter continued. "The Third Fleet is nearing the West Coast, ready to lend support to the relief effort."

The ships were replaced with a squadron of fighter planes in mid-air. A trio of missiles launched from the lead plane. More followed from the others. The image changed again, this time showing an explosion.

"There's no way that was caused by those missiles," Tom said.

"Military operations are underway," the reporter continued. "Civilians are asked to remain indoors so as to not interfere with the relief effort. Any military personnel on leave are to disregard all previous orders and report to the nearest civil authority…"

"It's propaganda," Helena said. "That's all."

"True." He pressed mute. "But someone took the time to edit all of that together. There's a plan. Someone is coordinating it. The question is, who." He picked up the telephone. "It's been disconnected."

"What about the sat-phone?"

"Got to wait for it to charge," he said. He glanced at the progress bar. "A couple more minutes."

"Right. Right."

"It's strange to be waiting," he began. "It's like—" He stopped. "Do you hear that?"

A knocking sound came from somewhere nearby. Tap-tap, tap. Their eyes turned to the two doors leading from the office.

Tom grabbed the shotgun, aiming at the nearest closed door.

"Open it," he whispered.

Helena took a tentative step forward, grabbed the door, wrenched it open, and took a sudden leap back. It was a storeroom, filled with cleaning materials and nothing else.

"Other door," Tom whispered, but Helena was already there. She leaned her ear against the wood, listening. She shook her head, and opened the door. It led into the living room of an apartment.

"Hello?" he called. There was no reply. He stepped through the doorway, tracking the shotgun left and right. The room was a mess. Empty bottles, dirty dishes, and a pile of mildewed clothes told of someone who'd been living like it was the end of the world long before February 20th.

"You hear that?" Helena whispered. He had. Tap. Tap-tap. Then silence. Tap, tap, tap-tap. Silence. It came again.

Four doors led from the room. The sound could be coming from behind any of them. He pointed at one, then the next, and gave a shrug. Helena replied with the same. He raised the shotgun, pointed at her, and then at the nearest door. She raised the gun, lowered it, checked the safety was off, raised it again, breathed out, and nodded. He took a step forward. She crossed to the door. The tapping came again.

"Ready?" she mouthed.

He nodded. She threw the door open. It was a bedroom. It was empty, and looked less lived-in than the living room. He gestured to the next door. She opened it. Another bedroom, with a bed with a mattress still covered in plastic. The next door led to a small kitchen. He aimed the shotgun at the final door.

"One," Helena mouthed. "Two." She threw the door open and jumped back. Tom stepped forward, jabbing the barrel into every empty corner of a small bathroom. The tapping came again. He lowered the shotgun.

"It's the cord from the blind," he said. The window had been left open, allowing the chill breeze to knock it this way and that.

"There's a photograph," Helena said, picking it up from the table by the couch. "Folded in half so only a man and a boy are visible. His son, I suppose. Maybe that empty bedroom was meant to be for his kid. Do you think he got the job managing the motel, thinking it would save the marriage, but in the end, he came here alone? That would explain the smell of despair about this place. But maybe, when the outbreak began, he went looking for his son."

"Yeah, maybe." He went back to the office. The phone had enough charge for a call. Moving back to the doorway so he could find a signal, he dialed Nate's number. It connected.

"Nate, it's—"

"You're alive! I knew you would be. What happened? No, wait, can you call back in an hour?"

"Nate, I—"

"I can't talk. Not right now. Are you safe?"

"Safe? I guess so," Tom said.

"Great, can you call back in an hour?"

"One hour? I guess, but—"

Nate hung up.

Tom frowned. "You heard that?" he asked.

"He sounded happy," Helena said.

"So I guess we assume everything's okay."

"What is it they say about assumptions?" Helena asked. "But if we've got to wait, then I'm having a shower. Maybe something to eat." She walked back into the apartment. "Except there's nothing here except cereal." There was the sound of the fridge opening. "Milk's very off. Ah, well. Shower first, but not in there. Who knows what I might catch."

She came back out to the office, opened the door to the storeroom, and grabbed a box of paper towels and a transparent bottle filled with a hideous pink liquid. The label said it was soap. Tom wasn't sure he believed it. She walked over to the old-fashioned rack by the counter and took down a key. "I'll be in room… wait, no, don't want to tempt fate." She put it back and took another. "Room one-oh-two. What about you?"

"I'll see what those other buildings are. Maybe one of them's a diner. I'll call Nate, and come and find you after."

"Okay. Good. One hour? That'll give me time to wash and have a quiet scream. I think I need that."

"Sure," Tom said, and forced a smile. She left, and he collapsed into the chair. She was acting like they'd achieved something, as if getting to the motel was a victory. Maybe she needed to think that, but all they'd done was find somewhere with power and, hopefully, running water. It was a temporary refuge. Good for a few hours that they could probably stretch to a night, but not much longer. If he could speak to Nate, and if the kid let him say more than a few words, perhaps he could talk to Max. Perhaps an extraction team would be sent, and he'd spend the night on a bunk in a military complex, or even back at the White House. What was more likely was that resources were stretched so thin no one would be sent. He would pass on his warning, and then, once more, be on foot. What then? Where, then, would they go?

"Worry about that in an hour," he murmured. Through the open door and the wide glass window of the reception area, and across the parking lot, he saw Helena climb the stairs. She reached a door, glanced left and right, opened it, and went inside. A moment later, she came out, waved in his general direction, went back in, and closed the door. Maybe she had the right attitude in pretending the nightmare was over.

He picked up the remote and surfed the channels. Most weren't broadcasting. The rest showed a variation on the same theme; fighter planes, military convoys, roadblocks, and soldiers forcing entry into buildings. He stopped, went back a channel. It wasn't a variation. It was the same footage, but the channels weren't broadcasting it simultaneously. There were no zombies, no lines of refugees, and no civilians at all that he could see. It was all stock footage, he guessed. Clips filmed during training exercises to be used in recruitment ads.

Out of idle curiosity, he opened the desk drawers, and found a bundle of keys, though none were for a vehicle. Underneath was a map of the area. He grimaced. They were only forty miles from Dr Ayers's house. The rest of the drawer was filled with delivery notes. The one underneath contained pamphlets announcing that the motel would open in March. Hoping that would mean the restaurant would already be fully stocked, but suspecting it wouldn't, he pocketed the keys, map, and a pamphlet, and went to check.

A padlock and chain had been attached to the doors at the front. The padlock was intact, but someone had hacked a hole through the wooden door, cutting the handle free. Inside, tables and chairs, still covered in plastic, were stacked in the dinning area. The bar hadn't been stocked, and the only delivery the kitchen had received was for crockery.

He went back to the manager's apartment and collected the sat-phone. It had enough charge for the call, and there was something about the twitching curtains that made him uncomfortable not having it on his person.

Like the restaurant, the gas station hadn't yet opened. The underground tank had been installed, and the filling cap removed. From the complete absence of any fumes, he guessed it had never been filled. The echoing clang of a pebble dropped through the opening confirmed it. The small store behind the pumps had the blue and red sign of an outdoor pursuits company he'd seen in a few of the larger towns in the northeast. A poster in the window advertised the latest in low-price, high-quality, all-weather clothing, but when he pushed the broken door open, he found nothing inside except empty racks.

He still had twenty minutes until he was due to call Nate. There was a ladder behind the store. He propped it against the gas station's flat roof and climbed up. There was nothing to see on the road in either direction. No cars, no people, no signs of life. No zombies either. That was a blessing, but he knew it was only a matter of time before they arrived. His eyes fell on the vehicles in the lot, and he mentally debated the relative morality of stealing one until, finally, it was time to call Nate. The call connected.

"Nate, listen," he said, and before Nate could interrupt, he gave the name and address of the motel.

"The Sunset View Inn? Sounds nice," Nate said. "I'll pass it along, but I wish you'd called ten minutes ago. You could have spoken to the president."

"You said an hour."

"Yeah, I know, but it's busy here." There was enthusiasm in Nate's voice.

"Nate, what's going on?"

"You won't believe it. Or maybe you will. Someone was sabotaging… well, everything. They think it was a cyber attack launched specifically at the White House. It cut off communications and slowed the relief effort. And you know who did it? North Korea."

"Korea?"

"Yeah. They were behind Air Force Two going down and everything. But it's okay now. It's all been fixed. There's been… hang on, something's going on. Okay, I have to be quick. If you called, I had to take your address. They're going to send someone to get you. It won't be until noon tomorrow. Will you be safe until then?"

Tom looked around at the empty landscape. "Probably."

"Great. President Maxwell is going to address the nation in the morning. The country's going to be divided up into zones, each with its own localized military command. Tomorrow's broadcast is the signal. Like, forty-eight hours afterward, the plan gets put into place. I'm filming it. It's going to be a proper documentary and we're going to broadcast it at the weekend."

"What do you mean?"

"You know, footage of the president at work, that kind of thing. It's pretty cool." The kid sounded genuinely excited. "Then there's going to be massive conscription," Nate continued. "Everyone will be enlisted. The truckers, the farmers, everyone. It's… it's huge."

"A cyber attack doesn't make sense," Tom said. "It would cut off communications, but doesn't explain how orders were being given elsewhere."

"Okay," Nate said, not sounding as if he was listening. "Maybe we can talk about it tomorrow. You'll be safe until then. Noon, right?"

"Probably. Yes, noon."

"Great. I have to go." He hung up.

Tom stared at the phone. Any relief at the prospect of escaping this hellish road-journey was tempered by the fact that the conspirators were clearly still at work. A cyber attack? North Korea? No. Perhaps they were desperately trying to hide their tracks now that their plans were in complete disarray. Perhaps. He hoped so. He'd find out tomorrow, but noon seemed a very long way off.

Chapter 23 - Rent
Clearfield County, Pennsylvania

He knocked for nearly a minute before Helena opened the door with the pistol in her hand.

"I was in the shower," she said, though as she was wrapped in a sheet and her hair was damp, there was no need for explanation. She headed back to the bathroom. He followed her inside, propping the shotgun by the door.

"The water's tepid, the soap's foul, but I almost feel clean," she said. "Did you speak to him?"

"I did," he said. "They're sending a helicopter. It'll be here tomorrow at noon."

"For you, or us?" she asked.

"Honestly? I didn't mention you, but when they come, and if there's an issue, I'll say you're an expert in virology who might have the cure for all this. By the time they know the truth you'll be somewhere far safer than this."

"Assuming I go with you. I still haven't decided. What else did he say?"

"They think there was a cyber attack, and that the zombies and the downing of Air Force Two are all linked, but that North Korea is responsible."

"But it's not, right?"

"Unlikely. There might be some truth to some small part of it." He crossed to a chair on the far side of the bed and sat down. "But I doubt it."

"But they're getting a handle on things?" she asked, stepping out of the bathroom.

"Yes. There's going to be a broadcast tomorrow, and there's some sort of plan in the works. He said something about zones and… and I didn't get any more from him."

"You'll find out the rest tomorrow, so cheer up," she said. "From the sound of it, the worst is over. I'm going to sleep for a bit. You should have a shower. And… maybe see if there are some clothes in the manager's office you can steal. One of the piles in there looked like they'd been washed."

Tom took the hint, forced himself to stand, and went back outside. A few minutes later, a random assortment of clothes in his hands, he was heading back up the stairs. He saw the curtains in the ground floor room move. Should he tell these people that a helicopter was coming? Would they mob it?

It was a problem to which he didn't find the answer in the shower. He dressed, piling on the layers. The clothes smelled faintly of mildew, but they were cleaner than what he'd been wearing. He collapsed into the chair, and decided that if the other people in the motel wanted to be left alone, he was more than happy to acquiesce. He could only hope they would return the favor.

He was woken by a knock at the door.

"We're sorry to bother you," a man's voice came through the thin plywood. Tom found himself smiling. For once, sleep had been interrupted by a human.

"We saw you come in," the man continued. "We were… um…" There was a pause.

"We wanted to know where you came from," a woman said. "What it was like there. We're going to leave, but we don't want to drive into danger."

Helena was looking at him. She was dressed, wearing the overlong blazer, and with a bag in her hand. She looked like she'd been about to go out. "Shall I?" she mouthed.

Tom shrugged, and pushed himself up in the chair, looking around for a clock. Helena opened the door. To the left of the frame was a man, to the right a woman.

"Hi," the man said. He gave a grin missing three teeth. His arm came up. In his hand was a revolver. He shoved it into Helena's face. "Don't try it," he said to Tom, as Helena backed into the room. Tom didn't move. The shotgun was by the door. There was no way he'd reach it.

Helena continued backing into the room until she stood against the wall. The woman came inside, closed the door, and picked up the shotgun.

"Got it," she said.

"Good." The man shifted aim, pointing the revolver at Tom as the woman aimed the shotgun at Helena.

"Sit on your hands," the man said.

Tom shifted his legs and slid his hands underneath them. With his legs spread and covered by his thighs, the man couldn't see him curl his fingers around the chair's seat. He glanced at Helena. She seemed oddly relaxed. He looked back at the man.

"Why?" he asked. He didn't think there was a need to ask anything more.

"This is our motel. You want to stay here, you have to pay."

"How much?"

"Half of what you've got," the man said. "Food, cash, ammo."

"That's robbery," Helena said.

"Hell if I care what you call it," the woman said. She grabbed the bag still in Helena's hand, backed off a step, looked inside and dropped it. "It's empty." The shotgun came back up. "Where's your food? Your ammo?"

"What do we get in return?" Tom asked.

"How about you get to live?" the man said.

Tom doubted it. He'd seen the man's expression before; the eager, desperate nervousness that was part fear, part glee at a bad job half done. The man was so full of adrenaline and anxiety he'd be easy to disarm. The problem was the shotgun. He glanced at Helena. She met his eyes. They flicked toward the bed.

"If we work together," Tom said, raising his voice, "we can make this motel safe. Keep the zombies away. Help one another stay alive."

"Maybe. Maybe, but the rent's due. Where's your bags? We saw you come in with them."

Tom made a point of leaning forward and looking around the room. On the table by the bed, he saw the shotgun shells lined up in a neat row. He looked back at the man, but didn't lean back in his seat.

"It's all in the bag. You can have half. No more. Agreed?" he said, nodding his head toward the side of the bed currently hidden from the man's view. The man took a step forward, his eyes turning toward the floor. He was five feet away. Another step.

Pushing at the chair with his hands, and the floor with his feet, Tom launched himself forward. His head slammed into the man's chest. The man staggered back. Tom swept his arms up. There was a gunshot as he grabbed the man's wrist. His other hand jabbed at the man's kidneys as he kept pushing with his head and twisting at his wrist. He slammed his forehead down on the thief's nose. As the man stumbled, Tom changed his grip on the thief's wrist, using the man's own momentum against him. There was a snap as bone broke. The fingers went limp. The gun fell. Tom brought his hand back, jabbing it like a blade at the thief's throat. The man went down, gasping for air. Tom scooped up the gun and turned to face the woman. She was on the ground. Blood pulsed from a wound in her chest. She was dead. Helena had the pistol, half raised in her hands, a look of disbelief in her eyes.

"You had to," Tom said, taking her arm. He steered her away from the body, to the door, and outside.

"I… I…" she began.

"I know," he said. Before he could say any more, he heard a curse from inside the room. The man was trying to draw a hunting knife with his broken hand. Tom swore, went back inside, and kicked the man's hand clear. He pressed the revolver against the man's head.

He wanted to kill the man yet he knew he shouldn't. Self defense was one thing, murder another. Even now, especially now, there had to be laws. Justice had to be done. As to who would administer that was a problem to be resolved later. He forced his inner rage back into its box, ripped the curtain cord down from the wall, and roughly bound the man's hands. He screamed. Tom said nothing as he pulled the man's knife from his belt. The blade was covered in dried blood.

"Whose blood is this?" he asked, his voice low.

The man spat. It didn't matter. Tom could guess. He backed away to the door.

"How are you?" he asked.

"Fine. I'm fine," Helena said. She didn't sound it.

"Can you watch him?"

"What? Why? Where are you going?"

He wished there was a way he could avoid telling her. There wasn't. He held up the knife.

"That's blood. That's..." Her eyes widened in understanding.

"I need to check," Tom said.

She raised the gun, pointing it through the open door at the man.

The set of master keys which he'd taken from the manager's office was still in his pocket. Tom took them out. He started with the nearest room. It was empty. So was the next. He found the first body in the room second from the end on the upper floor.

The victim was an older man, at least sixty. On the table next to the TV, he'd placed a family portrait. Taken at least ten years before, he stood next to a man and woman, with four children in front. To his right, in the center of the picture, was a young woman wearing a graduation gown.

The man had been stabbed, and his throat had been cut. Tom assumed it was in that order. There was a bag in the room, and it had been opened. The contents were strewn about the floor. He closed the door and went to check the other rooms.

Downstairs in a slightly larger room at the end of the building with a clear view of the road, he found the killers' stash. It was a meager haul, some canned food and a few packets, some loose shotgun shells but no gun to fire them, a half-empty bottle of bourbon and a half-full box of . 357 rounds, a stack of bills that couldn't amount to more than a few hundred dollars, and car keys. Those were lined up on the table. There were five sets. He guessed that one must belong to the victim upstairs, and one to the pair of killers. He was wrong.

He found four more rooms containing bodies. Couples, individuals, and one family. He looked inside long enough to confirm they were dead, and wished he hadn't seen even that.

"What did you find?" Helena called from where she stood on the balcony above him.

"Bodies. Not zombies," Tom said, and left it at that. He'd only checked one third of the motel. Opposite, he could see a man at a window, watching him. A curtain above and to the left twitched. Otherwise there was no movement. He'd have to deal with those people and check the other rooms. First, there was something else he had to do.

Wearily, he climbed back up the stairs.

"How many?" Helena asked.

"It doesn't matter. You don't want to know."

"They killed them?"

He suspected the man had done worse to the pair of girls in one of the downstairs rooms. "Yes," he said. "Swap." He held out the revolver.

"Why?"

"I want a gun I know that works," he said, and took the pistol from her.

He walked back into the room. He pushed the door closed. The man had rolled onto his back. He stared up as Tom raised the gun.

"It wasn't me," he said. "It was her. It was all—"

Tom fired. Once was enough.

Chapter 24 - Refuge
Clearfield County, Pennsylvania

"Why?" Helena asked. "Why did they do it?"

"I don't know," Tom said. He stood next to her on the balcony, looking down at the parking lot, and the other rooms. "Because it was easy. Because they were evil. Because they enjoyed it. Or, maybe they were people like you and me, but the horrors of the last week broke something inside them. I really don't know. Sometimes there aren't any answers. Sometimes the ones you get aren't an explanation. It doesn't matter. They're dead. We're alive."

"That's how it's going to be now? Alone, fighting and killing one another?"

"For a while, maybe."

"Well, it shouldn't be. It doesn't have to be."

Tom didn't reply. The man was gone from the window opposite. Tom was dreading checking the other rooms, but it had to be done. And then there were the rooms with their twitching curtains. He wouldn't be able to sleep until he'd found out who the occupants were, and whether they were in league with the two murderers.

"Noon tomorrow seems like a long way off," he said. "Why did you unload the shotgun?"

"To see if I could," she said. "I couldn't sleep. I couldn't stop thinking about…" She trailed off. "I thought I'd go and see if I could find…" She trailed off again. "I wanted a new life. It was more than that; I knew I needed one. A new town, new friends, a new job. I had to put the past behind me. And this is…" She trailed off again. The next time she spoke, weary frustration had been replaced with angry fear. "Tom. Look."

On the road to the south, still three hundred yards away but heading toward them, came a lurching, shuffling figure.

Tom sighed. "Better save the ammo, I suppose."

In front of the reception and office were two raised flower beds. Plastic sacks of soil had been dumped in one, and the other was half-full. Next to them, left out to rust, were a pair of shovels. It wasn't a good weapon, far from it, but the long handle would keep some distance between him and his foe.

Resting the shovel over his shoulder, he walked toward the zombie. Male, he thought. Wearing a hat, a scarf, but only one glove. The other hand was missing two fingers. Was that how he'd become infected? It didn't matter.

He gripped the shovel two-handed. When it was eight feet away, he swung, smashing the flat of the blade into its face. The force of the blow knocked it from its feet. He twisted the shovel and brought it down edge-first onto the zombie's face. Skin broke, and red-brown fluid oozed out, but its arms still thrashed. He swung again, this time breaking through bone, the shovel biting deep into its brain. It was still. Leaving the shovel there, he went back to the motel.

Helena hadn't moved from the balcony, but she wasn't watching him. A man stood in the doorway of a room on the opposite side of the motel. He was around Tom's age, though with a few less inches in height and a few extra in girth. In his hands was a rifle. Tom reached for the pistol he'd stuck in his belt, but forced his hand down by his side. Despite the weapon, there was something not immediately threatening about the man. Tom walked toward him, stopping thirty feet away, and two feet from the cover of a brand-new, high-end silver town car.

"Hi," Tom said.

"We heard shooting," the man replied.

Tom couldn't see anyone else behind the man. "You saw the man and woman come to our room?" he asked. "They wanted to rob and kill us. That was their plan for everyone in the motel. It looks like they were halfway done. You can check those rooms if you want." He jerked his thumb over his shoulder.

The man didn't turn to look. "You killed them?" he asked.

"The woman was killed in self-defense," Tom said. "The man? That was justice."

The man nodded, but Tom couldn't tell if he disapproved or not.

"Where are you from?" Tom asked.

"Cleveland. You?"

"New York," Tom said.

"You were there when this began?" the man asked.

"We got out of Manhattan before it was cut off."

The man nodded again.

Tom had had enough. "So," he said, " how do you want to do this?"

The man blinked. "What do you mean?"

"You saw the zombie? More are going to come. If you want to leave, go. If you want to stay, you've got to help."

"We're out of gas," the man said. "Otherwise we wouldn't've stopped."

"There's probably some in these cars," Tom said. "You can take what you want."

"But you're staying?"

"Until tomorrow," Tom said. He was growing increasingly frustrated. There just wasn't time for them to stand around trying to decide if they could trust one another.

He heard footsteps. It was Helena.

"Hi," she said. "My name's Helena. What's yours?" She wasn't speaking to the man, but to a child Tom hadn't noticed standing just inside the room. The boy slid around the door and grabbed hold of the man's jacket.

"I'm Lawrence," the man finally said. "This is Noah."

"Hi, Noah," Helena said. "I teach boys who are about your age."

Tom wondered how old that was. The child was about three feet tall, but Tom's limited experience with children only narrowed that to somewhere between five and ten years old.

"I know you're scared," Helena continued. "I am too. But if we help one another, we'll all be okay." She looked at Lawrence.

"Help each other how?" Lawrence asked.

"There's a—" Helena began. Guessing what she was going to say, Tom interrupted.

"Check all the ground-floor windows are closed," he said. "Then block off the parking lot with the vehicles we don't need."

"And split the fuel in the tanks?" Lawrence asked.

"Sure. And the food. Then take turns to stand sentry through the night."

"Agreed."

Chapter 25 - Here We Stand
Clearfield County, Pennsylvania

There were twelve vehicles in the lot. Five matched the keys found in the killers' room. Of the others, one car belonged to a murdered couple, found in a room three doors down from the one Helena had claimed. The pair had been dead for at least two days. Tom had found no more victims in the motel, though there was still one room that he was sure was occupied. Lawrence owned a mid-sized minivan, but that still left five other vehicles. Four had local license plates, and nothing inside. The fifth was the luxury silver four-door that even Tom would have thought twice before buying.

As he was sizing up the cars' windows, debating which one to break, the door to the other occupied motel room opened. Two women came out. Both carried long kitchen knives. In their early twenties, on the unkempt side of fashionably dressed, each was pushing the other as if neither wanted to be in the lead.

"Is this your car?" Tom asked trying to disarm the situation before it escalated.

"Yeah. It's ours. Leave it," the one on the left said, taking a step back as she spoke.

"We're putting up a barrier to stop the undead," he said. "If you plan on leaving, you should move it onto the road."

He turned away from them, and went to a smaller family car, pausing to throw a glance toward the room where that dead family now lay. He tried not to look at the toys in the backseat as he shunted it into place. When he got out, the two women were standing nervously by their car.

"I'm Tom," he said.

"Monique," the taller of the two said.

"Amy," the other said.

Tom smiled. "I'm trying to work out what to say now. The usual small talk doesn't seem appropriate."

"You're going to wall us in here?" Amy asked.

"Not exactly," Tom said. "We want a barrier in case the zombies turn up. Though it's more likely to be when, not if."

"And then what?" Monique asked.

"Kill them, I suppose," Tom said. "If you want to leave, now would be the best time. Where were you going?"

"Home," Amy said.

"New York," Monique added.

"Ah. We came from Manhattan. You won't make it there."

"We wanted to get to Brooklyn," Amy said.

Tom shook his head. There wasn't time for this. He tried to keep his tone polite. "If you're not sure of your plans, move the car onto the road while you work them out."

Five of the sturdier vehicles joined the silver sedan, so there were three pointing in each direction. The keys were left in the ignition in case of an escape he hoped wouldn't be necessary. The other six were shunted, bumper-to-bumper, across the entrance to the motel. They didn't quite stretch across. The gap at the northern end was filled with mattress frames and other furniture from the rooms.

Leaving Lawrence, Amy, and Monique to add more furniture on top of and around the cars, he and Helena walked the perimeter of the motel to check that the windows and doors were closed.

"Do you trust them?" Helena asked.

"I don't think they were involved in the murders," Tom said. "That's not the same thing, but it's enough for tonight. Lawrence will protect Noah. As long as we're assisting him with that, he'll be reliable. As for Monique and Amy, I think they can be trusted, but I don't know if I'd want to rely on them."

"They're beauticians," Helena said. "Not that they call themselves that. They say they focus on inner beauty rather than conforming to someone else's ideal, but it's still more about clothes, hair, and makeup than about diet and exercise."

Tom grunted, noncommittally.

"I think they knew what those two… murderers were doing," Helena said. "They weren't surprised when I told them. I was… angry. Not sure why, I mean, what was I expecting them to have done, call 911?"

"I tried," Tom said, pushing at a fire door. It didn't move. "Do you think we should upend the beds in these rooms so they cover these windows?"

She rapped her hand against it. "Seems solid. It's probably a waste of time. Did you really call 911?"

"Yeah. I thought someone should report what had happened. Not sure what I expected. I guess I wasn't thinking clearly."

"No answer?"

"No, just a recorded message saying that I should listen to local television and radio broadcasts. Obey the civil authority. Instructions would follow. That's what it said. Instructions. Not help."

She tried another door. "Noon can't come soon enough."

"You don't want any of this fuel?" Lawrence asked, as he pulled the tube out of the dented hybrid's now empty gas tank.

"No. Won't need it," Tom said without thinking. In his mind's eye, he could see a clock counting down until noon. He was debating whether, if the undead came in too great a number, it would be better to wait for the helicopter on the roof of the filling station rather than risk driving off into the unknown.

"Why don't you go and help the nice ladies sort the food," Lawrence said to Noah. The boy had been the man's dogged shadow for the last two hours. "It's all right, go on," Lawrence said. Reluctantly, the boy left. The man turned to Tom. "What happens tomorrow?" he asked.

Tom had sensed the question was coming. He thought of lying, but his life had been full of too many lies. Telling the truth, or most of it, seemed beguiling.

"There's a helicopter coming at noon," he said. "A government extraction."

"For you? You some kind of scientist or something?" Lawrence asked.

"Something, yes."

"You've a cure for all this?"

"I doubt there is one, but no. I do have some information I'm trying to get to the president."

"Ah." Lawrence screwed the cap on the bourbon bottle in which they'd syphoned the fuel. The only empty and sealable containers they'd been able to find were the bottles littering the absent manager's apartment. "How big a helicopter?"

What he was really asking was obvious. "I don't know. I imagine there'll be room for your son."

"But you can't promise anything?"

"I can't even get in contact with them." He kept trying every time his hands were free. The number wasn't connecting. There could be many reasons for that, but he couldn't help but think it was something sinister.

"Hmm." Lawrence looked north, and then south, not at the road, but at the miles of land either side.

"Where were you heading?" Tom asked.

"Originally?" Lawrence sighed. "Noah's my nephew. His parents were... they're going through a rough patch. Noah was staying with me while they tried to sort things out. I was trying to take him back there when all this happened. Became clear I wasn't going to get him home and wasn't going to get us back to mine. Hard to know what to do, or where to go. I've a friend who has a place in Montana. Doubt we'd get there now. Taken us a week to travel two hundred miles. And where are we? Nowhere. Kind o' hoped I'd meet someone who knew where safety lay."

"I'll take him with me," Tom said. "I can't offer more than that."

"I understand. Trust to the kindness of strangers? What a world. How much ammo do we have?"

"Eighteen rounds for the 9mm, twelve for the shotgun, seventy-eight for the .357." Despite finding some ammunition in the killer's stash, the revolver was the only firearm. That explained, at least in part, the murderers' actions. The other, evil part was best left unexplored. "How many do you have for your rifle?"

"Seventeen. It was a lot more five days ago." Lawrence raised a hand, rubbing thoughtfully at his stubble. "The zombies will come," he said. "If we stay."

"And if we leave, the helicopter won't find us," Tom said.

"Hmm." Lawrence stared off into the distance again. "This isn't a great place for a siege. If the helicopter comes, there won't be room for all of us."

"Probably not," Tom said.

"At which point, we'll have to flee. Seems a shame to waste a day." The cogs clicking into place were almost audible. "But Noah might get out, and there really is no refuge to which we can flee. Fine. But we'll need more weapons."

The motel had few to offer. Other than the Amy and Monique's knives, three more shovels, and a rusting pickaxe too cumbersome to contemplate, the closest they found was a fire axe.

"We'll need something heavy," Helena suggested. "Like the metal railings for the balcony?"

It was make-work, and Tom left them to it. He climbed to the roof of the filling station so he could survey the countryside. When he'd last checked the television, it was still broadcasting the same variation on *stay inside and stay tuned for more information*. It wasn't comforting. Nor was the lack of traffic. Compared to what he'd seen in the last week, there should have been a steady steam of refugees traveling past. The internet was collapsing, but the radio stations were still broadcasting. That there were still people out there had offered some comfort, even if their messages were full of desperate hope and fearful despair. So why had they seen no vehicles?

It was possible that they were so remote that little traffic passed this way. That idea was dispelled as soon as he considered that they were in a motel, not something likely to have been built off a completely beaten track. The logical alternative was that the roads to the north and south were now blocked somewhere out of sight. He could take a car and check, but what would he do if he found them blocked? What if he found the undead? Knowing would do no good unless they had to escape, in which case they would have little choice in the direction they went. His eyes fell on the track leading into the woods. There was no way of knowing if it led out again, and with less than an hour until sunset there wasn't time to check. That didn't mean there was nothing he could do. They'd parked six vehicles on the road. They didn't need one for each of their odd partnerships. Nor, realistically, if they had to flee, was it likely that all six of them would be alive to escape. Wishing he'd not had that last thought, he climbed down from the filling station, and headed for the road.

"Where are you going?" Helena asked, as he climbed into the cab of a pickup truck.

"I'm going to move the two trucks to the track. If the zombies come down this road that'll be our way out."

Helena glanced up and down the road. "You think that's likely?"

"Probably not," he lied.

He was maneuvering the second truck into place when there was a shout from the motel. It was one word. "Zombie!"

Tom was halfway back to the motel when he heard the crack of the rifle. The second came as he was letting himself in the backdoor of the manager's office. He heard the third as he ran out into the parking lot. Lawrence stood, legs braced, in the middle of the road. Amy had tight hold of Noah, though it looked as if it was as much for her comfort as his. Monique was by her side. Helena stood on the roof of a car, her eyes on the road, her fingers curling around the stock of the shotgun.

"Wait!" Tom yelled, as the man fired again. "Stop!"

Lawrence ignored him, chambering another round.

Tom pushed the barrel down. "Wait."

"Look," Lawrence replied.

Four zombies were down – all with headshots. The nearest was forty yards away. There was no time to be impressed with the man's skill. Behind them, another fourteen staggered along the road toward the motel.

"Wait," Tom said again.

"What for?" Lawrence raised his gun. "The rifle will be useless when it gets dark." He fired. A zombie fell.

"And in the morning?" Tom asked.

"Got to survive the night to worry about that," Lawrence said.

The mass of arguments against wasting ammunition died when they met the logic of his reply. Tom raised the fire axe, and backed off a pace, letting the man work. He was a good shot, but when he fired his last round, there was still one zombie left.

"He's all yours," Lawrence said.

Tom walked slowly toward his foe. It wasn't a he, but a she. A woman in a green skirt and jacket, a white blouse stained red, and jet black hair on the right-hand side of her head. On the left was nothing but an oozing scab where her scalp had been ripped away.

He tested the weight of the axe, mentally rehearsing the blow, but his eyes kept going back to the woman. Who was she? Where had she come from? It didn't matter. She'd turned. She was dead. She wasn't a woman. It was a zombie, a monster from nightmares, in which no humanity remained.

Ten feet. He raised the axe to his shoulder. He couldn't pity the dead, not now, perhaps never. It was the living with whom he had to be concerned. The zombie snarled. He swung the axe. The blade sang through the air, chopping through the creature's knee, slicing through bone and tendon, muscle and flesh. As the zombie toppled forward, he skipped back two paces, and was already bringing the axe up as it hit the ground, face first. He was grateful for that. It meant he didn't have to look into its eyes as he swung the axe down onto its skull.

He wiped the blade clean on the zombie's coat. Was it a uniform? None of the other bodies were similarly dressed. The next nearest wore a padded jacket, the one behind, nothing but a T-shirt. He could check them for I.D., but to what end? Knowing where they'd once called home wasn't going to help him survive the night.

"Tom!"

He glanced behind and saw Helena pointing down the road. He could guess why, though the dip in the road meant he couldn't see the creatures coming.

"How many?" he called back.

"Two."

He raised the axe and waited for them to come.

Chapter 26 - A Long Night
Clearfield County, Pennsylvania

He punched the axe-head forward. Bone broke, and wood cracked as the axe shaft split. He dropped it and drew the revolver.

"Light! I need light!"

There was no reply. He raised the gun, pivoting left and right, trying to peer into the darkness.

They'd turned the lights on in the motel, and in two of the cars they'd parked outside. They could see for twenty yards around the building, but had blinded themselves to anything beyond. Monique was meant to be bringing out lamps from the rooms in the hope they could push the shadows further down the road, but there was no sign of her.

A shape staggered out of the darkness. He raised the revolver. Bracing his hand on his wrist, he waited. Waited. He fired. The zombie fell. Was that the tenth? The twentieth? He'd lost count.

When thirty seconds passed without any more hideous faces appearing out of the darkness, he backed away until he reached the wood and vehicle barricade. It had seemed so sturdy at sunset. Now, it seemed little more than a taunt, a signpost to these creatures as to where they were.

"We should have left," Helena said. "Right after we killed those two murderers." She dropped the metal bar from her hand. Her arms were covered in gore.

"I was thinking the same thing," Tom said. "But where do we run? It's clear those roads were blocked by something." Vehicles filled with the undead was his first thought, and he tried not to let it become the one that dominated his mind. It was bad enough not being able to see what lay outside the meager pool of light without imagining it filled with hundreds of snapping, gaping mouths.

"We can't leave now," he said. "Not in the dark when we can barely see a few feet ahead of us."

"Amy! Weapons! Hurry!" Helena snapped. Amy had been left in charge of weapons and Noah. Her hands shook too much to be trusted with anything else. "That wasn't what I meant," Helena added as the young woman passed through another iron bar, one end wrapped in a torn sheet. Tom grabbed a bottle and splashed water on his hands before wiping them dry on his jacket. He could feel the skin tightening as cold bit into his damp flesh.

"What did you mean?" Tom asked.

"That we shouldn't have stopped. We should have kept on, but we didn't. When that helicopter comes—"

"If it comes," Lawrence said coming up to join them. He dropped the broken handle of the shovel.

"If," Helena agreed. "There's not going to be room for all of us. We can ask a soldier to give up their seat for Noah, and perhaps for Lawrence, but not for all of us. Sooner or later, we have to make a stand, right?"

Lawrence laughed. "You're not saying you believed Maxwell when he gave that speech?"

"I dunno," Helena said. "But here and now, it's true. Some of us will be left behind. We should have left, but we didn't. We're here, and we have to make this place a refuge."

"How?" Lawrence asked. "There're no weapons. Barely enough food to get us through the week. There's water, but no well, and we're on a hill. When the power's cut, the pumps won't work, the water will stop. This isn't a refuge. It's not even a fort."

"Tom can get them to send supplies. And troops, right?"

"Maybe. I can try."

"He can ask," Lawrence said. "He can't even guarantee they'll listen, let alone do anything about it."

"But they might," Helena said. "If we drive off into the unknown, they won't know where to send them. But if we stay here, they can. There needs to be refuges, places people can come, places they can be safe. The alternative is that we all wander the countryside until we're each attacked, infected, and we turn. We'll all die."

"Maybe," Lawrence said. "If we survive tonight."

"North!" Monique called. "North!"

215

Tom dropped the water bottle and grabbed a metal bar. They walked wearily out into the road to meet them. One, then two, then four lurched into the beams of light from the car. He shifted the metal bar to his left hand and drew the revolver. He fired. He was tired. His aim was off. The bullet slammed into the zombie's shoulder. He fired again. The bullet hit its forehead. It collapsed. He tracked the barrel to the next creature, pulled the trigger, and the hammer hit a spent round. He was *very* tired. He'd forgotten to reload and now there wasn't time. He stuffed the revolver back into his pocket.

"The shotgun!" he barked and realized Helena hadn't been carrying it. He swore and stepped forward, swinging the metal bar low. It crunched into a leg. The zombie went down. He stepped back, but there wasn't time to swing at its head. Another zombie lurched into the gap. He swung, aiming at the skull, but the zombie's flailing arms were in the way. Bone broke, but the zombie kept on. He punched the bar forward into its face. The metal bit into flesh, tearing away skin. The zombie kept moving. It was too much. Something in him snapped.

He screamed. Swinging the bar up and down, no longer aiming, just beating at the creature until it stopped moving, then on to the next. He no longer saw the faces of the zombies in front of him, only Farley and the other conspirators who'd betrayed the people they'd sworn to protect.

Something tugged at his leg. Reflexively, he tried to jump back, but a great weight prevented him. It was the zombie he'd knocked down, and its hands were curled around his leg. He stamped his heel down on its skull. It cracked open, oozing brain onto the road. A wave of dark satisfaction washed through him. He screamed again, turning it into a yell, knowing that this here was death and that he would meet it head on.

Something glowing tumbled through the air. There was a whoosh, and the ground in front of him lit up. Another flaming light, and this time he heard the breaking of glass before the eruption of flames. Someone was throwing the glass bottles that they'd filled with gasoline.

Hope blossomed with the flames, and the momentary wave of relief cleared the berserk rage from his mind. The flash of triumph was extinguished when a third bottle smashed into a zombie's chest. Flames engulfed the creature, but it didn't stop. It didn't scream. It staggered on, arms flailing, a living torch, getting nearer, nearer, not just to him, but to their barricade which was as much wood as it was metal.

The rage was gone now, replaced with exhausted fear. He raised the metal bar, dreading what would come next. The shotgun roared. The zombie fell. Arm still raised, Tom looked around, but there were no more zombies. The world had gone suddenly silent, except for the bubbling of twice-dead flesh. And there was something else. Someone was sobbing. He turned around. It was Amy. She was cradling Monique's head.

"What happened?"

"She came to help," Amy said.

"Let me see." A chunk of flesh had been ripped from her arm. Blood poured from the wound. "We need a bandage, quick!"

"Why? She's dead already," Amy howled.

Tom picked up the wounded woman. "Keep watch," he yelled at Helena and Lawrence, and carried the girl over the barricade.

A few of the vehicles had had first-aid kits. They'd left them with the meager store of food. Tom grabbed a bandage, ripped it open, and slapped it on Monique's arm. What else was he meant to do? Should he elevate the wound above the heart? He had no idea. He felt Monique's neck. There was a pulse, but it was weak.

"She wanted to help," Amy said.

"Sure. Of course," Tom murmured, unable to think of anything more comforting to say. He looked around. "Where's Noah?"

"Here," the boy said.

"Take Noah, and some food and water, go up to the roof of the filling station," Tom said. "Wait there. Both of you. Keep watch, understand? You keep watch and you shout out if you see anything. Go. Now."

The only safety that roof offered was as a refuge until the helicopter arrived. If it arrived. Dawn was a long way off, and noon an eon after that, but there was nothing else he could do, nowhere else they could go. Amy grabbed Noah and backed away. Tom looked down at Monique. Her pulse was weakening. He took out the revolver. The spent rounds tinkled to the floor. He'd tried to save the world, and he'd failed. There was no

217

way of knowing what would have happened if he'd not discovered the cabal's plans. He couldn't imagine that it could have turned out worse. For the first time in thirty years, he wished he'd never come to America.

Slowly, methodically, he reloaded. He reached for Monique's throat. The pulse flickered. It was gone. He aimed at the woman's forehead, but he waited. He had to be sure. Monique's eyes flicked open, absent of all life. He fired.

He stood. He wished that there was something more, some ceremony he could perform that would give meaning to this senseless death.

"Tom! They're coming!" Helena called. Tom took one last look at the dead girl, opened the revolver, replaced the spent round, and then headed back to the road.

Chapter 27 - The Final Address
February 27th, Clearfield County, Pennsylvania

They'd killed their last zombie at three a.m., but spent the rest of the night waiting for more. When dawn came, he saw the carnage they'd wrought. For many reasons, he couldn't believe it. Bodies lay twisted, burned, and broken. Limbs had been smashed, skulls split, and the roadway was coated in the dark slime of necrotic fluids. Yet it was the number that was most surprising.

"I was sure there were more," he said.

"Forty. Forty-five," Lawrence said with a shake of his head. "Yeah, it felt like more."

Tom's eyes fell on Monique's body. He went into the nearest room, and found a sheet with which to cover her.

"Now we wait for noon?" Helena asked.

"I guess," Tom said, peering into the distance. "It's not like they're going to stop because it's daylight. I suppose we could drive down the road and find out whether it's blocked or not."

"If I start driving," Lawrence said, "I won't be coming back. Go and wash. I'll keep watch."

A tepid shower didn't help, and he felt guilty standing under the running water for so long. The borrowed, mildewed clothes only heightened how detached from reality he felt. He went back to the barricade. Lawrence went to be with Noah. Helena went to shower.

It all felt wrong. This was America. A week ago everything was normal. Now he stood in a motel that had become a battleground, and one that would never be remembered. Certainly, he had no intention of bringing the place to mind. He turned his eyes to the rising sun, breathed in deep, and then wished he hadn't. The smell of singed flesh made him gag.

"Tom!" Lawrence called. He was pointing to the south. Tom clambered onto the roof of the nearest car so he could get a better view though he knew what he'd see. A soldier lurched toward them. Not a soldier, not anymore. He jumped down, picked up a metal bar, and went to wait in the road.

"Nate?"

"I can't talk. Not now. The president's about to address the nation."

"We've been fighting zombies since last night. There are five of us here. We'll all need to be evacuated."

"Right. Fine," Nate said impatiently. "I'll pass it along, but I have to go."

"You heard that?" Tom said to Lawrence.

The undead had continued drifting in during the morning, never more than one at a time, but always in a slow, constant trickle.

"If any more come..." Lawrence said. He didn't finish. He'd made the threat to leave a dozen times since sunrise, even going so far as to put food into one of the cars. He hadn't left yet.

"We should watch the president's address," Helena said. "I mean, we might as well, right?"

They dragged a television as far out of the room as the power cord would allow, and turned the set on. To the background of an orchestral piece that Tom vaguely recognized but couldn't name, a flag fluttered in an unseen breeze, overlaid with the text: Stand by for the President of the United States.

They waited. Tom paced away, looked down the road. It was clear. He turned back to the television, and then back to the road. The TV. The road. The music abruptly stopped. He turned around.

It wasn't the Oval Office, but the lawn in front of the White House. A podium stood there, empty. Behind it were arrayed dozens of people. To either side, watching them, almost as if they were guarding them, were Marines in uniforms that looked like they'd seen recent use.

"That's not right," Tom said. "It makes them look like they're prisoners of war."

"Shh."

The president walked to the podium. "My fellow Americans," he began.

"He looks sick," Tom said.

"Shh!" Helena shushed him again. Max did look sick, pale, drawn, tired, and as if he'd lost a few pounds in the previous week. That was to be expected, wasn't it?

"We are not at a crossroads," Max said. "There are no choices, no alternative paths. We have each come to face a terrible horror in this past week. It may seem unimaginable, yet it is terrifyingly real…"

"Who told him to say that," Tom muttered. It was the wrong thing to say. As the speech went on, Tom's brow furrowed further. Max wasn't a great speechwriter. He'd excelled at town halls and debates, and had a way of coming up with instantly quotable, off-the-cuff remarks. However, when he consciously tried to write a speech it always turned out wrong, like it was now. He peered at the faces behind the president. Nate had been right; all the familiar ones were gone. Who were these people?

"More instructions will be given to you over the coming days," Max continued. "You must listen to your local authorities. Together we can defeat this foe. Our nation is not lost, nor will it be as long as we stand together. God bless America, and… God—"

There was a scream. A figure lurched through the crowd toward the podium. There was a fusillade of gunfire. The screen went blank, before being filled again with the image of that fluttering flag.

In the courtyard of the motel, there was absolute silence.

"That was Washington," Amy said quietly. "The White House."

"Tom?" Helena asked.

He shook his head, not sure what to say.

"Noah, come on. We're leaving," Lawrence said.

"No," Helena said. "You can't."

"Amy's right," Lawrence said. "That's the White House. Do you know what that means? It means that all the military in the world can't stop these things. Washington's gone. Any chance of stopping them is gone. Any helicopters, any soldiers, they'll be deployed to save the capital, and it will be too late. It can't be done. It's over."

"You don't know that," Helena said.

"What do you think's going to happen next?" Lawrence asked. "You think people are going to stay in their homes? Whatever we've seen so far, it's going to get worse. We can't stay here, and we can't wait on the chance this helicopter will arrive."

"But... Tom?" she turned toward him.

"He's right," Tom said. "Despite how many people we saw on the roads this last week, most *were* staying in their homes. How many of them will be hungry, desperate? They'll see this as a sign it's all over. They'll take to the roads. There'll be too many for the military to stop, and far too many for them to protect. You saw what happened here yesterday? Thousands more people will be infected by nightfall. Tens of thousands by tomorrow. The whole nation will be in ruins by the end of the week. It's why you have to wait, Lawrence. There's no safety out there. Wait. The helicopter *will* come."

"Call your man and see," Lawrence said.

Tom dialed the number. Nate didn't answer.

"We're going," Lawrence said.

Tom tried to think of something he could say that would stop him. He couldn't, and he wasn't sure that Lawrence was wrong. He picked up the shotgun and handed it to the man. "Good luck."

Lawrence nodded. One hand on Noah's shoulder, he led the boy to the car. After the briefest hesitation, in which she glanced at Monique's shrouded corpse, Amy followed.

Tom and Helena watched the car drive away. Tom headed to the filling station.

"Want to see if they make it," he said. But by the time they got to the roof, the car was gone. He sat down.

"What does it mean?" Helena asked.

"Farley. This must have been his plan all along."

"What?"

"Or his plan for the last week. The White House was guarded by an army, and a phalanx of the best-trained bodyguards in the world. A zombie didn't manage to get through that cordon."

"You mean it was brought in?"

He took out the tablet. "I mean that someone inside was deliberately infected."

"But... why?"

"So that when the president addressed the nation, a whole week after the crisis began, people would see that attack. It doesn't matter how it happened, or what happens in Washington now. Chaos will take hold. Everyone who saw it will take it as a sign the government is gone, and no help will come. They can broadcast whatever they like on the television and the radio, and it won't matter. No one will believe it. Here, look. Nate said he was uploading footage. He must have been recording the speech."

"He uploaded a video?"

It took an age to load, and wasn't worth the wait. It showed exactly what they'd just watched, except that it continued for another few seconds, long enough for them to see the president bundled off the stage by secret service agents.

"Why? Why would Farley do that?" Helena asked, as Tom put the tablet away. "How does it help him?"

"It makes it easier to seize power. Maybe he plans to hide in a bunker until this is all over. It will be over, some day, and when it is, he wants to emerge from his nest at the front of an army of thousands. He won't need more than that to take over what's left of the world."

"But... why?"

"Because the cabal wants power. Nothing more. They want to rule, and to them it doesn't matter how many subjects they have."

"We have to stop him."

"Yeah."

"No, I mean we really have to stop him," she said. "I mean, if I survive all of this, I don't want to end up as some kind of feudal serf living in his twisted dystopia."

Tom sighed. "That's pretty much how I've felt for the last few years. Yet here we are."

"Oh." Helena deflated. "Is there a way of finding Farley?"

"Not that I can think of."

"He won't be in Washington?" she asked.

"He might be."

"But he might already be in Cheyenne or somewhere?"

"Possibly."

"Well, what *do* we do?"

Tom looked down the road, then up at the sky. "We could try to catch up with Lawrence and help keep Noah safe, but we might not find them. And if we did, what could we do beyond keeping him safe today?" And they might find they were already dead. "We might as well wait for noon. See if the helicopter comes."

"If it doesn't?"

"Look for Max." Assuming that Air Force One hadn't met the same fate as the vice president's plane.

"I can't imagine we'll find him, either," Helena said. "Not now."

She was right, but he wasn't going to give up, and he could think of nothing else to do and nowhere else to go. Nowhere? An idea came back to him, a memory of the escape he'd planned when he thought his adversaries were entirely human. He could leave the country. No doubt Julio had long since fled the airfield, and Sophia would have taken her boat somewhere safe, but perhaps not. He thought of calling them, but resisted the urge. "Wait until noon," he said.

"Noon," Helena agreed.

They sat, waiting, watching the road.

"Zombie," Helena said.

"I see it." He took one look at the sky, then at the tablet. "Half an hour." He turned it off and climbed down the ladder.

By the time they'd clambered over the barricade, the creature was sixty feet away. He looked at the metal bars dotted along the ground. "I don't think I have the energy," he said, drawing the revolver.

"You want me to?" Helena offered.

Fifty feet. Forty. "No." He raised the gun. Aimed. Lowered it. Sighed. Aimed. Fired. The shot echoed across the landscape. Birds erupted from the trees nearby. He'd not noticed them flocking there.

"We should go," he said. "North or south, I suppose it would be better to… to… You hear that?"

"No. What?"

He cricked his head, but the sound had gone. "I must have imagined it. Wishful thinking, I guess." It wasn't. He heard it again.

"It's an engine!" Helena said. "Safety! I can't believe it!"

They both turned their faces to the sky. As the sound drew nearer, he realized there was something wrong with it.

"It's not a helicopter," he said, climbing up onto the barricade. "It's coming from the north."

"A car? It sounds too large."

"Green. Military," he said, peering into the distance. "Thinking about it, Nate didn't say it would be a helicopter. I assumed—" He stopped, staring. "Run. Go. Go now."

"What?"

"Hide. Or drive away. It doesn't matter. Go."

"What? What is it?"

"A BearCat. It's a green-painted BearCat, just like the one that Powell was driving when he abducted Dr Ayers. That's only forty miles from here. Go."

"And you?"

"I'm going to kill Powell."

How? There were few choices. The road was littered with bodies and debris. Powell would stop, he would get out, and that would be his chance. He dropped down from the barricade, and ran along it, looking for the best spot. He wished he still had the shotgun. Better yet, Lawrence's rifle. He had the revolver, and that would have to do. The engine noise grew louder. He looked around for Helena. She'd gone. There was a twinge of regret at that, but it was for the best. There was only one logical outcome to this confrontation.

The vehicle rumbled up the dip. He could see it clearly now, one hundred yards away. He moved to his left, so he was better concealed. Ninety yards. He'd chosen the wrong spot, his angle of fire was restricted, but it was too late to change it now. Fifty. Forty. It would stop any second. It bounced over the first of the corpses they'd killed during the night. Thirty. It wasn't slowing. Twenty. Bones cracked, dead skin burst as those thick tires rolled over the bodies. Ten. It wasn't going to stop.

The APC slammed into the flimsy barricade. The air filled with the sound of wood splintering and metal scraping against metal. Tom sprinted for the only cover he could reach, the staircase that led to the motel's upper floor. He rolled to the ground, coughing and wincing as the noise subsided. The engine cut out. A moment later, bullets flew, smacking into concrete, ricocheting off metal. He hugged the ground.

"Cease fire," a voice drawled.

Tom raised his head. He thought he could see a rifle barrel, and the corner of a helmet behind it, but that was all.

"Mr Clemens, you mind if I call you that?"

Tom couldn't see who was speaking. "Is that you, Powell?" he called.

"Powell? Ah, yes. Agent Powell. Call me… Herold."

"Powell? Herold? What's your real name?" Tom called.

"Oh, you're hardly one to talk. Clemens? Finn? *Sholto*? Do you get all your names from books?"

Tom glanced up at the sky, hoping against hope that perhaps the helicopter might arrive. What Powell said next disabused him of it.

"You wanted an extraction, didn't you, Mr Clemens? Well, here we are, ready to pull you like a rotten tooth."

He was one of those, Tom thought, the kind of man who liked the sound of his voice. He wondered how long he'd spent working on the line. Still, it did confirm no help was coming.

His options were limited. He was fifty feet from the manager's office. That was the only door that was unlocked. In front of the office were the raised flowerbeds. They would probably stop a bullet from an automatic rifle, but that still meant a dash across nearly forty-five feet of exposed ground. He supposed he could dive through the ground-floor window of one of the rooms, assuming he could break the glass, but then what? The only escape were the trucks on the track behind the motel. He might get to one, but what if that track led nowhere? Better to attack and get it over with.

"Who sent you?" he called back.

"Does it matter?" Powell replied. "There'll be plenty of time for questions later. Throw out your weapons, come out with your hands up. You know the routine. Quickly, Mr Clemens, it won't be long before we have company of the most *un*pleasant sort."

Tom caught the inflection. He peered around the corner. He could see the assault rifle, the helmet behind it, and behind that… yes, he could make out the edge of a face with white-blond hair.

"Okay," he said.

Shoot the window. Two shots and hope it broke. They'd think he was going to run through it, and so that was where they would aim. That would be his chance to fire the other four shots and hope they hit.

He breathed out. Aimed at the window.

"Hey!" someone yelled.

There was the sound of glass breaking. A whomph. A scream. He peered around the corner of the stairs. The front of the BearCat was in flames. The soldier's arm was on fire, and he was beating at it with his other hand. Tom raised the revolver. Where was Powell? There, he saw him.

Another bottle sailed through the air, landing on the vehicle's roof. A sheet of flame washed over it, and Powell was lost from view. Tom pulled the trigger twice before he truly understood what was happening. Someone – it had to be Helena – had thrown the remaining Molotov cocktails at the vehicle. He couldn't see her, but when a third bottle didn't come he hoped she'd decided to run. It was time for him to do the same. He ran across the motel parking lot, trying to get sight of Powell. Automatic fire sprayed across the asphalt. He rolled, fired, and changed direction. The shooting recommenced, though this time the bullets went nowhere near him. He reached the manager's office, pointed the revolver at the vehicle, and pulled the trigger. The hammer hit a spent round.

"Tom!" It was Helena, calling through the door on the other side of the office. She had her bag across her back, her pistol in one hand, and a glass bottle in the other.

Bullets sprayed the window. She ducked out of sight, as he raised his hand to protect his face from the falling glass.

"Tom!"

"It's Powell," he said, reloading. "I've got to kill him."

"The zombies, Tom. They're coming. All of them."

He paused. "What do you mean all?"

"They were following the BearCat. Didn't you see? There are hundreds of them."

He heard more shots, but no sound of impacts. Gingerly, he raised his head. Flames licked along the wood of the barricade and toward the motel rooms. He could make out the shape of the armored car, but not of the people beyond it. The gunfire intensified, but it wasn't aimed at them.

"Tom, please," Helena said. "While we still can."

There was a scream. The gunfire slackened. A figure staggered through the gap in the burning barricade. It wasn't wearing a uniform. He raised the gun.

"Tom!"

Another figure lurched through the barricade, and then a third.

Reluctantly, Tom stood and followed Helena outside. They jogged away from the motel toward the woods. When he turned back, he saw movement. He stopped, raising the revolver. He lowered it again. There was no point wasting bullets on the undead.

By the time they reached the two trucks he'd moved to the track the day before, the motel was an inferno.

Helena pulled a lighter from her pocket. "Get in the truck. Start the engine," she said, opening the door of the second vehicle.

Tom stood by the lead truck's door. He wanted to know that Powell was dead. The zombie that had followed them from the motel was getting nearer. There were other figures behind it. None wore uniforms. Reluctantly, he got in the truck.

Helena lit the rag sticking out of the top of the bottle. "I want to make sure they can't escape," she said, dropping it into the rear-most truck. "Go!" she yelled, running to the passenger-side door.

He didn't need the encouragement. He put his foot on the gas, and drove away. When he glanced in the rear-view mirror, he saw a plume of dirty black smoke pouring upward from the motel and flames engulfing the truck behind them.

"Thank you," he said. "For not leaving."

"Yeah. Sure," she said. There was a tremor in her voice.

"Thank you," he said again.

"Do you think Powell's dead?" she asked.

"Maybe."

And maybe he was, but there were other conspirators in the cabal. They wouldn't stop. Farley wouldn't give up. Not now. Not ever. Not until he was dead. America was crumbling. The world was on fire. Nonetheless, as the truck bounced along the unpaved track, he thought there was hope. A small one, sure, but it was there. The slimmest of chances that maybe the world still might be saved. Maybe.

To be continued…

21666213R00137

Printed in Great Britain
by Amazon